STEALING RENOIR

A Mystery Thriller Where Art,
Crime, and History Converge.

Stephen Allten Brown

Singing Rock Publishing

SINGING ROCK PUBLISHING

ISBN-13: 9798463721334

Cover design by: Art Painter
Library of Congress Control Number: 2018675309
Printed in the United States of America

About the Cover. On September 8, 2011, Madeleine Leaning on Her Elbow with Flowers in Her Hair by Pierre Auguste Renoir was stolen during an armed robbery in a Houston home.

FBI TOP TEN ART CRIMES
ART CRIME TEAM

BOOKS BY

STEPHEN ALLTEN BROWN

Shadows of Chaco Canyon
A Promise Moon
Mystery Island

For More Information:
https://singingrockpublishing.mailerpage.com/

F ACT:

It was the largest art theft in history. Between 1940 and 1944, Hitler's Nazi regime looted approximately 100,000 works of art from Jewish citizens in occupied France. The initial shipment of stolen artifacts from France to Germany filled thirty railcars. Between 1933 and 1945, the total number of works plundered from museums and citizens in Austria, Czechoslovakia, Poland, Belgium, Luxembourg, Denmark, Yugoslavia, Greece, Germany, Russia, Norway, and the Netherlands has been estimated at between 650,000 and 1,000,000.

Two stolen Renoirs hung in the living room of Carinhall, Herman Goering's country retreat near Berlin. Included among the personal collection of over 1400 works of art he amassed as Hitler's second-in-command were masterpieces by Sandro Botticelli, Jan Bruegel, Claude Monet, Alfred Sisley, Georges Seurat, and Vincent van Gogh.

C hapter One:
   Thursday, Halloween Night: Key Biscayne, Florida

D r. Elizabeth Moynihan sharpened the focus on a tele-scope aimed at Richard Pendleton III's security detail. Elizabeth thrived on tension; whether appearing on live television or breaking into a mansion with the best alarm system available on the market—both had their rewards. Adrenaline remained her preferred drug, and the rush from stealing valuable art delivered the ultimate hit. An educated woman could have it all and it was faster to steal it.

Elizabeth rubbed her hands on her tights to wipe the sweat off her palms. Four surveillance cameras swept the back of Pendleton's house, while security guards spent more time fending off trick-or-treaters than patrolling the grounds. She had arranged for pallets of toilet paper to be drop-shipped to strategic intersections in the neighborhood, and it took two guards to defend the formal entrance against teenagers armed with toilet paper. Trees, traffic signs, and security fences wore two-ply streamers that added a festive air to the occasion, a clever way to interfere with the security cameras' sightlines while occupying the attention of Pendleton's security detail. She swiveled the telescope to survey the gathering crowd.

Gaily costumed partygoers had reached the gridlock stage because of her orchestrated media blitz on social media. Students from the University of Miami retweeted the party invitation. Digital natives forwarded the thread and the event went viral. Using crowds of people to provide cover for a robbery wasn't an original idea, but Elizabeth liked to think the Halloween costumes added a bit of flair. The largest art heist in recent history had occurred at the Isabella Stewart Gardner Museum in Boston during the Saint Patrick's Day parade.

The *Chácara do Céu* Museum in Rio de Janeiro suffered similar catastrophic losses during Carnival, losing paintings by Picasso, Matisse, Monet, and Dali.

Elizabeth preferred Renoir—specifically, *Portrait of Señorita Santangel,* painted by Pierre-Auguste Renoir in 1876, and an illicit addition to Richard Pendleton III's collection. But not for much longer . . .

Elizabeth rolled her shoulders to loosen her muscles. She slipped on flesh-colored gloves with a liberal application of fake warts on their backs to give the appearance of an integral part of her costume. Tonight, Elizabeth was a witch—a very bad witch. Her witch's broom, bound in brown and yellow crepe paper, masked the spear gun. A pointed witch's hat covered much of her distinctive blonde hair. Her black cape hid her tool belt and climbing harness. A dull orange bag with a smiling jack-o-lantern on the side held additional tools and a rope ladder beneath a surface layer of candy.

She began to snap her fingers softly, alternating hands to increase the tempo as her excitement built. She wiggled her toes, vibrating with energy. She kneaded the muscle cramp building near her Achilles tendon when her adrenal glands started the rush, elevating her respiration and heart rate, turning the surgery scar pink. She slowly raised one foot above her head to stretch her core muscles, regulating the surge of adrenaline. She had lost some flexibility but little of the core strength that had made her an Olympic-caliber gymnast. She wasn't nervous; she was fully actualized, at that rarefied competitive level where all senses heightened to a razor-sharp focus. Only the achievement of her goal existed.

She tapped her phone and called the fireworks team. The crisp diction of her privileged upbringing emerged. "You may begin."

Trick-or-treaters paused in their quest for candy or debauchery to look skyward. The security guards turned away from the fence they were supposed to be guarding to stare at the unexpected display.

A volley of dry ice pellets created a dense blanket of low-lying fog that drifted through the formal gardens and softened the focus of the four security cameras sweeping the back of the mansion. Every fourth rocket carried dry ice pellets in various combinations of primary colors to replenish the fog and further muddle the video images.

Elizabeth scaled the perimeter fence surrounding Pendleton's estate while a blaze of vibrant colors trailed behind each pyrotechnical explosion. She crouched beside a statue of a Greek goddess and pulled the crêpe paper off her spear gun; the southwest corner of the mansion was a ten-second sprint from her hiding place. She had six minutes and twenty-seven seconds before the blitz ended and the fog lifted.

The next volley of fireworks launched a glittering shower of gaily-colored streamers and confetti. Elizabeth was an art thief with an environmental conscience; the fireworks cannons used biodegradable ice crystals colored with vegetable dye instead of shredded paper or strips of plastic. A flurry of falling ice created enough background disturbance to defeat the radar sensors mounted on the perimeter of the estate. Every monitor in the guardhouse filled with static as reflective ice crystals scattered the radar beams. The disturbance gave her twenty seconds to climb above the limited range of transmitters directed outward from the mansion's perimeter, not upward.

She aimed the spear gun at the wooden molding of the third-floor bay window and pulled the trigger. A sudden whoosh of compressed air rocketed the harpoon into the soft wood below the glass. She yanked on the cord to set the barbs and sprinted for the rope ladder hanging from the shaft of the spear, her shadowy form lost amid the background clutter of falling ice crystals. For someone who had learned to turn cartwheels and somersaults on a balance beam—a glorified four-inch-wide piece of wood—running across roofing tiles came easy.

The main power lines tied into a junction box near the chimney. Though the control module for the alarm system had a direct connection to the utility company's power grid, Elizabeth knew how to bypass the failsafe. She had been rehearsing on the same alarm model for two weeks, an investment that had allowed her to practice bypassing each circuit board necessary to gain access to the interior of the house. The last red light turned green: three seconds faster than her previous best time.

The alarm had a cellular backup that notified the security service every time the alarm was disabled. There was no way to beat it. Since there was no one home to answer the phone, the next call would be to the guard house. It should buy her another thirty seconds.

High-pitched whistles from ascending rockets masked the squeak of the diamond-tipped glasscutter she used to cut a small hole in the window. She reached inside. The clasps hadn't been opened in years. The sash ground to a halt after she raised it a few inches. She wedged her shoulder into the opening and arched her back to force the window pane high enough to crawl through. She landed on her hands and knees as the primary barrage of fireworks exploded. The guards covered their ears.

The next eight rockets carried powdered magnesium that burned with the white-hot flame of emergency flares. It was enough light for Elizabeth to see the far wall. And there it was: *Portrait of Señorita Santangel,* perhaps the most valuable Renoir ever painted. She grabbed the nearest chair and sprinted across the room, leaping over an ill-placed ottoman with gymnastic grace. She stepped onto the chair and pressed her cheek against the wall. She tilted the top of the frame forward and used her flashlight to illuminate the upper edges.

There!

In the upper left-hand corner and burned into the back of the wooden frame—an indelible mark that had proven impossible to obscure: the intertwined Yiddish characters *Beis* and *Hei* which formed the Santangel Coat of Arms.

"Thank God for Baruch Hashem," she muttered. She wasn't

Jewish or particularly religious; she was well on her way to becoming the world's first billionaire art thief. Her elaborate con was in play and some of the marks still thought they were partners. She'd planned for everything except aging parents and the return of Ben Abrams.

F riday, November 1, 10:30 a.m., Key Largo, Florida

Chapter 2

Ben Abrams pressed a button to open the rental car's power locks—once to actuate the feature, again to make certain all four switches were in the unlocked position; the final time to satisfy his compulsion. A long line of forgers and art thieves were out of business or behind bars because of his obsessive/compulsive need for order. One elongated crack in an artificially aged veneer or a bent link in the ownership chain was all it took to make him uncomfortable. He opened the car door to the same sense of impending doom he evoked in criminals.

His reflection in the sideview mirror revealed red hair and freckles. He needed a haircut. Small, pitted scars disfigured his lower jawline from teenage acne. Contacts had replaced the magnifying lenses he once wore for glasses—otherwise Ben looked much the same as he had fifteen years ago in high school, back when his mother had merely seemed absentminded, losing her keys, forgetting to cook supper, or putting a potholder in his lunchbox instead of a sandwich. His father's obsession with family art had been full-blown by then; he had already been too distant to notice her gradual decline.

A blanket of tropical heat and humidity smothered the last gasp from the car's air conditioner. Ben's shirt reattached itself to his back. Twelve hours ago, he had been at the National Gallery of London, using the Santangel Coat of Arms to authenticate a masterpiece painting that had been missing since the 1930's. The intertwined Yiddish characters, *Beis* and *Hei* burned into the back of the wooden frame, had formed an impression that was impossible to obscure. Ben longed to be in London, looking for the surviving heirs of a masterpiece painting, not visiting a house that wasn't a home, returning to a place he'd sworn to leave behind forever.

"*Oy, vey.*" He leaned forward until his forehead rested against the steering wheel. "Give me strength." He reconsidered the odds and downgraded his wish. "Or a sense of humor."

Sun-bleached cypress boards curled away from the eaves of his father's house. Rust spots instead of nails anchored the front steps and a board was missing from the front porch—the latest in a series of repairs he had already paid for—his younger brother having cashed the checks to buy liquor, probably.

His father still lived on Key Largo, occupying the house Ben and his brother Alexi had grown up in—old enough to have been built when $500 down could buy a three-bedroom home on two acres. The densely wooded land abutting the original plot was part of an old-growth forest that extended to the edge of the beach and was the only good investment his father had ever made.

His mother had checked out of her unhappy homelife decades ago. Dementia accelerated her retreat: death had merely completed her escape.

Ben looked at the sagging pier and saw rotted pilings and missing boards. He had written a sizeable check to Alexi for pressure-treated lumber. He closed the car door and redirected his gaze toward the house like a burn victim confronts fire.

The doorbell hadn't worked for a decade. The tear in the screen door was new, and the old man who opened the front door looked different. When the edge of the door struck his walker, he cursed in Yiddish and Ben recognized the sandpaper texture of his father's voice, worn thin with curses.

"Took you long enough."

Jet-lagged and a world away from where he belonged, now that Ben was in a foul mood and willing to fight back, the old man was too weak to mount a suitable defense. He reached through the torn screen and unlatched the door from inside, instead of arguing. "I got here as soon as I could."

"Wrong turn?"

"An ocean."

"Didn't take you this long to leave."

"More motivation." The truth slipped out—from disuse, mostly. Ben hadn't intended to resume hostilities within the first thirty seconds of his arrival. Bickering formed the core of family dynamics, runner-up to holding a grudge.

"Not too late to run away." His father glared at him from beneath bushy eyebrows gone completely gray. "Again."

Which his father, Abraham Isaac Abrams, had done long ago, by moving upstairs. Only the distances were different. The old man lived in the past and chased rumors of the family's lost art collection, although there was enough shared guilt to go around. His mother had checked out from reality and his brother was a drunk.

"Where's Alexi?"

"Sleeping in," his father said, a familiar euphemism for "sleeping it off." The same way he had called their mother's affliction, "Wisenheimer's," adhering to the family tradition of using humor to avoid emotion.

"When's the funeral?"

"How the hell should I know?"

His father followed family tradition by assigning his middle name to both sons and left the remainder of parenting duties to Ben's mother. Maybe he expected her to take care of her own funeral, too.

"Not that it matters." Although his father had visibly weakened, his ironic tone was strong as ever. Nothing wrong with his timing or delivery, either.

"Meaning she'll be late for her own funeral?"

"What else?"

A glimmer of life remained in the old man; his sense of humor had survived. Ben's mother had been chronically late for everything. Her tardiness had moved from legend to lore.

Ben and his father acknowledged the irony by making eye contact for the first time in fifteen years. Touching was out of the question, a hug: unknown. A shared joke was a major step toward a conditional ceasefire: a provisional olive branch bereft of leaves, a small twig, perhaps, yet remarkable progress.

His father turned away first and struck a bookcase in his haste. Free-standing shelves lined both sides of the hallway. The impact dislodged a year's worth of dust and a refrain of traditional curses. A table lamp tipped onto its side and rolled off the top shelf. The bulb burst with a hollow explosion.

"Ah! I've been looking for this." The lamp had been sitting on top of a thick book featuring color prints of Renoir's early work. A clean spot on the cover bore an octagonal imprint of the lamp's base and revealed a swatch of vibrant color punctuated by distinctive brushstrokes. His father blew the dust off and peered inside. Once a bathroom had been added to the second story of the house, his father seldom left his personal library. Now every room in the house bulged with research material and held enough clutter to embarrass a hoarder.

His father turned his back on the chaos and left his walker at the base of the stairs. He grabbed the railing and struggled up the stairs one heavy tromp at a time, favoring his right leg and pulling with his left arm. It was painful to watch and forbidden to offer help.

Ben picked up the big pieces of glass and swept up the rest. He opened the hall closet and selected a black hooded sweatshirt to cover the mirror in the hallway—not exactly kosher, but it would have to do for now.

He had survived this tumultuous upbringing by spending weekends with *Grossmutter*—his grandmother—a superb storyteller with a gift for animating memories, and a quick wit that delighted in embellishment. But not about her escape during *Kristallnacht*—the Night of Broken Glass.

"As serious as life and death," was how she prefaced any recounting of family history. "I remember the riots. How our Gentile neighbors looted every Jewish house and business. The army used our home as a collection point for stolen paintings."

The missing art explained his father's obsession, Ben's career, and to some extent, the animosity between them. It was more rewarding to catch art thieves than follow rumors of family paintings that had disappeared long ago. His brother had not been so lucky; Alexi struggled to create art and mostly found disappointment and blackouts.

Ben used a sweater to cover the mirror in the living room. One of Alexi's *avant-garde* sculptures supported a precarious stack of additional books featuring pieces from Renoir's early work with porcelain. A three-car garage held his father's exhaustive collection of coffee table books devoted to Impressionism. Ben's great-grandfather, who hadn't believed in spanking children, made an exception when Ben's grandfather had nicked the frame of a Renoir with an errant Dreidel on Chanukah. The retelling became family legend and explained his father's obsession with the family lore of an original canvas that had been stolen from Ben's great-grandparents. He used a towel from the bathroom to cover the mirror next to their portraits. There weren't enough towels to cover an entire wall of ancestors and their failed dreams. His father had been running from the ghosts of his past: doomed to lose an unwinnable race.

He draped a towel over the mirror in his old bedroom. The dinosaur curtains his mother had sewn him for his eighth birthday were all that remained of the original furnishings from his childhood. Bookshelves filled two walls and stretched to the ceiling. File cabinets stuffed with research material filled the rest of the available space. His room had been the first bedroom converted to a library, followed by the den, dining room, and ultimately the pantry after his mother had scorched the walls while boiling water.

A clay iguana clung to the wall beside Alexi's door. The teal body featured bright yellow armored plates along the spine and looked more like a mutant dinosaur than a reptile. Ben had used two weeks of his vacation-time to help his younger brother convert the back porch into an apartment after he lost his trailer in a messy divorce. He gently turned the knob in either direction. Locked. A bad sign.

Ben opened the backdoor and walked down to the dock

where cellphone reception was strongest. He checked his email. Still no response from multiple attempts to contact his boss. He tried calling his personal cell—no answer. It had been his boss's idea to institute a company policy offering a "no questions asked, ten-percent reward based on the insured value of stolen art." Profits were up and now his boss was on the short list for CFO of Coastal Insurance Company, but thefts were up, too, along with an increase in recently issued, risky policies. Ben had been working overtime and the thieves were winning.

F riday, November 1, 2:30 p.m.

Chapter 3

The theft of Renoir's *Portrait of Señorita Santangel* posed a serious enough claim against Coastal Insurance Company to explain why Ben proceeded to Richard Pendleton III's mansion, instead of staying on Key Largo and taking the remainder of his bereavement leave. A Bentley, several Mercedes-Benzes, and more Range Rovers than on an African safari were all jockeying for the right-of-way at the traffic circle near the Key Biscayne Yacht Club, where tiny houses made with concrete blocks in the 1950s sold for a million dollars apiece. The claimant, Richard Pendleton III, had bought two of the adjoining historic landmarks and had them torn down before the local preservation society could get an injunction to stop him.

Ben pulled the appliance-white rental car into a narrow, private driveway. The antiquated road was an illusion, a defensive tactic employing a sharp curve to deny perpetrators enough speed to penetrate the reinforced gate. He checked his email while waiting for the guard to open the gate. Several new messages appeared, but still no response from his boss for additional information about Pendleton and his unusual policy. Coastal Insurance Company was headquartered in Manhattan, so Ben's boss was 1300 miles away—a personally ideal situation unless he needed something in a hurry.

Ben changed screens on his phone and checked the FBI's Art Loss Register. A stylized question mark filled the space where the image of Pendleton's stolen Renoir should be. The theft of *Portrait of Señorita Santangel* was front-page news, but there hadn't been a picture of the canvas online, either.

The tires thrummed on the cobblestone lane. The right

quarter panel of the car squeaked. Ben felt the impact from each stone through the thin padding of the cheap seats. He parked beside a Rolls-Royce with "RPIII" on its prestige plates. Ben recognized the discreet barcode on the back window. The leasing company specialized in providing prestige autos on a temporary basis and their insurance premiums were astronomical—as were their fees.

The ocean breeze carried a mixture of Miami hydrocarbons and oleander blossoms that smelled like expensive perfume on a sweaty drag queen. Fluted marble columns supported a portico above a tiled landing; gargoyles jutted from the balustrades. Matching fountains with stylized ocean nymphs sprayed colored water with a chlorinated tang. Amid such opulence, the stainless-steel deadbolts looked incongruous mounted into intricately carved doors predating the Industrial Revolution.

A stylishly thin young man opened the door as Ben reached for the knocker. Pale skin and a fair complexion gave him the look of an anemic waif from the moors of Scotland. He wore an unbleached cotton tunic and linen pants from the same era as the house, yet his accent was full of the stressed consonants of a Slavic country short on vowels, so "Come in" gathered an extra syllable. Ben followed him inside.

A 17th century French Antique Louis XIV Walnut Armoire stood next to a Hepplewhite sideboard with original hardware. A Tiffany lamp sat atop a Shaker end table. Victorian hand carved barley twist parlor chairs lined the opposite side of the entryway. After he stopped tabulating dollar amounts, he realized the works lacked a defining theme; the overall effect was clutter and a predictable garishness unique to the *nouveau riche*.

The waif tried to shunt Ben to an over-decorated sitting room filled with Chippendale tables bearing assorted baubles executed in silver and gold.

"No thank you." Ben had been around rich people for most of his life, so he knew better than to take orders from servants or let them herd him into a holding corral—no matter how richly decorated. He could gain valuable insight about a claimant by examining their living space when they weren't around to stop him from being nosy. The room to the left, the one the servant had tried to steer him away from, looked promising.

He exited the foyer and gazed upward at stained-glass windows from a demolished gothic church. The remarkable antique glass stretched three stories toward a ceiling featuring a frieze populated by Greek goddesses and New Testament disciples, as if the painter had converted to Catholicism midway through the commission. Three couches with matching loveseats and side tables occupied the open area, which seemed more suited to an automobile dealership than an art collection, although natural lighting helped counter the imposing space, while the stained glass overhead further softened the direct sunlight with subtle tints of red and blue.

An empty frame hung from a wall that positively begged for a masterpiece from the Impressionist Era. His shoes sank into the lush Persian rug as he approached the hardwood flooring that formed a line of demarcation between the massive room and the wall where a Renoir should be hanging.

"What the h—?" He noticed a scratch on the lower left-hand corner of the frame. "It can't be."

Ben had been raised on the same family stories responsible for his father's compulsion. Of a Renoir stolen from his great grandparents on *Kristallnacht*.

"*Look at the frame; it's the scratch I've been telling you about.*" For a moment, Ben thought he heard his grandmother whisper the start of her saddest story. *Grossmutter* had been a little girl in 1938 when Nazi's vandalized Jewish synagogues, homes, and businesses. Both her parents were among the 30,000 Jews sent to concentration camps after the mass arrests following *Kristallnacht—The Night of Broken Glass*.

Dramatic sweeps of textured plaster filled the empty space where a canvas should have been. The natural lighting highlighted a distinctive scar on the bottom left corner of the frame.

He moved to within an inch of the frame to study the unusual mark. It could have been caused by an errant Dreidel. The gouge in the wood extended to within a millimeter of the linen mat. It was easy to see how a noted pacifist such as his great-grandfather might have made an exception to his moratorium on physical punishment.

"*I could still see the handprints on his tuches myself.*" Grossmutter had a distinctive laugh—like a cow with hiccups. Ben could still hear her laughing at her own joke.

He pressed his cheek against the wall and peered behind the frame, his nose close enough to smell the distinctive aroma of a previous era. Aged wood, oil and lacquer, even the dust carried the scent of antiquities. He had spent his early childhood being dragged to estate sales by *Grossmutter,* who loved finding bargains. A widower's closet, a spinster's jewelry box, the musty odors of a house furnished with antiques—these were the formative experiences of his early sensory development. Aged canvas, crudely distilled oils saturated with pigment, even the long-dead trees used in the frame had a unique odor—each component contributing an ingredient to the combined scent emanating from the masterpiece. He pulled a pen from his pocket and used it to gently tilt the frame away from the wall.

The waif tugged on Ben's sleeve to get his attention. He pleaded. "Please. I insist. You must wait in the sitting room."

"Go right ahead." Ben forestalled the hired help with diplomatic misunderstanding and used a pen to gently tilt the empty frame away from the wall. He kept his cheek away from the wall to avoid contaminating the crime scene. There, in the upper left-hand corner, written in Ladino—the Spanish form of Yiddish from the fifteenth century: *Beis Hei,* two intertwined characters that formed the Santangel coat of arms, Louis de Santangel's way of honoring Christopher Columbus for keeping his part of the bargain, discovering the New World and saving their families from the Spanish Inquisition.

"*Baruch Hasem,*" Ben muttered, and with these words renewed a broken family connection with the ancestors.

"Beg your pardon, sir?"

"*Beis Hei,* a discreet abbreviation for *Baruch Hasem,* or

16

thank God."

Richard Pendleton III swept into the room and curtailed Ben's inspection of the upper left-hand corner of the suspicious frame.

Chapter 4

If Richard Pendleton III wasn't careful, his frown and wrinkled brow were going to necessitate another facelift. The blond highlights, the tan, the capped teeth were meant to take ten years off Pendleton's chronological age, but Ben wasn't easily fooled; the lack of elasticity in the skin on his temples and around the eye sockets implied recent plastic surgery.

"Serge, you idiot." Pendleton scowled at the waif and risked another wrinkle. "I told you the sitting room."

"I tried. He wouldn't, I . . ."

Ben heard a tremor in the man's reply. Serge's eyes widened and he looked scared. Was Pendleton that difficult to work for?

"That will be all." Pendleton dismissed the man with a belittling flick of his fingers.

Ben raised Serge's status from domestic help to personal assistant, although the leash was looking a little too short and the gold collar too tight. Serge blinked with the deliberate sort of closure favored by birds of prey when hunting for their next meal. Or peering through keyholes, more likely, since there were plenty of them in Pendleton's garish mansion and he didn't act like the sort of man who inspired loyalty among his staff. It took Serge three tries to remove the loathing from his expression, although the scowl went no further than his eyes. He slinked off in the opposite direction from his arrival. The servant's quarters or the doghouse, Ben supposed.

"I'm sorry for the theft of your Renoir," Ben said, instead of "hello," or "have you run background checks on your employees, recently?"

Pendleton turned his right hand sideways and waved off

Ben's comment with a repeat of the same disdainful flick of fingers used to dismiss Serge. In this harsh light, the start of an extra chin formed an unflattering mirror image to the cubist nudes in Picasso's later works.

Ben ignored the insult and focused on business. "You are understandably upset about the theft of your Renoir: *Portrait of Señorita Santangel.* I don't recognize the title; I wasn't able to find any record of the work. It's not listed as part of Renoir's *oeuvre.* That's unusual."

"Many things are."

"And exceedingly rare."

"You are not already knowing this?"

"Just now learning about it. It's a new policy. New enough to still be on my boss's desk or locked in his personal safe."

"You don't use computers?"

"Passwords."

"Or phones?"

"I've called, texted, and emailed." Ben held up his phone as proof.

"Then why are you here?"

"It's a new policy with a 170 million-dollar claim against it. Most clients—" Ben stopped talking but kept thinking. He had flown through six time zones after investigating the *reappearance* of a similar masterpiece painting with suspicious provenance—covered by a similar policy, also recently written by his boss and equally unavailable. Ben saw a coincidence and suspected a con.

"Coming unprepared is hardly an attribute," Pendleton added disdain to his voice and matched his peevish expression.

"Then let's get started." Ben adopted the same casual wave Pendleton had employed and deflected the insult. "Who was the previous owner?"

"They couldn't have done it."

"Nobody is beyond suspicion." Ben spoke from experience.

"They're all dead."

"They?"

"Many previous owners."

"Fine. Then *they* won't mind you telling me."

Pendleton looked down his nose at Ben with the condescending expression typically reserved for dimwitted stepchildren. "It can't possibly be relevant."

"It's critically important. Most recoveries involve connections to prior owners. Ex-spouses and family members are in second and third place."

"But all three are impossible."

"Try probable. I can think of two recent investigations where that was the case."

Pendleton crossed to the furthest loveseat and sat on the edge facing away from Ben. He reached for a bell to summon a servant.

Ben took a seat across from him instead of acting on his initial impulse, which was to put the man in a headlock and pry a straight answer out of him. "Again. Who did you buy *Portrait of Señorita Santangel* from?"

"Would you care for some tea?"

"No." Ben softened his tone to hide the distrust. "No, thank you." Pendleton was a client, after all—the sort of client who had underlings lodge complaints against disrespectful insurance investigators. Fortunately, Ben closed cases; he liked to think his success rate at catching criminals kept him insulated from petty grievances issued by insufferable prima donnas like Pendleton who occupied the rarified world of collectable art. Still, Ben liked to think—and original thought, along with the corresponding questions it raised, weren't always welcome in these circles.

"What's taking so long with that tea?" Pendleton rang the bell again; three short tones followed by a long raucous clanging —as if additional decibels would make the water boil sooner.

Serge returned, bearing a worried expression, and carrying a manila folder instead of a tea service.

"*Ratzooi,*" Pendleton dismissed him. "Not now."

Serge disobeyed with a shake of his head that pained both

men, although Pendleton was better at disguising his discomfort.

Serge handed him the folder. Pendleton placed it on the couch without looking inside and shooed him away with minimal effort and twice the disdain of his previous dismissal.

Serge shifted his weight from foot to foot like a sprinter anxious to escape the starting blocks. He certainly looked ready to leave, yet ignored a second dismissal—a serious transgression judging by the scowl currently making age lines in Pendleton's unnaturally tight face.

Pendleton opened the folder with an exaggerated effort and began to read.

"I'll check on the tea," Serge said, as soon as Pendleton's expression turned murderous.

"Bad news?" Ben asked.

Pendleton didn't answer, although he unintentionally acknowledged hearing Ben's question by glancing at him and quickly averting eye contact. The first news clipping came from the New York Times and was a brief recap of one of Ben's recent cases:

> *The Garden of Monet's House in Argenteuil* (1874) by Claude Monet will remain in The Metropolitan Museum of Art, after a fair and reasonable settlement was reached with the heirs of Henry Percy Newman, of Hamburg, Germany. Terms of the agreement remain confidential.

Ben watched the skin across Pendleton's forehead resist the habitual muscle contractions of wrinkle-inducing stress. The uneven elasticity between skin grafts and connecting tissue formed minute patches of shiny tissue that only the dramatic lighting of such an incredible room could have revealed. It wasn't the plastic surgeon's fault, it was unwelcome news of the worst kind. For Pendleton to react so violently, Ben figured it must be about money.

> *Shepherdess Bringing in Sheep*, by Camille Pissarro, formerly hanging in the president's office at the University of Oklahoma, is now hanging in the *Musée D'Orsay*. As part of the agreement, the sole surviving heir, who wishes to remain anonymous, received fifty percent of the auction proceeds.

Pendleton folded the paper in half, printed side facing inward. He glanced at Ben, looked away, and tore the offending sheets into smaller pieces. He tucked the pieces into his pocket rather than leave the evidence in a nearby trashcan.

Ben raised his level of distrust to match Pendleton's evasive actions. Each shredded piece of paper in Pendleton's pocket represented bad news or a loss of money. Collusion and a coverup were in the mix, somewhere.

Serge returned with a tea service. The ritual became an elaborate production, complete with stalling, staging, and proper place settings.

The first sip of tea triggered memories of a Passover spent in the Mediterranean. The brew left an exotic aftertaste of anise and mint. Better than strychnine which had also seemed like a possibility. Ben leaned against the cushions. Raised the cup to his lips periodically and tolerated the standoff until the last sip turned muddy.

"So . . ." Ben pushed his cup to the center of the table.

Pendleton stiffened, getting the message: the interlude was over.

"You were telling me about the previous owner of *Portrait of Señorita Santangel.*"

"I was not." Pendleton's pretentious tone returned. "I have time trials and a yacht race to prepare for."

Ben nodded. Blinked so Pendleton wouldn't see him roll his eyes.

"*The* race," Pendleton added, like he expected more than a token sign of disinterest.

"Good luck." The only race Ben was interested in winning involved the recapture of a stolen Renoir.

"The America's Cup Trials. It's two weeks of trials against the world's best sailors." Richard Pendleton III was a multi-millionaire who wanted to be a billionaire. Yachts were big boys' toys and he was playing out of his price range.

"Explains the traffic." Ben wasn't impressed. Another of his clients built 12-meter racing yachts and he knew how far Pendleton was behind on his payments. "Back to your Renoir. Who did you get it from?"

"You should already have all this."

"Indeed." *Finally, something we agree on.*

"It's confidential."

Not for long. Especially since you don't want to tell me. Ben changed tactics. "What about the appraisal?"

"What about it?"

"Who did it? Can I see your copy? What is the provenance? Where is the documentation that accompanies any masterpiece? But you already know all this. I'll need to see everything. This isn't your first policy—or your first claim."

"Some woman, a local." The dismissive wave returned; the evasive tactics remained. The wrinkles in Pendleton's forehead, the tightening at the corners of his eyes—these were signs of furious thinking—or outright lying.

Pendleton looked down his nose as if an odor was attached to his memory of the appraiser. "Your insurance company knows all this. Your boss handled the details. Let me speak with *him*. Your questioning grows tiresome. I'm busy."

He didn't look busy; he looked complicit. His answers were evasive and his body language had all the adjectives associated with lying. "This woman—the appraiser—who was it? She might have some information about the theft."

Pendleton shrugged. "Only the Renoir was stolen."

"*Only?*" Something in Pendleton's casual tone didn't jibe

with the astronomical value of the theft.

Pendleton patted the sides of his carefully coifed hair. He examined his manicured nails while somehow managing to look increasingly bored. Not a bad act, but obviously affected.

"You said 'only.' It's a Renoir. That's not enough?"

Pendleton didn't answer.

"About the appraiser . . .?" Ben asked a leading question so he could judge Pendleton's level of evasiveness.

"What about her?" Pendleton's eyes darted to his left.

Did you bribe her? Ben wondered. *And what are you lying about now?*

Pendleton studiously avoided eye contact. He drew himself into an erect position on the couch and radiated disdain.

"Back to the appraiser . . . do you have her name written down? Somewhere? Stored in your phone, perhaps?"

"She wrote a book the university felt obligated to publish." Pendleton's accent got thicker as his temper got hotter. The long vowels and nasal consonants returned to their origins in South Africa, with the clipped speech patterns of Dutch Colonials who insisted on referring to the independent nation of Zimbabwe as Rhodesia.

"Do you remember the book title? I can search for her name that way, if necessary."

Pendleton refilled his nearly full cup of tea. He used the silver tongs to rearrange the scones but didn't transfer one to his plate. He adjusted the pleats in his pants and swept an imaginary speck of dust from the front of his polo shirt before commenting.

"Coastal Insurance Company has issued to me a bona fide policy." The hard "c's" in "Coastal Insurance Company" drew a fine mist of saliva that left a small white dot at each corner of his mouth. "Your superior handled the details. From now on, I wish to speak with him only."

"Oh." Ben kept a neutral tone instead of saying what he was thinking: *I'd like to speak with my boss, too. Give him a chance to explain himself before I add his name to the list of suspects.*

Serge returned with reinforcements: a butler who had formal training in the diplomatic school of dealing with insurance investigators asking unwelcome questions. The two men entered the room from a long hallway connecting the gallery with a greenhouse, an indoor swimming pool, and other rooms too distant for direct viewing. The elderly man wore the black suit and starched white shirt from a previous era, when live-in staff were common. He bowed at the waist with a fluent demeanor and waited with an unspoken request for further directions.

"Show Mr. Abrams to the library." Pendleton ordered. "Serge, stay here."

Serge looked like this was the last place on the planet he wanted to be. It also looked like he was busy with financial computations, weighing the cost-of-living versus the prideful expense of quitting, but that could have been Ben's prejudices. His meeting with Pendleton was clearly over. There was no advantage in refusing to leave or creating a scene.

The servant tilted his head in Ben's direction and gestured toward the upper stories by opening his palm and bending the fingers of his right hand with a polite and dignified motion. "There's an elevator, sir."

"I prefer the stairs." Truthfully, Ben preferred to avoid small, enclosed spaces tethered to cables manufactured by the lowest bidder. It had taken hypnosis and psychotherapy to deal with his fear of elevators. The result was a temporary reprieve. He took the stairs in any building with less than ten stories.

Two flights of steps and a lengthy hallway later, they entered a study filled with the pungent aroma of leather and polished wood. Floor-to-ceiling shelves packed with old books from the days of leather bindings and moveable type encompassed an entire wall. A neat hole had been cut in the window. A pressure sensor dangled from beside the opening.

"Will there be anything else, sir?"

"Maybe. Unless you're anxious to see if Mr. Pendleton needs something more."

"Always, sir." His voice was respectful, but his tone was as subtle as a brick through a window.

"Once a bully, always a bully?" Ben guessed.

"As you say, sir."

"Why wasn't anyone home?"

"The party, sir."

"What party?"

"*The* party. Mr. Pendleton gives all staff the night off."

"Like '*The* Race.' A Halloween party, I'm guessing?"

"Oh, much more than that, sir. *The* Halloween Party, the social event of the season. By invitation only. Mr. Pendleton rents the villa. It's an annual event."

"*The* annual event, I'm guessing?"

"Yes, sir. On South Beach. At 1116 Ocean Drive."

Ben shrugged. Halloween on South Beach in Miami was like Carnival in Rio de Janeiro, only with better weather and fewer clothes.

"*Casa Casaurina*, sir," he added, a name drop with significant impact.

"Ah . . . Gianni Versace's old house—where he was killed by his young lover."

"Andrew Cunanan, yes sir."

"Those headlines in the Herald were bigger than when they announced the end of World War II, or so I've heard."

"And the coverage more intense. Now it's a private, members-only party mansion."

"Creepy."

"Tis the season."

"Are you the one who discovered that *Portrait of Señorita Santangel* was missing?"

"And the rope, of course." A brief smile enlivened his solemn expression and revealed a sense of humor lurking beneath the placid surface. "A rather ingenious solution for a high-tech alarm, wouldn't you say, sir? No one foresaw the use of a rope ladder hanging from a harpoon."

"The fireworks were a clever distraction."

"A bit of élan, that."

"Just careful planning." Ben's pragmatic nature reduced most choices to the economics of profit and loss.

"More like exceptional planning, sir." He paid Ben a priceless compliment in polite currency, with a respectful silence that credited Ben with enough intelligence to connect the dots and recreate the crime.

Ben moved to the window and stuck his hand through a hole cut in the glass. He opened the window to envision the burglar—someone with exceptional athletic skills—disabling the alarm on the roof, climbing down the rope ladder, returning to . . . where?

"The groundskeeper?" Ben pointed at a statue of a Greek Goddess. "Did he notice a flat spot behind that statue?"

"Very good, sir."

"Where the thief waited for the dry ice."

"Dry ice, sir?"

"I checked with the fireworks company. Every fourth rocket held dry ice." Ben leaned out the window and continued reversing the robbery sequence. "I can see it. Fireworks to distract the guards, dry ice to fool the cameras . . . over the fence after the fireworks started . . . back to Crandon Park . . ." He reversed the order of how the crime was committed so he could begin tracking the criminal. "Last night's party in a rented house filled with kegs of beer, all charged to a stolen credit card . . . toilet paper streamers . . . a parade . . . I can see all of it. Halloween was a nice touch."

"Very interesting, sir."

"It's more than interesting; it's a pattern."

"Yes, sir."

Ben heard the subtle shift in his tone. An unasked question lurked beneath his diplomatic response. "And the alarm, of course."

"Very *good*, sir." The sense of humor resurfaced in the tone of his response.

"Yes, it is." Ben said, appreciating the subtlety. "The alarm.

It's too good. The thief had help."

"Then I wish you good hunting, sir."

"Any ideas on where I should start?"

"You might contact Dr. Elizabeth Moynihan. She authenticated the painting and performed the appraisal—not that you heard this from me, of course."

"Very good, sir," Ben said, treating him as an equal.

F

riday, November 1: 4:30 p.m.

Chapter 5

The University of Miami issued Ben a parking pass, but it was more of a hunting license. Commuting students hunted in packs, with the most elusive trophy being a vacant space. Ben was driving a rental, so he parked in an alley behind a dumpster.

Dr. Elizabeth Moynihan's office door was closed. There was a narrow window beside it, however. Ben peered inside and knocked on the door.

She looked up from a textbook. "Come in," she called.

Ben reintroduced himself and handed her a business card. Their paths had crossed but never on a personal level. Elizabeth was a media figure and Ben avoided the spotlight. "Thanks for waiting. Sorry I'm late; stuck in traffic."

She nodded. "I hear the same thing from my students."

Maybe an insult. He let it pass.

There was nothing in her serious manner or stiff posture to suggest she had ever been called Liz, or Beth, and certainly not Lizzie. Elizabeth Moynihan had television personality hair—thicker and larger than average. Perfectly styled, no single curl would dare get out of place. Her skin tone and green eyes suggested strawberry blonde was her natural hair color. Although they'd never had a personal conversation, he almost felt like he knew her from her weekly appearances on the local television station. They'd spent hours together, separated by an electronic box. She was prettier in person—like a coral snake requiring extreme caution.

Elizabeth's healthy tan emphasized a smile worthy of a toothpaste commercial. She was ten pounds too thin as demanded by television and had the muscle tone of an athlete or swimsuit model. Everything about her was conventionally blonde until she spoke. All stereotypes about dumb blondes vanished when she discussed art. Elizabeth was a rarity in the academic world, an expert with charisma and the communication skills suited to mass media. Nobody suspected the master thief beneath her polished veneer.

Elizabeth was on her way up—unlike most of the artists she skewered on her weekly show. "That's not painting, it's coloring outside the lines," was one of her more memorable reviews. "Like someone vomited up tubes of cheap acrylic paint," had become a catch phrase among her legion of dedicated followers.

Ben still cringed whenever she lambasted pretentious hacks, although he didn't disagree with her assessment that hype and hypocrisy dominated modern art. Elizabeth was accurate and unrelenting in her evaluations. She brought superior knowledge backed by unassailable fact to her insightful conclusions. Her trademark was a stylized dial which she used to rate local exhibitions and the artists who comprised the dynamic art colony that flourished in Miami. The meter was seventy-five percent red, with a small pie-slice of yellow and a sliver of green. A positive review on her show could launch an artist's career, guaranteeing gallery space in the prestigious Wynwood Art District and a healthy flow of investment-minded patrons with disposable income.

The downside of an appearance on Elizabeth's show was landing in the red zone, exposed as a no-talent *poseur* and banished to the netherworld of obscurity. Her visit to a gallery featuring Alexi's works pegged the meter in the red zone. Elizabeth had compared his pottery to "undercooked lumps of dough." His drinking, already chronic, steadily worsened after the negative review on her show.

"Have a seat." She gestured toward a chair that was too nice and looked too comfortable to be standard university issue. Same with the solid oak bookcases, antique end tables, and matching lamps. Framed pictures of Elizabeth with the governor and both state senators hung on the wall behind her desk; local celebrities, television personalities, a pop diva, and a bona fide movie star known for her art collection completed her personalized "wall of fame."

"Thank you for seeing me."

"Certainly. Anything to help." For someone who wielded such power, she seemed remarkably gracious in person. Which was the real Elizabeth? The mean-spirited slayer of pompous no-talent artists or the courteous, somewhat aloof woman seated before him?

Ben stood in front of the bookcase instead of sitting in the chair opposite her desk. The shelf at eye-level featured the two books she had authored: *The Art of Appraisal,* and *Searching for Renoir.*

"I'll be brief. Sounds like you already know about the theft of Richard Pendleton III's Renoir: *Portrait of Señorita Santangel.*"

"Indeed. Not the first time it's been stolen. Besides, I wrote the book on stolen Renoirs," Elizabeth gestured toward the bookcase.

"Oh?" *One of them, anyway.* Ben reached for the copy of *Searching for Renoir.* "I've used this book." He flipped to the flyleaf. It was from the initial printing, like his father's copy. He turned to the index to give the impression he needed to refresh his memory. "There's no mention of *Portrait of Señorita Santangel.*"

Elizabeth rearranged the pens on her desk. She straightened an already straight laptop and moved the mouse aside. There wasn't anything else on the desktop to fool with, so she swept her palm across an already clean surface and checked for dust that wasn't there.

A childhood stutter meant Ben had developed into an exceptional listener. He waited for her to continue, knowing better than to interrupt someone who was having trouble answering a simple question.

"There are certain," Elizabeth searched for the appropriate euphemism, "delicate matters, that I'm not at liberty to discuss."

"Oh?" Successful investigations favored listening rather than talking—one of Ben's core strengths, along with an insatiable curiosity about crimes and criminals. He motioned for her to continue.

"That's all."

"Not quite. A stolen Renoir is international news."

Elizabeth waited for him to continue.

She was better at remaining silent than he had given her credit for. "*Portrait of Señorita Santangel* is a major find. The sensationalism of the theft, plus a whiff of suspicious provenance—with the 'Publish or Perish' mentality of academia, it's an opportunity. A gold mine. Worth a magazine article, at least. Play your cards right, you could parlay this into a new book. Maybe ride this theft all the way to the Holy Grail: a network special. It's a gift."

"Not the kind that's given."

"But it's there for the taking." *And you didn't get your own television show by missing opportunities.*

"See for yourself." She rolled her chair away from the desk to offer him an unobstructed view through the window of her power office in the coveted Ivory Tower.

He came around her desk, enjoying the proximity. He was acutely aware of her scent, the subtle shifts in her posture, the primal awareness of mutual attraction.

Elizabeth used her sexuality to further distract him. She moved to the window and stood beside him, nearly touching.

The view was spectacular. The scenery outside the window wasn't so bad, either. Ben kept his peripheral vison focused on Elizabeth. She looked taller on television. He watched her body language, admired the fluency, began speculating on the more personal aspects of nonverbal communication.

She moved closer until they were touching. "The private, invitation-only preview is Wednesday night," she said.

"Huh?"

"I'm broadcasting my show live to help promote the venue." She rested her hands on the window ledge.

Ben looked at her fingers: *no ring.*

"See the banners?"

He shifted his gaze away from her curves. Lake Osceola and a shallow canal meandered through the University of Miami campus and flowed past her office to Biscayne Bay. Banners hanging from the light post in front of the Lowe Museum fluttered in the offshore breeze. Gaily colored standards announced the imminent arrival of a special exhibition: *Impressionists and the Sea.*

"The local buy-in has been spectacular," she said. "The University Museum is hosting the special exhibit to coincide with the America's Cup Trials."

"'*The* race,' according to Richard Pendleton III."

"He's got an outside chance to win," Elizabeth said.

Unless the boat builder repossesses his racing yacht.

"And why I didn't say anything about his questionable acquisition." She pointed at the ceiling.

Ben looked at the acoustical tiles above her desk, not getting the implied message.

"The president," she said.

He shrugged.

"Of the university. He has the office above mine."

"Ah . . ." From its humble beginnings in three empty University of Miami classrooms, the Lowe Museum had become a major player in the art world. *The Impressionists and the Sea* exhibition was a public relations coup and destined to be a gold mine for the university. The event was drawing international attention. Ben had been following the publicity in the *London Times.*

"The president vetoed your plan to expose Pendleton as a trafficker in stolen paintings?"

"Alleged trafficker. There's no proof."

Ben considered possibilities for corroboration—difficult, at best. Nearly impossible if she was complicit, and Elizabeth appeared to be part of the equation. "Not yet, anyway."

"If ever. Until then, do you have any idea how much

money the America's Cup is going to bring to the city?"

"Millions?"

"Times ten. Plus all the exposure and tourism generated by the exhibition. Besides, Richard Pendleton III sits on the museum board because he's a major donor."

"And you don't have that much tenure."

"I don't have a lot of things."

"Not an exclusive club. Doesn't change the fact that *Portrait of Señorita Santangel* has been stolen," he nodded in her direction. "More than once, according to you. Most recently from Richard Pendleton III. And the first time?"

"Professional secret."

"We're in related professions."

"More like fifth cousins." She used both hands to change the subject. "Speaking of millions, there won't be enough room at the regional airport to park all the private jets, or enough slips at the marina for the yachts."

"Big money—and lots of it. Got it the first time. Doesn't matter if it's 'Old Money' or 'New Money,' every second that goes by without a recovery moves *Portrait of Señorita Santangel* closer to being lost forever."

"That sounds like one of my lectures."

"Then we understand each other. Since you're the one who appraised the painting, I'd like to see your copies of Pendleton's documents—if you don't mind, of course."

"Where are yours?"

"In my boss's briefcase, maybe. Could be inside his safe or buried in digital form within his password-protected computer. Doesn't help me with my investigation . . ."

Ben's mind caught up with his mouth—finally—so he shut it. Elizabeth was leaning forward, her mouth slightly open, her eyes locked onto Ben's face with the penetrating gaze of a fortune teller. The epidemic of ill-advised policies on suspicious works explained his missing boss. But why was Elizabeth so interested?

She appeared to be holding her breath.

Something had shifted in their conversation to sharpen her focus. He replayed the conversation in his mind and came up with a test question. "The missing documents?"

Elizabeth drummed her fingers against the desk with a staccato beat.

Ragtime, maybe? Ben wondered if she played the piano. "About those missing documents . . .?"

"What about them?" She shifted her gaze to the left.

Typically, a sign that someone was lying, but not conclusive. He waited for her to answer his question about the documents.

Elizabeth avoided eye contact and straightened an already neat pile of folders lying on top of her desk.

"Are the copies of Pendleton's documentation in there?"

"No. Why?"

"He's part of the problem."

"He has the originals and copies. Look at his set."

"He was even more reluctant to share them than you are—which I didn't think possible. How come?"

She stared out the window and didn't answer. The rhythm of her breathing changed when she shifted her gaze.

He waited. Shouldn't take long. Elizabeth was a television personality and a university professor—she was used to talking, enamored with the sound of her own voice.

One Mississippi. Two Mississippi. Seven seconds of silence was enough elapsed time to make a hermit anxious to speak. Ben silently counted and avoided eye contact by examining the wear patterns on her reference books. The spine of her own book, *In Search of Renoir*, looked especially worn. The cover was missing from the book shelved it.

Elizabeth began drumming her fingers on *five Mississippi*. Ben ignored the percussion, although the syncopation reminded him of *Maple Leaf Rag*, by Scott Joplin.

Hidden talents. Ben watched her keep perfectly still, as rigid as someone holding their breath underwater. When she finally relaxed enough to exhale, her unconscious sigh was as incriminating as the spike on a polygraph test. She was hiding something or lying—probably both.

On *eleven Mississippi*, Elizabeth unlocked the filing cabinet. The folder she placed on top of her desk was too thin to make more than a whisper of noise upon impact.

He opened a manila folder with only three pieces of paper inside. "This is it?"

"Enough for an appraisal."

The first page was a copy of a handwritten receipt that he read aloud. "'Sold. August 2, 1938: *Portrait of Señorita Santangel*, painted by Auguste Renoir in 1876.' Why is that date so familiar?"

"I don't know." The words sounded strange coming from Elizabeth Moynihan, Ph.D.

Ben noticed her troubled expression—wondered if it was the first time she had ever admitted to not knowing the answer. "Really?"

She nodded.

"No information about the seller, the buyer, or even how much the purchase price was." Ben listed the inconsistencies.

"Sufficient for an appraisal."

He assumed her clipped tone reflected impatience. Until he looked up and recognized her tight-lipped expression. Pendleton had worn a similar, aloof-yet-guilty look, and used the same curt responses when Ben had inquired about provenance. More than just curt, evasive.

He examined the next piece of paper in the folder, a receipt. "Paid in full. November 11, 1939."

Elizabeth hid her expression by turning to look out the window.

Ben noted her discomfort. Her posture had stiffened, with knees slightly bent as if bracing for impact.

He double-checked the date on the receipt. "That was the day after *Kristallnacht*. The Nazis torched synagogues, vandalized Jewish homes and businesses, and arrested 30,000 Jewish people who ended up at the death camps—my great grandparents among them."

"I'm sorry."

"Thanks. A real tragedy. My grandmother was the only family member to survive." He laid the receipt aside and examined the last document in the folder. "An affidavit, signed by you. It says here that Solomon Santangel commissioned the work in 1876. It means the painting remained in the family's possession until . . ." He used his fingers to count the months between the dates on both receipts. "These dates are off by fifteen months. A lot can happen in a year and a half."

Her tacit silence implied consent.

"Maybe a lot did happen. Explains why there's so little documentation."

"Which *might* explain the lack of documentation," she countered.

"Which also makes it just about impossible to verify authenticity and validate provenance."

"Not entirely. Lead isotopes in the white paint are an exact match to two of Renoir's documented works painted in the same year."

"That would do it. And the lab reports?" Ben used his phone to take pictures of both documents.

She mentioned the name of a respected laboratory and downplayed her contribution, returned the papers to the file cabinet, tugging on the door to make certain it locked. She picked up her purse, sending a clear message she was ready to leave.

He ignored the hint. Her defensive posture implied she was more interested in avoiding further questioning rather than leaving. She adjusted her stance to remain behind her desk—a subtle shift behind a barrier and an increasingly protective position. She was hiding something.

Ben stalled for time and reached for her book: *Searching for Renoir.* "Any plans for a sequel?"

"I don't know."

A lie. As a tenured professor and internationally known

art critic, "I don't know" wasn't part of Elizabeth's vocabulary. She was overdue for a new book in the competitive "publish or perish" world of academia. Besides, he could tell she was lying by the self-protective shift in her posture. The flirtatious animation disappeared. The epicanthic fold at the outer corners of her eyes tensed. She clutched her purse to her chest. Was she hiding something in the purse?

He flipped the page. Searched for something he could use to chip away at her evasiveness. Maybe a compliment would reverse the sudden change in her attitude. "This is a great book."

She glanced at the book and quickly looked away.

That was more suspicious than her defensive attitude. No author could resist a second glance at their own work—like a doting parent with a child prodigy. Ben watched her resistance wane, her gaze drawn to her book like a junkie to a fix—until she noticed he was watching. She averted her eyes. Shifted her position slightly toward the window so her gaze naturally flowed away from her desk and the full-color plate featured in the book —a trifold, no less.

He spun the book around so it faced Elizabeth and unfolded the page to the detail of *Madeleine Leaning on Her Elbow with Flowers in Her Hair*. In Renoir's portrait, Madeleine's dark hair was anchored by a pink flower, although the elbow mentioned in the title extended past the edge of the canvas and wasn't pictured. The broad brush strokes, with their distinctive pastel-like appearance, were typical of Renoir's later work when rheumatoid arthritis had crippled his hands and made holding a brush agony.

"Stolen from a Houston residence on September 8, 2011," Ben added. He tilted the magnificent color plate until the view was irresistible to an adoring author. "The painting was insured by Coastal Insurance Company—one of my few unsolved cases. I've stared at this painting more than any other person on the planet."

"Maybe."

"Definitely."

"I doubt it. Any leads?"

He shook his head. "Unproven."

"Sorry to hear that."

She was lying—no inflections in her voice.

"Not as sorry as I am." Ben watched her body language for additional signs of deceit. "The frame is interesting, though. What did you think about the back of it?"

She didn't respond; she rested her elbow on the table, cupping her hand to support her chin, perhaps unintentionally replicating the pose of the woman in the stolen painting. It might have been discomfort or coincidence—possibly guilt, given her fascination with stolen Renoirs. The palm of Elizabeth's right hand masked her expression.

"On the back of the frame?" Ben repeated his question and gave her another chance to deflect his suspicions.

She pretended not to hear.

"The Yiddish characters *Beis* and *Hei*, which stand for *Baruch Hashem*, or—"

"I know what it means."

"It's also incorporated into the Santangel coat of arms." He waited, giving her another opportunity to demonstrate superior knowledge.

She glanced out the window instead of proving how smart she was.

More suspicious than an outright lie. When she didn't respond, he created another opening. "Any insights about the water stains on the frame ?"

When she didn't respond, he silently began counting *Mississippi's.*

Clack, clack, clakity-clack. Elizabeth drummed her fingers, alternating between her nails and finger tips.

Peacherine Rag, or maybe Elite Syncopation. Both Joplin tunes. One more leading question ought to do it: "Any thoughts on the gaps in ownership . . .?"

She shrugged, pretending ignorance.

Ouch. Painful to watch, nearly impossible to bear, Ben

knew how much it hurt Elizabeth to leave a question un-answered—especially since she was used to being the expert with all the answers.

"Just a couple more questions—"

"No time."

"Worth the wait. This one might interest you. It has to do with your book." He drew her attention to the color plate of *Madeleine Leaning on Her Elbow with Flowers in Her Hair.* "Why steal the frame? Whoever stole Pendleton's Renoir left the frame behind—like most art thieves."

"Is that a riddle?"

"More of a puzzle," Ben said, "with pieces that don't fit."

"I was never very good at games. Comes from being an only child."

As a college professor, published author, and recognized expert with her own television show, it was obvious Elizabeth loved to be the smartest person in the room and have everyone know it. Yet she had just passed up several opportunities to prove it. *Strange.*

She brushed past him and rested her hand on the door-knob. "I've got a class waiting."

"I'll walk with you."

"No thanks."

"Just one more thing—"

"—No time. I'm late for my class."

On a Friday? At 5:00 p.m.?

She placed the palm of her hand on his back, ushered him into the hall, and ducked into the elevator—putting an abrupt end to his questions.

The stairs were faster and safer. He took them two at a time, ran out of the lobby, and took refuge behind a thicket of Yaupon Holly. The white blossoms smelled like grape bubble-gum.

Elizabeth exited the building, walking with the motions of a woman on autopilot, adopting the rote, mindless sort of gait of a person who had followed the same route for years. Her shortcut led to the Pavia parking garage next to the museum and a prestige faculty parking space at ground level. She got into a red two-door Mercedes-Benz sports car. Ben snuck close enough to recognize the distinctive yellow-on-blue decal of Coral Gables Estates, an exclusive, gated community within walking distance of her office. She accelerated out of the garage and rolled through the first stop sign, ran a bleeding yellow light at the exit and kept her foot on the gas pedal.

F riday, November 1: 8:30 p.m., Key Largo

Chapter 6

Ben followed two meandering ruts of matted grass and wild sea oats that served as a rudimentary driveway connecting his father's property to the main road. The normally indistinct path showed signs of recent traffic; the tires kicked up pieces of gravel that pinged against the fenders of the rental car. Flashing lights from a Key Largo Police car spun disjointed circles of kaleidoscopic red and blue lights that disappeared into the forest surrounding the rusted gate and sagging fence. He slammed on the brakes. Crime scene tape stretched across the palm trees flanking the entrance. A police officer stood guard.

"You can't go any further, sir."

"I live here," Ben said. "Is it my father?"

"And you are?"

"Benjamin Abrams."

"I.D.?"

Ben dug his license out of his wallet for the third, fourth time today? He'd lost count.

The officer shined a flashlight on his license and in his eyes. She leaned her head toward her left shoulder and spoke into the microphone attached to her uniform shirt.

"Is it my father? My brother Alexi? What's wrong?"

The radio squawked a reply. "Just a minute, sir. The chief detective will be right out."

"Lauren?"

"Detective Welles. Yes, sir."

"That's her maiden name."

The officer shrugged. "I'm new, sir."

"What happened?"

"I don't know. Detective Welles will be with you, shortly."

Lauren Welles wore the lightweight khaki shorts and uniform shirt of the Key Largo Police Force. The steel-toed boots would have looked incongruous on someone without the toned legs of a runner, but she managed to pull off the look by folding over her socks to taper the abrupt change between her shins and the padded tops. She could probably still wear the same dress he'd pinned the corsage to when they went to the Senior Prom fifteen years earlier.

"Ben. Hi. Relax. Your dad and Alexi are fine."

"What is it?"

"You'd better see for yourself." She turned to the officer. Her fluency in sign language helped explain the connection between Lauren's expressive hands and her inability to talk without using them for punctuation. "It's okay. He's with me."

If someone held Lauren's hands still, she'd have to lie on her back and kick her legs to talk. Her older sister had lost her hearing in childhood from a virulent strain of mumps. The two had been inseparable, so sign language became Lauren's native tongue. The unsolved homicide of her sister explained Lauren's decision to pursue a career in law enforcement, as well.

"I heard you were back. What's it been? Ten years?"

"More like fifteen. You haven't changed much." The compliment came easily since there was no lie involved.

"Your hair is curlier," she tilted her head, "and even redder. I didn't think that was possible. Sorry. Not much of a reunion."

"Now that we're caught up, want to tell me what's going on?"

"A body. Looks like murder. I was afraid it was you. Same height. Same build."

"You couldn't tell?" Ben's imagination had been fueled by the special effect's capabilities of Hollywood. He assumed the worst.

"We found him next to your dock. It's bad, but . . ."

"But what?"

"I'll need you to take a look. With a murder, we don't want

to waste any time getting an ID."

"You're sure?"

"About the murder? Definitely. Puncture marks on his neck. Probably from a taser gun that shoots barbs. Looks like he drowned. Probably unconscious when somebody threw him in."

Ben followed her around the side of the house and down to the dock. She knelt beside a body bag. The creases were still sharp from the original folds; outgassing plastic carried the pungent chemical odor of cheap hydrocarbons. "Brace yourself," she said, and grabbed the zipper. "He's been in the water long enough for the fish to have taken a few bites."

The smell was bad, the damage from bite marks worse. He closed his eyes and spun away, staggered a few steps upwind until the odor subsided. The nightmare image remained. A stiff breeze coming off the ocean and the lack of a recent meal saved him from vomiting but dry heaves left him bent over, hands on his knees, head dizzy.

Lauren consoled him with a hand on his shoulder. From an old habit, her fingers came to rest against the tender skin at the base of his neck; one of the few ticklish spots on his body.

He leaned his head toward her touch without thinking— muscle memory, or nostalgia perhaps.

Except a disfigured corpse was in a body bag near their feet. Lauren removed her hand, and Ben tilted his head in the opposite direction. The moment passed. He concentrated on taking shallow breaths.

"Made any enemies lately?"

"What?" Ben felt faint but wouldn't admit it.

"Sorry. I don't mean to scare you, but maybe someone thought that was you."

"You're kidding—right?"

"Did you get a good look at him?"

"Unfortunately."

"Same build as you, same age, height, weight, and found on your dad's property right about the time you show up." Lauren used her fingers to list the reasons he should be worried.

"Wearing a nice suit." She used her thumb to mark the fifth similarity. "Any recent cases come to mind? Someone nursing a murderous grudge, maybe?"

"I've put a few folks in jail, sure. But most of them are fences or forgers. A few lawyers and businessmen. Not really the sort of criminals who go around killing people. Although . . ."

"Although what?" Lauren tensed.

Ben felt the intensity of her stare all the way through to his spine; he wouldn't like Lauren hunting him if he was guilty of a crime. "I've got my suspicions about the 'what.' *Portrait of Señorita Santangel*, a Renoir. Everything about my latest case is suspicious."

"As suspicious as a dead body? How about taking a closer look? I'd rather you didn't wash up on the same beach."

"Oh? Sounds like you're taking a personal interest." Ben could still feel the soft caress of her fingers on the back of his neck.

"Can't handle the additional case load."

She didn't sound completely serious. *Encouraging.* And he hated to appear weak. He peeked and then couldn't look away. "You're right. That was a nice suit." Crabs or carnivorous fish had helped themselves to a buffet. "I don't think his own mother would recognize him."

"But do you?"

"Enough of what's left of him—mostly the yellow bowtie. *D'Erve*: a guy who used to be the best middleman for stolen art in the world."

"Are you sure?"

"When there's a stolen Renoir, he's the guy I look for."

"Looks like you found him," Lauren deadpanned. "I'll run the fingerprints and confirm your ID tomorrow."

"I'm sitting *shiva*."

"I won't ring the doorbell."

S
unday, November 3, 6:18 a.m., Key Largo

Chapter 7

The ocean sighed and sent a gust of wind to flutter the dusty black tarp beneath Ben's feet. Palm fronds clacked above his head and sounded like a gunshot. A cold emptiness in his chest expanded, moving from iceberg to glacier as he cupped his fingers and dredged a handful of dirt to throw on his mother's coffin. She had begun fading away for five years before anyone realized part of her was missing. Alzheimer's: a slow death by incremental amounts, a forgone conclusion, and yet he had been dreading this moment since her prognosis.

He waited until the last three stars from Saturday night faded from view. He approached her grave; he held his hand over the unstained wood of his mother's simple casket and pressed his fingers together instead of letting the dirt fall into the gaping hole. A few grains of sand swirled free and slowly spiraled into the void.

She had been alive just two days earlier, although her mind had predeceased her. She wouldn't have recognized him if he had taken the time to visit. Now it was too late, and he had the rest of his life to grieve.

He relaxed his grip and let the soil filter between his fingers. A pebble, then a small dirt clod struck the wood with a dull thud—the hollow sound of permanent loss. He knew it would sound like music to her ears, if she could hear—if she could remember to listen.

He brushed his hands together to remove the dust and didn't turn away until the last grain of sand settled onto the casket. His mother was finally free and he was happy for her. Death *and* asylum; relief mixed with loss and formed guilt.

He caught a whiff of alcohol when Alexi joined him grave-side. His brother looked like he'd slept in his clothes; he had the bloodshot eyes and flushed cheeks of a fulltime drinker. His arm shook. He spilled some of the dirt before he moved close enough to hold his hand above the coffin. Alexi looked in danger of falling into his own mother's grave—or joining her within the year unless he stopped drinking. Three empty spaces to the right of the pit meant there was plenty of room in the family plot.

He put his arm around his brother's shoulders. Alexi instinctively leaned away from his touch, so Ben unwound his arm and turned to watch the sunrise. A storm front had stalled at the edge of the world where the ocean and horizon met. A thin band of light peeked beneath the edges, turning the dark black bottoms of rain clouds a yellowish gray. His mother had died at daybreak on Friday. Jewish law called for burial within twenty-four-hours, but because of *Shabbat*, and rules against burial on the sabbath, she remained true to form and was late to her own funeral.

His father shuffled forward. He needed both hands to maneuver his walker and looked as unsteady as Alexi. He grabbed a handful of dirt and had trouble letting go of it.

Ben stepped forward to help. Together, they began *El Malei Rachamim,* the chanted prayer using the traditional Hebrew name of the deceased . . .

Sitting *shiva*: Ben placed a pitcher of water on the front porch of his father's house so visitors could show respect for the dead by washing their hands before entering. The doorbell was already broken, so he unlatched the screen. It was warm enough to prop the front door open to allow visitors to enter peacefully and quietly without performing any labor or distracting those in mourning. There was no need to lower the chairs in his father's house since they were already uncomfortable or piled with books; the traditional mourning ritual of sitting on a box or a stool would have been an improvement. Alexi was in the kitchen preparing the condolence meal. So far, so good, but tradition called for the family to light a candle and keep it burning for seven days after the funeral. A vanilla-scented candle was all he could find and the house smelled like a bakery.

Family tradition required an argument about something —anything, when humor could no longer forestall grief. The choreography might change but the same two-step dance around loss remained the same. Both brothers blamed each other for a shared pattern they refused to admit. Alexi preferred humor to sadness and Ben was more comfortable with anger. Fortunately, the police intervened before the inevitable argument escalated.

"Hello?" Lauren called.

"In here." Ben recognized her voice.

Lauren was in uniform. The file folder she carried looked thick enough for bad news. "Where's your father?"

"Where else?" Alexi tilted his head and glanced upstairs.

"Working?"

"Dreaming," Alexi said. "Still chasing the same dream— not any closer to catching it. Good luck getting him to come down."

Ben nodded. "Might take a warrant."

"Or a pry bar." If Alexi meant it as a joke, his tone betrayed him.

Lauren raised her eyebrows.

Ben saw the unasked question and formulated a diplomatic answer. He pointed at his father's walker. "He has a hard time coming downstairs."

"That hasn't changed." Lauren was no stranger to the household quirks. "I—we, need to speak with him."

"Right. Probably be a lot easier if we all go up there."

"Deal me out." Alexi turned the burner to simmer and escaped to his room, his normal refuge when a conversation turned serious.

There was compassion in Lauren's knowing look, and sadness, too. She used her hands to help translate uncharitable thoughts into tactful English phrases. "In my job, you learn to recognize patterns. Sometimes there's not much we can do other than let things play out."

"Are you referring to Alexi or my father?"

"With families, there's always more to the story." Raised by mortician parents, Lauren was too polite to speak ill of the dead or slander the survivors, present company included.

It was a quality that made him nervous. Ben had never quite felt like he measured up to her standards. She also brought out the best in him, a compassionate side he typically set aside from fear of being hurt. For the first time since he stepped off the plane, he was glad to be back.

"What's in the folder?" He changed the subject and told himself it was diplomacy instead of habit.

"A rap sheet and some photos."

"The floater?"

She nodded. "*D'Erve.*"

"Let's go upstairs, then. "First my mom, now the floater. This is a day for disposing of bodies."

Ben and Lauren invaded his father's inner sanctum, despite the upstairs having been off-limits for thirty years. Shelves lined every wall and sagged beneath books and mounds of paper. A layer of dust softened the edges; additional stacks of research material covered the bare spots in the carpet. The clutter ended at the ceiling, where his father had replaced the original fixtures with high-intensity lights. A shadow didn't stand a chance near the desk in the corner, where all three lights from a floor lamp illuminated a framed object attached to the wall.

"You framed an old key?" Despite contact lenses, Ben had trouble reading fine print. It didn't help that he was color-blind and the stylized script at the bottom of the frame was written in gold leaf. "*La llave de oro abre todas las puertas.*"

"The golden key opens every door," his father provided the translation without correcting Ben's mispronunciation—an unexplainable departure from tradition. Lauren's stabilizing presence helped. His father credited his recently departed wife, whose spirit had been hovering upstairs since her entombment. The ancestors retained their morbid sense of humor and chose a skeleton key to serve as common ground.

"It still unlocks the gate to our estate in Madrid." His father tapped his fingernail against the glass.

"Spain?" Ben asked.

"Of course."

Ben ignored his father's annoyed tone and brushed aside the implied insult. Maybe it didn't rate a burning bush on the miracle scale, but his tolerance toward his father's prickly nature was monumental in its own way and proof of divine intervention. The golden key had never faced a more resilient lock. The ancestors were working overtime brokering a ceasefire and earning their pay.

"I've never seen this. The wooden box is unusual." Ben moved beside him until they were almost touching. His father smelled like an old man, a stale combination of worn clothing and trace elements of pipe smoke. And he had shrunk. For the first time in his life, Ben was taller than his father. He noticed the slight stoop to his shoulders and the papery-thin texture of the skin on his hands. His veins formed a purple spiderweb.

"Your grandmother made the box. Read what's engraved on the shaft." His father pointed to the archaic script on the key.

Ben leaned forward until the small print came into focus. "I recognize the Yiddish characters: *Beis Hei.*"

"An abbreviation for *Baruch Hasem.*" A faint tremor passed through his father's arm. He had curled the other three fingers of his hand into his palm and was using his knuckles to remain upright by leaning against the wall. His wrist was almost too weak to support his weight; he compensated by resting his other arm against a stack of books.

"Praise God," Ben translated for Lauren. "It's Yiddish."

"So was your floater," she said. "His alias, anyway. *D'Erve.*"

"The Fence?" His father chuckled.

"Did I say that wrong?" Lauren asked.

"No. No. Just that it also has a deeper meaning." His father took off his glasses.

Ben recognized the prelude to a professorial discourse and made a discrete cutting motion with his hand to stop her from asking a follow-up question.

"Besides being a middle-man for stolen goods?"

Stop. Ben held up both palms.

His father untucked his shirt tail.

No more questions. Ben mouthed.

"Something else?" She missed the signal.

Too late.

His father began polishing the lenses: the point of no return. When the pedantic professor emerged, there was no stopping him.

He held his glasses up to the light for inspection and peered myopically through the lenses. He cleared his throat with a deliberate, "*Ahem.*"

The idiosyncratic sound triggered the very warning that Ben had been trying so desperately to communicate. Lauren's eyes grew wider as her memory got better. She recalled previous lectures prefaced with the distinctive sound and looked to Ben for an intervention.

There was nothing he could do except lean his shoulder against the wall and get comfortable. He met Lauren's gaze, shook his head sadly, and directed her attention to the only available chair.

"The first letter Christopher Columbus sent back to Spain from his exploratory voyage in 1492 was addressed to his primary financial backer, Louis de Santangel..." His father inhaled. The oxygen machine clicked and delivered enough for him to finish the sentence, "a Jewish merchant who agreed to loan the royal court the money for Columbus's journey . . ." He waited for the next puff, "in exchange for a special charter granting his family protection from the Spanish Inquisition." His father stopped polishing his glasses and returned them to his nose.

Ben's shoulder hadn't turned numb and the lecture was already over? He turned his head to look at his father, watched him anticipate the mechanical click and how he inhaled at the exact moment the machine delivered another burst of oxygen. After two cycles, he continued.

"Hand me . . ." He ran out of breath and pointed to the key.

Ben took the frame off the wall. "I just saw these same characters on the frame of Richard Pendleton's stolen Renoir."

"*Beis Hei.*" His father inhaled greedily and held out his hand for the key, timing the request to coincide with the next burst of oxygen. "Inscribed on the back of every painting in the Santangel collection."

"What does it unlock?" Lauren asked.

"Many secrets," he waited for a burst of air.

"She was being literal," Ben said.

His father's grin faded into a frown. He lowered his head so the dirty look he sent in Ben's direction was unobstructed by his glasses. The portable oxygen machine huffed. It took three bursts of air for the proper sarcastic tone. "I know that."

Lauren stepped between them before Ben could deliver an impertinent response. She raised the manila folder and opened it with the same motion as the parting of the Red Sea.

Ben bit back his antagonistic response.

His father waved his hand in a vague, apologetic gesture.

With this final intercession, the ancestors were out of miracles, taxed beyond the limits of spiritual intervention. The rest was up to Lauren, who had prior experience with family dynamics and had brought two extra copies of the police report—one for each headstrong man.

"Your floater, Harold Feinstein, a.k.a. *D'Erve.*" She opened her own copy of the rap sheet. "Plenty of arrests. Very few convictions."

"Insurance fraud, possession of stolen property, extortion, bribery," Ben read from the lengthy rap sheet. "Not exactly in a rut."

"No wonder he ended up dead," his father said. "As to why he had to wash ashore beneath my dock—*oy gevalt*."

"Woe is me," whispered Ben in translation.

"Maybe this is why." Lauren pulled two photos from the folder and laid them beside the key.

"*Beis Hei*. I knew it. This is a photo of the back of the frame that was around Pendleton's stolen Renoir: *Portrait of Señorita Santangel*." Ben reached for his phone to take a picture.

"Where did you find this?" His father's hands shook as he reached for the photo. The strap from around the oxygen machine slipped off his shoulder.

"In a waterproof money belt."

"No. This painting." He cursed and waved the copy hard enough to make it bend in the middle.

"No painting. Just the photo of the back of the frame," Lauren said. "Tucked away in a hidden compartment."

"It's the painting that was just stolen," Ben added. "It's got to be. *Portrait of Señorita Santangel* was stolen on Halloween. From Richard Pendleton III."

"I know that!" His father jabbed at the photo with his finger, struggling for breath. "Same characters." He waited impatiently for the next puff of oxygen, "as on the key." It took two more more oxygen doses until he could continue. "The Santangel coat of arms." He used the same finger to scan a lifetime's worth of books, moving left to right along each shelf with the fluency of a master librarian. His finger stopped and he lurched forward in the same direction, without waiting for his body to catch up with his mind. He stumbled and clutched at Ben's forearm for support.

His father's grasp felt unnaturally warm—almost hot—like the Devil's touch endangering a true believer's soul. It was the same spot his father had so violently avoided graveside and Ben's first impulse was to pull away.

"Over there . . ." He struggled for breath. "Under the window . . ." He pointed to the bookcase in the far corner, too impatient to wait for the machine to deliver enough oxygen so he might finish the sentence.

Ben followed the direction of his father's finger, as unerring as a compass orienting to true north. After two steps he recognized the cover: *Searching for Renoir*, by Elizabeth Moynihan. He tilted the book away from its neighbors and laid it on his father's desk. Dust motes danced in the sunlight when he opened the cover. It was a signed first edition.

His father removed his hand from Ben's forearm to lean on the desk. Both men pulled apart. Lauren moved beside Ben and gently leaned against him before the angle of separation grew critical and he lost his balance. He didn't shy away from *her* contact. She seemed content to allow the touch, encouraged it, even, pressing against him with a subtle pressure made noteworthy by implied consent.

The book naturally fell open to a full-color trifold of Renoir's *Madeleine Leaning on Her Elbow with Flowers in Her Hair*.

"I know this picture," Ben said. "The painting has been missing since 2001—one of my rare, unsolved cases."

"*Meh*. Look at the frame." Ben's father unfolded the insert and placed his index finger on the upper left-hand corner of the photograph. "Same dark wood as is *D'Erve*'s photo. Probably the same frame-maker, a Parisian carpenter who was popular in the mid-to-late 1870's."

"I can narrow the year down to 1876," Ben said. "Renoir used the same mistress as a subject in three of his paintings from that year. It makes sense he'd use the same frame-maker."

"See how the wood grain is almost identical to the painting in *D'Erve*'s picture?" His father used a magnifying glass to enlarge the detail. "*Beis Hei* is inscribed on the backing. I know it. If I could see the back of the painting, I could prove it."

"I know who might have a picture of the back of the frame," Ben said. "She wrote this book: Elizabeth Moynihan. Same lady who appraised the Renoir stolen from Richard Pendleton III: *Portrait of Señorita Santangel.*"

"How can this be?" His father asked.

"I don't know. Yet. I'll pay another visit to Elizabeth Moynihan tomorrow and find out."

M

onday, November 4, 9:00 a.m.

Chapter 8

The University of Miami Library was on the opposite side of campus from the lofty real estate occupied by Elizabeth Moynihan's office. Ben left his ink pen and pocketknife in a locker and donned linen gloves. A distinctly academic aroma—old leather and aged parchment—permeated the University of Miami's special collection. Wealth measured in knowledge lined the shelves; a card catalogue firmly anchored the room in the previous century. A series of maps with dwindling swaths of uncharted territory documented earlier centuries, and a staff member who looked like she had been eligible for retirement for as long as Ben had been alive sat at the information kiosk.

"I would like to see every book and all the research material that Elizabeth Moynihan has checked out in the last month." Elizabeth Moynihan's appraisal of Pendleton's Renoir had stretched the limits of unanswered questions beyond mere coincidence. Pendleton's insurance policy was new, so his acquisition had to be equally recent. Ben slid two fingers into his shirt pocket for a business card. He had expected an argument or a flat-out refusal for such a suspicious request.

"Certainly," she said, after looking at his card. "Glad to help."

"Really?"

"I knew your mother—from temple," Mrs. Goldsmith explained. "If there's anything I can do to help, just ask. And I will say *Kaddish* or *El Maleh Rachamim* for her soul."

"Thank you."

Mrs. Goldsmith—call me Goldie—returned pushing a cart piled with dusty catalogues and clothbound tomes. "Some of these were in the stacks."

"This is part of it—has to be." Ben rested his finger below the heading. "A June 29th, 1939 catalogue from the Degenerate Art auction at the Theodor Fischer Gallery in Lucerne, Switzerland."

"Theodor Fischer. Why does that name sound familiar?" She began transferring items from the library cart to Ben's table.

"*Entartete Kunst,*" Ben prompted.

"Oh yes, of course. Hitler's degenerate art exhibition. Quite shocking for the time." Goldie had a full head of pure white hair that must have taken a long time to turn from black to gray before losing all its color. She had the naturally thin physique of those who endure and looked old enough to have attended the *Entartete Kunst* opening in Berlin in 1937. Hitler, a frustrated artist, retaliated against the art institutions that criticized his work by having 16,000 modern paintings removed from German museums when he came to power. *Entartete Kunst*—Hitler's degenerate art show premiered in Berlin in 1937. Ultimately, more than 70,000 paintings were confiscated, stolen, or destroyed. A few found their way out the backdoor and into private collections.

Ben opened a facsimile copy of the June 29th, 1939 sales catalogue from the Degenerate Art auction at the Theodor Fischer Gallery in Lucerne, Switzerland. There had to be a discrepancy in the publication somewhere, otherwise Elizabeth Moynihan wouldn't have gone to the trouble of requesting a special copy.

Some people watch television to relax; Ben assembled jigsaw puzzles, turning them face-down for the added challenge. He spread the books and magazines on the table and sorted through every item Elizabeth Moynihan had requested until patterns and similarities emerged. Renoir was the common link between all the unanswered questions—specifically stolen Renoir paintings.

Like a jigsaw puzzle with an extra piece, a dusty textbook published prior to World War II appeared out of place among the collection of glossy catalogues and coffee-table books featuring full-color photographic plates of Impressionist paintings. Ben checked the index. A chapter on how to photograph art appeared insignificant until he cross-checked for featured works: *Madeleine Leaning on Her Elbow with Flowers in Her Hair*, stolen in 2011. There had been a smug knowing in Elizabeth's response when he had mentioned the theft, as if she was harboring an inside joke too personal to share.

He opened the book to a chapter on the best practices for photographing paintings—circa 1936, touting the advantages of color photography, made affordable with the emergence of Kodachrome film—and learned from someone else's mistakes.

A panel showing the effects of overexposure highlighted the intricate patterns of craquelure in the lower left-hand corner of an unexpected, uncatalogued painting: *Portrait of Señorita Santangel*. It hadn't been listed in the credits, yet had served as the subject for demonstrating improper lighting. As unique as a fingerprint, the minute variations and cracks in the surface of the painting were on prominent display—heightened by the example of how intense lighting can fade the natural coloration of a painting and produce a washed-out photograph.

"Find something?" Goldie was back from her search for Elizabeth Moynihan's recent book requests.

"A picture of *Portrait of Señorita Santangel*. The stolen painting I'm looking for, the same one Elizabeth Moynihan found." He turned the book around to show her the image of a striking young Sephardic woman wearing a low-cut blouse. A tiara anchored the raven-black hair atop her head. Luminous brown eyes below dramatic brows dared the viewer to look away, but it was impossible to stop staring at her compelling face. A fair complexion, a hint of color in her cheeks, the knowing expression of a shared secret—perhaps an illicit lover; all these attributes animated the painting with timeless beauty.

"Oh my." Goldie raised a hand to cover her open mouth. "Santangel. Why does that name sound familiar?"

"The *Santangel* family goes all the way back to the Spanish

Inquisition. They financed Christopher Columbus' first voyage until they were kicked out of Spain. Now they own banks in Vienna and castles in Europe. My great-grandparents owned a fine art gallery on the *Donaukanal* in Vienna, and the Santangels were their best clients."

"Hmmm." Goldie crossed the room to the information kiosk and wiggled the mouse to re-energize the screen. "Sounds like it's worth taking a closer at Elizabeth Moynihan's requests."

"That's what I've been doing."

"Only the books she's checked out to read. What about the books she's written?" Goldie tapped the side of her head. "I'm thinking like a research librarian."

"I own both of them."

"That you know of. What if there's more? Or magazine articles, maybe. Research papers, a blog post, interviews . . ." Goldie logged on to the computer. "Time for some serious searching."

Ben pushed his chair away from the table. He thought better on his feet. For exceptionally difficult problems, he resorted to pacing.

"Aha," Goldie rolled her chair away from the screen so Ben could see the results.

"Elizabeth Moynihan's Master's Thesis: *Missing Masterpieces*. Sounds interesting."

"Strange." Goldie clicked through several screens. "The library copy is reported stolen."

"A digital copy, maybe?"

"Students have to pay extra for that." She moved the pointer and clicked on a link. "Nope. Nothing in the database." She navigated to a different screen. "Here's her Doctoral Dissertation: *Presumed Missing*."

"Is it?" Ben asked. "Missing?"

Goldie switched screens. "Yes, to both. The print copy is missing and the digital copy has been removed on request."

"Sounds like she's uncovered some lucrative secrets she doesn't want to share. Making an appointment to see her is out. She's not returning my calls, texts, or emails. I need to find out what her office hours are so I can drop by unannounced."

"Why wait?" Goldie asked. "She's practically right next door—taping her show on campus."

"I thought she did that on Saturday mornings."

"It's a special—part of the festivities for the Impressionists and the Sea exhibit that opens tomorrow night at the museum." Goldie glanced at the clock. "If you hurry, you can catch the last ten minutes."

Elizabeth Moynihan taped her show at the Public Broadcasting station located on the University of Miami campus. It was a standing-room-only audience, with a waiting list for season tickets. Ben gave the security guard one of his business cards and a brief explanation. It worked so well, he wished he had thought to try it at sold-out concerts. He muted his phone and eased into the studio for the taping of the final segment: "Guess the Artist."

Elizabeth moved to the edge of the stage and swept her gaze across the entire crowd. These were her fans; many of them leaned forward in their seats. She put a hand to the side of her face as if sharing a secret with 300 of her closest friends. The inside story was guaranteed to be scandalous.

The lights dimmed. Stage hands dressed in black moved the furniture off the set.

"Guess the artist." The audience chanted.

A baby spotlight illuminated Elizabeth as she held a microphone to her lips. "Guess the artist who combined the body of his mistress and head of his benefactress to produce several landmark works. This despite them being, arguably, the two most important and influential women in his life."

The audience was too well behaved for anyone to shout out the answer or hazard a guess. A few of the more knowledgeable people whispered discretely among themselves.

Ben narrowed it down to three possible artists. Given

Elizabeth's fascination with Renoir, Pierre-Auguste certainly had the inside track. The back wall of the set was a giant screen. It flickered to life with a familiar deep blue. The outlines of a faint image appeared as the screen energized. When a photograph of Madame Charpentier materialized, he knew his hunch was right. Renoir's style and brushstrokes were too distinctive for Elizabeth to use any of his canvases as audience clues.

"This is the woman who introduced tonight's mystery artist to the wealthy social class, a woman who loved to dress up as Marie Antoinette. Her connections made it possible for him to evolve from being just another talented, starving artist to the darling of the art-buying set." Once again Elizabeth put her hand to the side of her face to deliver the salacious gossip—using the gesture as a comedian would employ a drumroll before delivering the punchline. "Behind her back, malicious gossips called her Marie Antoinette cut off at the bottom." The focus of the picture changed to a closeup of Madame's rather generous proportions which made her physique suitable to nude bathers in classical compositions.

"Well-fed" might have got Ben slapped had he uttered it aloud. *Zaftig* or calorically-challenged were other euphemisms equally hazardous to his health. None of these synonyms were remotely acceptable to the predominately female audience.

Elizabeth stepped away from the edge of the stage to deliver her condemning lines. The distance exacerbated the harsh tone and dramatic change in her demeanor. "I believe 'voluptuous,' is still used today, although 'Rubenesque' is the denigrating term currently in vogue with the artworld."

A collective protest swept through the crowd. Elizabeth joined them in mutual distaste of such prejudiced misogyny and used the emotion gathering in the room to launch her next lines.

"In a later portrait, the artist draped her in a 'voluptuous' black dress and posed her children on a couch beside her to hide her true feminine form. Of course, this canvas was widely accepted, attaining masterpiece status. Some double-standards never change."

Her fans voiced their disapproval. When she waved her arms to encourage them, the women in the audience raised the decibel level of their protest.

Special effects transitioned the image of Madame Charpentier into a kaleidoscope of prisms that filled the screen and pulsed as colored lights swept through the audience like reflections from a mirrored disco ball. The screen returned to blue. Black and gray pixels formed dots that solidified into a new photograph.

"The mistress," Elizabeth announced the next picture. "Featured from the neck down in several works until her untimely death." Her tone implied the woman's premature passing was the mystery artist's fault.

Ben recognized Renoir's favorite model from 1876, Marguerite LeGrand. Renoir wasn't responsible for her death. In fact, Ben had studied the painting Renoir gave Dr. Paul Gachet as a reward for his valiant efforts to save her. Renoir also paid for Marguerite's funeral, but Elizabeth knew how to push her audience's buttons . . . and plug her own book.

"There's more," she promised. "Much more, and you can read about it in *Searching for Renoir*!"

The cover of her book flashed onto the screen. The opening bars of the theme music associated with her show began playing. "Applause" appeared on the monitors above the stage although the cue wasn't necessary.

"I'll be in the lobby to autograph copies," she promised. Both of her books were for sale and everyone in the audience funneled past an assembly line of booksellers and cashiers before reaching the signing table positioned at the exit. Ushers held the audience to give Elizabeth a head start so she could reach the author's table before a potential customer managed to escape.

Thomas Benson joined the line of autograph seekers and book buyers. He watched Elizabeth Moynihan's show and had a thief's intuition about crooks, crooked artists, and crooked art dealers. Benson had been laundering money for organized crime figures for the past decade. Now he had expanded his services to dealing in stolen art for his cash-rich clients. Like morbid breadcrumbs, a trail of bodies linked him with his clients and their illicit activities. Benson catered to the newly rich—drug dealers with sacks of dirty money they wanted to invest. Since most of his clients weren't troubled by a conscience, Benson had expanded his portfolio to include masterpiece paintings. Since his clients were crooks, they were partial to stolen paintings. There were fewer questions about the purchases: no receipts. And it was easier to hide a valuable painting than an airplane full of drug money.

Elizabeth Moynihan occupied a unique position in the art world, with unparalleled access to the honest and dishonest elements in the rarefied world of collectable art. Someone with a mean streak that wide would naturally be drawn to the criminal element so prevalent in the big-money, small morality field of masterpiece art—a place where most of the appreciation was financial, and investment potential took precedence over provenance.

Benson tucked a business card between the cover and flyleaf of Elizabeth's newest book. His hands, despite their immaculate manicure, had simian hair that extended past his knuckles, and hinted at a missing link in his walk-in closet full of skeletons. His pink palms and soft fingers suggested a lifetime without an hour of honest work.

He approached the table. "I'm also a fan of your earlier work: *Missing Masterpieces* and *Presumed Missing*."

"Oh?" Elizabeth paused from her assembly-line approach to autographing books for groupies. Only her most adoring fans were familiar with her master's thesis and doctoral dissertation. "I'm flattered."

"Don't be." Benson had stolen his copies from the University of Miami Library. "You should be worried, instead." He opened the flyleaf and handed her the business card serving as a bookmark. "Call the number on the card. You'll be needing a new fence."

"I beg your pardon?"

"You need a replacement fence. Consider me your new 'General Contractor,' now that *D'Erve* is permanently out of business." He smirked at the deadly pun.

Elizabeth didn't know much Yiddish. She recognized the nickname of the world's premier dealer in stolen paintings, however. If *D'Erve* was dead, she could be next. "How do you—"

"Take the card. Call the number," Benson ordered. He lowered his voice to deliver a parting threat certain to give Elizabeth a sleepless night. "I know about *Entartete Kunst* and the Theodor Fisher Art Gallery in Lucerne. And then there's the Santangel coat of arms burned into the frame that was around *Portrait of Señorita Santangel*. Don't make me call Ben Abrams, unless you *want* to go to jail."

Tuesday, November 5, 8:00 a.m.

Chapter 9

Elizabeth Moynihan lived in the house built by her grandparents. Coral Gables Estates occupied a picturesque area of Historic Miami and formed an exclusive bastion against common urban sprawl. Stands of non-native trees and invasive vines ensured privacy for the rich while offering nesting opportunities for pine warblers, red-tailed hawks, great crested flycatchers, and an entire percussion section's worth of woodpeckers.

The elaborate entryway was the size of a large apartment, with a massive chandelier that hung from an anchor chain salvaged from an ocean liner. Twin staircases curved upward for three flights before connecting to a lofty balcony high enough to create its own cloud formations. A specialized key unlocked the door to a bedroom furnished with bird's-eye maple antiques; mirrored display racks of designer shoes filled the entire back wall of her walk-in closet. The fob on her keychain bore the iconic three-pointed star of the Mercedes-Benz logo, but when she pressed the button with the image of an open trunk, the display case opened like a clamshell to reveal a full-sized vault. The subterfuge amused her. She unlocked the vault door and stepped into her private gallery.

She sat in her custom-made viewing chair and stared at Renoir's *Madeleine Leaning on Her Elbow with Flowers in Her Hair* —stolen from the Houston couple who had hired her to do the appraisal. Elizabeth loved the risk of owning a stolen masterpiece—craved the connection to a timeless work of art touched by the masters. The dopamine rush from owning an original canvas was simply a bonus, a reminder of her personal link to immortality.

Her gaze traveled to the ultimate Renoir— an Impressionist canvas so few people had seen that it was almost unknown: *Portrait of Señorita Santangel.* Now it was hers and no thug like Thomas Benson was going to take it away from her.

The intruder alert sounded. A green light on the alarm panel turned to yellow. The light for the front-gate sensor started flashing.

"Hello?" The intercom reverberated with static when someone stood too close to the microphone. "Winged Sandal Courier Service. Delivery, ma'am."

Elizabeth pushed the intercom button to transmit. "I don't want to be disturbed."

The courier leaned closer to the speaker and mashed the call button. "It's marked urgent, ma'am."

Elizabeth slid aside a wooden panel. The recessed monitor displayed video feeds from her security cameras, and she recognized the courier's uniform. Verified he had an envelope in his hand. "I'll need to see some ID."

It was a bad picture, even by driver's license standards.

"Who is it from?"

"Isabella Santangel." He broadcast another burst of static.

"Who?"

"*Señorita* Isabella Santangel. I think I'm saying that right."

"Impossible."

He held the envelope up to the camera so she could verify the address.

"Very well." She entered a code to open the gate.

Elizabeth signed for the delivery and sent the courier away with an acceptable tip. She tore open the envelope. A prepaid phone, an unremarkable piece of printer paper listing five nearby locations, and a sheet of photo paper with troubling images had been stuffed inside.

She turned on the phone and waited for a call.

Thomas Benson stared out the window of his suite at the Miami Biltmore Hotel and watched a sleek black Labrador retriever splash into the canal, disappear beneath the surface, and then emerge with a bright yellow ball clenched in its teeth. It was unusual to see a small, dark-skinned child on the private grounds, but he recognized the child's protective detail, two immense men with the same distinctive tribal facial scarring of the deposed African dictator occupying the adjoining estate. He waited until the African contingent moved on before he headed south along the walking path paralleling the canal.

The phone was untraceable, stolen from a large retailer and bought with cash from the thief. Benson stood at the water's edge and inserted a SIM card into a throwaway phone. DEA, FBI, NSA—an entire alphabet soup of agencies—monitored phone calls and tracked cell phones by their distinctive electronic signatures, or Subscriber Identification Modules.

When the noise from a passing yacht masked his voice, Benson powered up the phone, waited for a signal, and then dialed the number to the companion phone he had arranged for the courier service to deliver to Elizabeth Moynihan.

"Hello? What do you—"

"Three," he interrupted. "In twenty minutes." Benson disconnected the call. Removing the battery ended his electronic exposure. He broke the SIM card in half and threw both pieces, along with the disassembled phone, into the water. It was a five-minute walk from the hotel, but Benson preferred to make his phone calls in front of the villa belonging to a Columbian drug lord in case a spy satellite was listening.

Elizabeth Moynihan drummed her fingers on the kitchen table, adjusting the angle to amplify the click of her nails against the hardwood surface. *Click, click . . . clickity-click.* A nail-biter by habit, it gave her great pleasure to hear evidence of her self-control. She had unconsciously raised the index finger of her right hand to her mouth during the phone call and could still taste the hot pepper extract she applied to the finish coat of her nail polish.

A courier envelope, a prepaid phone, and two pieces of untraceable printer paper lay on the table in front of her. She slid a fingernail beneath the first sheet of paper and flipped it over. Five numbered paragraphs, five separate locations, preselected, delivered anonymously, and communicated with four words: "three," and "in twenty minutes."

Number three was the Cocoplum Yacht Club near the terminus of Coral Gables Waterway. She had eighteen minutes—plenty of time to drive there but not long enough to formulate a defensive strategy. The directions were specific and printed on the sheet: Come alone. Drive the red Mercedes convertible.

Elizabeth set the alarm and stepped outside. The house featured a detached garage because her grandparents had considered automobiles to be rolling incendiary devices. She grimaced at the sound of sand crunching beneath the leather soles of her Jimmy Choo almond-toe leather flats. The chain-mail toe cap was susceptible to scratching and she cursed the sand, the beach that held so much of it, and the wind that insisted on coating every available surface with enough grit to mar a 1500-dollar pair of shoes.

Elizabeth accelerated through the security gates at the end of her private driveway as they opened wide enough to clear her side mirrors. Every street was a cul-de-sac in the planned development, guaranteeing privacy for the inhabitants but creating roadblocks for those facing a restrictive timeline. The main connecting street formed a dividing line for old and new money; stands of slash pine, acres of scrub oak brambles and windswept dunes anchored by sea oats offered additional layers of privacy between the secure compounds of her like-minded neighbors. Prado Boulevard terminated at the marina.

Elizabeth parked in the rudimentary shade of a palm tree. The envelope from the courier service and everything that had been inside rested on the seat beside her. The instructions were clear and concise. She despised following orders, but the color images on the second piece of paper were both intriguing and too dangerous to ignore. Nineteen minutes after the call, she locked her car and brought the envelope with her, as instructed. She had appraised artwork for movie stars and recording artists who had demanded far more elaborate terms before meeting. The arrangements seemed more suited to a ransom drop, although the concept of kidnapped art was familiar to her.

"Over here," he called.

Elizabeth looked left, toward the direction of his voice. A plane? The aircraft rested on strange-looking pods connected to bulky wings floating on the water. The propeller was attached to the roof and pointed in the wrong direction. She turned her head to the right and scanned the opposite side of the marina. Other than a young couple rigging the sail on a catamaran, the area was deserted.

"Come closer," the man demanded.

Which she did, but only a few steps. "What do you want?"

"For you to come aboard."

"Surely you can't expect me to get into that!"

"I do. If you want to see the originals on that second piece of paper, I sent you."

She put her hands on her hips and slowly began to shake her head from side to side. "No."

"Yes."

The plane didn't look any better from the end of the pier. "That's a glorified boat with wings. And it looks in danger of sinking. Do you expect me to bail?"

"It's an amphibious plane with retractable wheels." Benson sat in the pilot's seat, three feet away from the pier. "Which means it can land at a remote airstrip outside United States' jurisdiction."

"Bermuda?"

He didn't respond.

"The Caymans?"

He stared at Elizabeth without blinking.

"The British Virgin Islands?"

"Quit guessing and get in."

"Not until you tell me where we're going."

"To a gallery. The gallery of the missing."

"These? In here?" Elizabeth held up the courier service's envelope so the winged sandal logo faced the plane.

He nodded.

"You're lying."

"Not quite."

"This one?" She pulled out the sheet of photo paper. "This painting by Renoir?" Her finger tapped the first color photo. "*Portrait of Señorita Santangel*. This isn't well-known."

"You know about it. Directly and personally."

"Impossible." Her dismissive tap of the paper matched her skeptical tone.

"Don't pretend you haven't seen it before. At Pendleton's more recently." Thomas Benson collected information. He had an incriminating network of inside sources—he cultivated them, but if there was one thing he excelled at, it was delivering bad news. "You're not the only person researching the Theodor Fischer Gallery in Lucerne."

Elizabeth Moynihan was too smart to volunteer information. She waited.

"I have a business proposition for you."

"Just a minute."

"No. Not even thirty seconds. Get in."

She scowled and put one hand on her hip, reverting to a childhood pose signaling the onset of a temper tantrum. "When I said one minute, I meant each one of the sixty seconds."

"*Portrait of Señorita Santangel* is probably already hanging on the wall of your private little gallery."

"What?" Her indignant shout drew the unwelcome attention of the couple on the catamaran. "I don't know what you're talking about. I came here about an appraisal." She waved the envelope for emphasis, but her voice lacked conviction.

"Good. Let's discuss your appraisal of "*Portrait of Señorita Santangel* . . . and the subsequent theft from Richard Pendleton III."

"Coincidence," Elizabeth said.

"Conspiracy."

"Unsubstantiated."

"Not anymore. Shall we discuss Renoir's *Madeleine Leaning on Her Elbow with Flowers in Her Hair*, stolen from the Houston couple who hired you for the appraisal?" Benson let the threat fester. "Add Pendleton's *Portrait of Señorita Santangel* to your dubious resume and that makes it a pattern. You'd better hope Ben Abrams doesn't figure it out."

"More nonsense." Elizabeth pretended innocence, although she wasn't a good enough actress to be convincing. "I came here about a commission. I don't have to . . ." She stopped talking when the sun glinted off an object in Benson's hand. That wasn't a finger he was pointing at her, it was a gun, and she had inherited enough of her father's guns to recognize an automatic with an ambidextrous slide and a reversible magazine that held ten rounds. Maybe a .32 or a .38. It was tough to tell them apart but at point-blank range it didn't matter.

"Get in," he said.

T

uesday, November 5, Noon

Chapter 10

Elizabeth Moynihan tugged on her seatbelt and double-checked the latch when Benson began his descent. They had flown south from Miami for an hour and skirted the northern edge of the Bahamas. The landing was abrupt but professional. The island was so small that the runway had been constructed on a diagonal to use all the available space. Insects feasted on her exposed skin; the sun blinded her. A walkway of crushed oyster shells connected the simple airstrip to a generic, tan hangar. She was too busy trying to avoid damaging her 1500-dollar shoes to notice Richard Pendleton III lurking in the one spot of shade on the island.

"You?" She tilted her head and lowered her sunglasses for an unobstructed look. "Shouldn't you be playing with boats?"

"Being speechless suits you," Pendleton said. "Pity the surprise didn't last longer."

"What are you doing on this godforsaken flyspeck of an island?"

"I own it." Pendleton waved an elegantly clothed arm in the general direction of the hangar and the private plane parked inside. "Follow me."

"No." Elizabeth's typical response to any order was to refuse it.

"Yes." Thomas Benson carried small-caliber veto power hidden in his jacket. His plane was parked behind them on the runway, looking equally ill-suited to being on land as it had in water.

Pendleton pivoted on his heel and led them inside. Their

footsteps echoed off the hangar walls. Despite a massive exhaust fan spinning too fast to count the number of blades, the temperature was approaching triple digits inside the building. Starlings nested in the triangles of exposed metal rafters.

Pendleton altered course to avoid walking directly beneath their messy perches. He stopped beside a free-standing refrigeration unit occupying the far corner of the hangar.

"A freezer?" Elizabeth stopped walking and transferred her displeasure from Pendleton to Benson. "Is this some kind of joke?"

"It's inconspicuous, in addition to being well-insulated and easy to control both temperature and humidity." Benson adopted a bit of her pedantic diction to make his point. "Attributes conducive to the preservation of fine art."

"I recognize the words," she said. "I wrote them."

"No doubt plagiarized," Pendleton said.

"You'd know all about that." She glared at him, widened her stance, shifted her weight, and looked ready to take root. "You haven't had an original thought in your entire life."

Pendleton waited beside the refrigerator door. A diamond pattern had been stamped into the brushed aluminum. The outer walls gleamed and were spotless. He rested his hand on the heavy-duty curved handle of the industrial-sized unit.

Elizabeth didn't move.

Benson cleared his throat. "I can think of several million reasons for you to go inside, all of them in unmarked bills."

"There is, however, a more lucrative option." Pendleton unlatched the freezer door and opened it wide enough for Elizabeth to see inside.

"Stolen from *Entartete Kunst*?" She asked.

"I was told you were somewhat of an expert," Benson motioned for her to go inside. "It appears to be true."

"Via the Theodor Fischer Gallery." Elizabeth didn't need to ask, not after five years of post-graduate research into stolen paintings. She reached into her purse and donned linen gloves.

"What else?" Benson asked. "Prove to me you're as good as

you claim to be."

Her hands trembled when she touched the frame; her fingers quivered as she traced the intricate scroll work. She brushed her gloved finger along the back of the canvas with the delicate touch of someone reading a love sonnet printed in braille. Using the glow from her phone, she directed the soft light onto a Renoir with a dubious ownership chain. She blinked rapidly and reached back into her purse—not for a tissue, but to remove a jeweler's loupe. Holding the lens to her eye, she studied the unusual texture at the bottom of the canvas.

"It's a fake."

Pendleton's pained expression affirmed her suspicions.

"Excellent." Benson looked delighted. "I know about the insurance scam you two cooked up. You'd better hope Ben Abrams doesn't figure it out. My idea, however, takes it one step further."

"With fakes? No thanks," Elizabeth said. "Anyone can empty a vacuum cleaner and create a layer of dust that looks like it's 100 years old. How many people know to find dust that predates above-ground atomic bomb testing? If there's cesium-137 or strontium-90, it will always be suspect."

"My business proposition, however," Benson stepped forward. "Is both real *and* lucrative."

She heard the malice in his voice, turned and saw the aggression in his stance.

"Pay attention, unless you want to join *D'Erve.*"

"*The Fence?*" Elizabeth asked.

"No. The floater." Benson forestalled her question with his own form of ghoulish humor. "You two should have thought about the fallout before you teamed up to defraud Coastal Insurance Company."

Pendleton bit back a comment and shut his mouth with a snap of his teeth.

"Do you mean Ben Abrams?" She asked. "He was in my office. Asking questions."

"Let him ask," Benson said. "As long as he doesn't find any

answers. I'm about to give him something else to worry about."

Elizabeth was in favor of anything that would let her hang on to a stolen painting. Besides, Benson's hand remained uncomfortably close to the gun in his pocket. She searched for a diplomatic pathway to put some distance between her principles and the need for self-preservation. "I'm certain that client confidentiality applies in this situation."

"Then consider yourself hired." He moved his hand away from the gun.

"For what?"

"For a lot of money."

"How much?"

"A plane-load," Pendleton pointed at the plane occupying the hangar.

"You still owe me for my appraisal of *Portrait of Señorita Santangel.*"

"Money won't be a problem," Benson assured her. "Which is why I'm here. I can guarantee a plane's worth of cash, bigger than that one."

"Well . . ." Elizabeth shifted her gaze to examine the plane. "How much bigger?"

T uesday, November 5, 10:30 p.m., Miami

Chapter 11

An entire day's worth of grit had worked its way beneath Ben's contacts. He leaned his head back to endure the sting of eye drops. Now his eyes were blurry *and* tired. He rolled down the window so the fresh air would help him stay awake and headed south on Highway One. An SUV that had been following him all day pulled in behind. Despite a distinctive right front fender finished in red primer, he didn't recognize the vehicle because the headlights were all he could see.

The traffic light turned red. Ben eased to a stop. He heard an engine roar when the driver following him accelerated. He glanced in the rear-view mirror, didn't trust his blurry eyes, and leaned over for a better view. He watched a pair of headlights approach. He blinked. Tensed. The initial crash snapped him forward and his forehead shattered the glass in the rearview mirror before the airbag slammed him backwards against the seat.

Both impacts disoriented him. A dull headache formed behind his eyes. He touched the rapidly swelling bump on his forehead and felt warm, sticky blood. Worse, the cut appeared big enough to need stitches. His vison was blurred, although that might have been from the eye drops. Not the first time someone had run into him while he was waiting on a traffic light. Any carwreck that he survived—especially when it happened to a rental car, seemed like more of an annoyance than a catastrophe. The car behind him backed away.

Hit and run? Worse than being rear-ended.

He glanced at the side-view mirror and noticed it was an SUV—considerably heavier and higher off the ground. He upped the aggravation quotient from dealing with the rental car company to filling out police reports and a month of paperwork.

Still. Not my car—still not a disaster. Getting a replacement was going to be a nuisance, however. He unlatched his seatbelt, put his hand on the passenger seat, and leaned over to open the glovebox for the rental agreement. The SUV was still backing away. One of the headlights was busted. Ten, twenty feet . . . too far. He heard the engine roar as the driver reversed gears. The truck-based vehicle accelerated. The glare from the remaining headlight filled the side mirror, then the rear window. The driver wasn't turning. Ben didn't have time to brace himself. There wasn't time to . . .

The SUV deliberately smashed into his car.

The passenger-side airbag exploded. If he had been speeding, the device would have saved his life. If he had been observing the speed limit, the sudden inflation might have hurt his nose or given him two black eyes, but he could have walked away from a serious accident. Instead, the full force of an explosion traveling 200 miles-per-hour struck Ben in the chest. The impact bruised his ribs and stopped his breathing.

The recoil smashed the soft tissue of his brain against the inside of his skull. He lost consciousness. Involuntary muscle memory responded. He gasped and resumed breathing. With oxygen came awareness. Pain demanded the breathing process remain shallow. He tasted blood, followed the source, discovered a molar-sized indention on the side of his tongue. A haze of whitish smoke filled the passenger compartment from the deflated airbags. He smelled gasoline. Maybe the gas tank had ruptured. He felt dizzy, sleepy, closed his eyes since he couldn't see anything anyway.

He heard the gritty crunch of footsteps approaching on broken plastic and glass. The ominous sound played in stereo, and it took precious seconds for his muddled brain to interpret the anomaly. Two pair of feet meant . . . two people—carjackers. *Kidnappers?*

He opened his eyes and saw fireflies. Bright whirling bursts of intense white light spun in dizzying circles.

The footsteps got louder as his assailants moved closer. He couldn't see them; he could smell them. They carried the disorienting odor of rotting flesh—like the floater beneath his father's dock.

"*D'Erve?*" Ben muttered. *I thought you were dead. Or was that supposed to be me?*

He closed one eye and the blurry images transformed into an ogre and his sub-human sidekick. They were wearing masks. His concussed brain struggled to orient itself to time and space. *Halloween? No. That was . . . four days ago?*

The initial impact had dislodged one of his contact lenses. He closed one eye and opened the other. The remaining contact lens corrected his vision. Dislodged blood cells settled to the bottom of the vitreous fluid in his eye. He could see again. *Football players?* He blinked. Men wearing crash helmets. *Not Trick-or-Treaters. An attack. Planned.*

The larger assailant swung a hammer against the window in the driver's door. The first blow shattered the glass and dislodged a few small squares in the epicenter. The next blow pelted him with broken bits of safety glass.

Breaking glass. *Kristallnacht?*

The third swing knocked the entire pane loose from the window frame and the follow-through struck him in the hip. Two pair of hands reached into the open window and started pulling him out of the car. He grabbed the armrest on the passenger door. There was blood on his hands and his fingers started to slip. He heard gunshots—didn't feel the wounds. Maybe he was in shock; he was too afraid to let go of the armrest to check for bullet holes.

A Miami street devoid of oncoming traffic is as rare as a total eclipse. Good Samaritans are equally scarce. Well-armed citizens with itchy trigger-fingers, however, are common. No car accident in Miami is so remote that it doesn't draw lawyers. The distinctive crumple of expensive metal and high-priced plastic is an amplified invitation to lawyers trolling for lawsuits; the promise of a quick settlement is a powerful incentive to respond.

The ambulance chaser arrived before the ambulance; he mis-identified the two men as competitors and yelled at them to stay back. When that didn't work, he started waving his pistol. It got their attention; they were armed, too.

Ben heard more gunshots and ducked his head. A police siren sounded. Rapid footsteps . . . men running. He tightened his grip on the armrest. When the wail grew louder, the sound of running feet receded. He risked a peek through the side window. His assailants had returned to their vehicle; the driver had the presence of mind to turn off the remaining headlight, making the license plate numbers too dark to read when the truck roared past.

The lawyer stuck around long enough to slip a business card into Ben's pocket as the paramedics loaded him into the ambulance. Ben felt his touch as he drifted in and out of consciousness. He reached for the Samaritan's hand to thank him. The ancestors intervened.

"Who are you?" He mumbled, and felt the unfamiliar contact from generations of survivors who bridged the gap between strangers to complete their otherworldly journey. Past met present to ensure the future. Ben was a skeptic, so it was *Grossmutter* who took his hand. She took the younger hand of the connected child Ben had been, before fear and intelligence compromised his pathway to timelessness . . .

Grossmutter handed him the key hanging in his father's study, the golden key that opened every door. Ben's grandmother unlocked the barrier between a long line of men who shared the middle name of Isaac.

Ben felt the paramedics strap him to a gurney and stow him in the ambulance. The siren wailed, sounding like the braying of a mule. He heard indistinct voices. Someone shined a light in his eye. When he blinked and looked away, his grandmother let go of his hand.

"*Grossmutter*," he mumbled. He reached for her. He couldn't feel anything and looked up.

A stranger dressed in white blinded him in the other eye.

"Equal and reactive," she said, and checked for feeling in the lower extremities.

Ben heard the prognosis in *Yiddish.* Somebody was trying to steal his painting. No, that wasn't right. *Grossmutter's* painting!

Grossmutter hovered nearby. Her parents had refused to leave Vienna. After *Kristallnacht,* it was too late; her grandfather (*Grossvater*) had been among the 30,000 men who were arrested and sent to Nazi concentration camps.

"The canvas is gone," *Grossmutter* said. "Follow the frame."

Wednesday, November 6, 4 p.m.

Chapter 12

The Key Largo Quik Stop was one of the few places to buy gasoline on the island. The police substation was tucked into a small space that once held a bank of payphones. Now the alcove provided a place for officers to sip coffee while completing paperwork. Lauren Welles was the type of detective who didn't want to get too far removed from the people she was entrusted with protecting; she preferred the informal setting of the substation, a place where citizens felt comfortable discussing island happenings in need of police attention.

"Got your text." Ben leaned against the counter. He winced at the sharp pain and gently returned to an upright position. His ribs ached and it hurt to breathe.

"Two hours ago." She glanced at the clock. "At least."

"I'm headed off the island. There's a private showing of *The Impressionists and the Sea* exhibit. Figured I'd save myself a trip and stop by on the way to the Lowe."

"Museum? Are you sure that's a good idea? You look horrible."

"Thanks. I feel worse."

"Car accident?"

"No. It was deliberate."

"I heard from Interpol on—wait. What?"

"Hit and run. Or, technically, hit, hit again, and run. There was an attempted assault in there somewhere. Maybe kidnapping or car-jacking. It's all kind of hazy."

She put down her pen and swiveled her chair so she was facing him. "Are those stitches? What happened to your forehead?"

"Stopped at a red light."

"How'd you hit your head?"

"With my brain. Against the rearview mirror, maybe."

"Back up. What happened?"

"Woke up at the hospital. I swear I got there in a packing crate—I think *Grossmutter* was carrying it. It's all running together and some of it's in German and the rest in Yiddish."

"Are you sure you're okay to drive?"

"It's another rental. Much bigger. And I took the insurance upgrade." He described the attack which explained the replacement car.

"I heard from the FBI and Interpol. They're interested in the floater—the one we found under your father's dock. You were right about the ID. I think it's connected to your accident."

"I don't see how." His memory was coming back in bits and pieces. "Well, maybe."

"Try probably." She clicked the mouse and logged onto the national criminal database. She swiveled the laptop so Ben could see the screen.

"I recognize that address. Lower Manhattan and pricey real estate. My boss lives in the same building. It's just a few blocks from Coastal Insurance Company's headquarters."

"Have you heard from him?"

"My boss? No. He's still missing. And if he's got any sense, he'll stay that way. He's worked for Coastal Insurance long enough to collect retirement—except there might not be any money left to fund it."

"You're kidding, right?"

"Just barely. His new policy of insuring paintings lacking complete provenance has doubled my workload. His idea to institute a policy of, 'ten percent pay-out for the return of a stolen painting with no questions asked,' has created a boon in the art theft business. Now it's threatening to bankrupt the company. The way Coastal Insurance is hemorrhaging money, I may have to get in line to kill him myself when the stockholders find out how much he's costing us. Meanwhile, what's his neighbor, *D'Erve*, doing beneath the dock at my father's house in Key Largo?"

"Besides decomposing?" Lauren had been a detective long enough to develop the macabre sense of humor that comes with the job. She highlighted a link on the floater's rap sheet: an international conviction for fencing—dealing in stolen art.

"Might explain Elizabeth Moynihan's nervousness and the books she's been checking out from the library."

Lauren tilted her head away from the screen. She raised an eyebrow, got as far as framing the question before Ben volunteered his theory.

"*Madeleine Leaning on Her Elbow with Flowers in Her Hair*, missing since 2011. Still an open case and one I'm sick of working on. Elizabeth Moynihan turned our discussion into some strange kind of competition about who had stared at it more. She's the expert on missing Renoirs, but got nervous when I started asking questions. Then she turned defensive."

"Sounds a bit far-fetched. Not exactly enough hard evidence for an investigation."

"Close enough. She did the appraisal for the Houston couple that "Madeleine" was stolen from. Now with *Portrait of Señorita Santangel* missing after she appraised it for Pendleton, it's too much of a coincidence for me."

"And you never did believe in coincidences."

"Still don't. With a coincidence, there's usually a *con* in there somewhere. If Elizabeth Moynihan is dealing with stolen art, Harold Feinstein, a.k.a. *D'Erve*, is the sort of guy she'd need. And if my boss is involved . . ." He opened the manila folder he was carrying and laid it on the counter. "Look at this."

"Bad pictures?"

"Research by Elizabeth Moynihan. An undocumented picture of *Portrait of Señorita Santangel*. The FBI Art Loss Register and the news outlets don't have it—or anybody else judging by the big question marks on all the online articles."

"And this helps me, how?"

"Explains the theft." He turned the page to a map.

"The United States, Great Britain, the Soviet Union, and France," Lauren read the countries listed clockwise, her voice slowing with each additional geographical discrepancy. "With common borders? Impossible."

"You're looking at occupied Germany after World War II. Elizabeth Moynihan is something of an expert on missing art. Maybe she's better at finding it than I gave her credit for."

Lauren turned the page to a map of Switzerland, which bordered the Allied Territory, and began to read about the flow of art to a neutral country—the world's storehouse for wealth. Art from all of Europe poured into Switzerland for safekeeping before World War II. After the fighting started, stolen art poured into Switzerland for the same reason.

"Under Swiss law, after five years, artwork belongs to the possessor if 'bought in good faith.' The victim has to reimburse the wrongful owner if they want their own painting back?" Lauren's indignation was professional. "This can't be right."

"The economics of neutrality," Ben said. "The Theodor Fischer Gallery in Lucerne was a revolving door for stolen art. A place where 'no questions were asked' and everything was 'bought in good faith.' I've dealt with them before—unsuccessfully. Their idea of 'good faith' would shame an agnostic." He opened another folder and handed her a facsimile copy of the June 29th, 1939 catalogue from the Degenerate Art auction at the Theodor Fischer Gallery in Lucerne, Switzerland.

"Van Gogh, Matisse, Picasso . . . Lauren turned to her laptop and opened a new window to search for information about the Theodor Fischer Gallery. She clicked on a link. "Is that a typo? The Nazis confiscated 70,000 paintings?"

"And burned a lot of them. The others were sold or stolen. The really valuable works were hidden in Switzerland."

"Any Renoirs?" Lauren brought Ben the history buff back into the current century. "You're still looking for a missing Renoir, right?"

"Quite a few Renoirs are unaccounted for. But you're right, the one I'm most interested in right now is Pendleton's missing

Portrait of Señorita Santangel."

"There's that Santangel name again. Any connection to the key in your father's study?"

"*Grossmutter* seemed to think so; she was trying to tell me something." Ben recounted his experience in the ambulance.

"You mean after you hit your head and suffered a concussion." Lauren sounded skeptical.

"I was knocked unconscious, not crazy."

"Debatable."

"Then you definitely aren't going to like this next part. I don't, either, but it's too real to ignore. My memory is coming back. There's a long, unbroken chain of ancestors and each link is a dead man with the middle name of Isaac."

Lauren was too polite to scoff and too well-trained as a detective to trust circumstantial evidence. "What does this have to do with Pendleton's Renoir?"

"Everything, if Solomon Santangel's middle name was Isaac. Pendleton's stolen Renoir is missing fifteen months of provenance from when the Theodor Fischer Art Gallery was auctioning off *Entartete Kunst* paintings. I think Pendleton's Renoir was part of those twenty-five canvases that weren't listed. Nobody knows what happened to them—or even who the artists were. Except . . . maybe they were part of the Santangel collection, hence the name: *Portrait of Señorita Santangel.*" Ben rubbed his hands together with anticipation. "I have an idea for a trap, and the Lowe Museum will be the perfect place to spring it."

"Be careful what you use for bait."

"Not *what*," Ben said. "*Who.*"

"Even worse," Lauren's skeptical glance focused on the stitches in Ben's forehead. "Remember your hit and run."

"I won't stop at any traffic lights. And if I get pulled over," he joked. "I'll say it was your idea."

"Won't work." She lowered her gaze to the way he held his arms around across his stomach to support his aching ribs. "What if D'*Erve*'s murder was a case of mistaken identity and that was supposed to be you? That means the hit and run was the second attempt on your life. Three strikes and you're out."

"I'll be careful," he promised, underestimating the violence a billion dollars in stolen art generates.

Wednesday, November 6, 4:45 p.m., Miami

Chapter 13

Elizabeth Moynihan thrummed her fingers against the hard-plastic door panel. She began to wiggle her toes as the adrenaline surge built. The van was new and rented for nineteen dollars and ninety-five cents a day plus seventy-nine cents per mile. A temporary wrap with the Custom Caterers logo covered the garish lettering that advertised the van's availability. A handwritten note claiming car trouble was as fraudulent as the catering company letterhead it was written on, and she planned to place it on the dashboard to explain leaving the vehicle parked overnight near the Lowe Museum's service entrance. She preferred alternate escape routes with unremarkable vehicles staged at key exit points. The van satisfied both basic needs while offering a secure hiding place for additional equipment. Breaking and entering required a wide range of tools—more than she could realistically carry.

She had already stashed an inflatable raft with an electric trolling motor and additional batteries in the opposite direction within dragging distance of Coral Gables Waterway. A powerboat was moored at the deep-water terminus of Mahi Waterway adjacent to the University of Miami campus. A rental car in the parking garage, a rusty work truck parked on a nearby side street, and a bicycle chained to a tree near the edge of Lake Osceola—when she returned to the museum later tonight, there were going to be plenty of avenues for escape.

She slipped out of the van when nobody was watching. A portico with fluted columns offered cover from prying eyes, while assorted statuary by Hans van de Bovenkamp and John Henry provided an excuse for choosing the atypical path connecting the service area with the formal entrance. Elizabeth nonchalantly stepped into the shadow of the largest statue: Poseidon with Trident, a marble statue imported from Greece before modern trade restrictions. Some of the anchoring bolts were so rusty that a cold chisel and a few well-placed blows from a hammer would break them in half. "Hmmm . . ."

She savored the casual stroll past marble statues most criminals would prefer to hide behind and started planning her next heist. Stealing a statue was the easy part, the challenge was in moving it. She paused to admire a bronze of Sisyphus and kept her adrenal glands primed. Despite an overwhelming urge to look over her shoulder or sprint for cover, she sauntered across the plaza with an outwardly confident veneer and an inner rush that was habit-forming.

Ben stood beneath a portico at the entrance to the University of Miami's Lowe Museum. He was there in an advisory capacity, not exactly welcome or invited, but entitled to full access by the considerable risk Coastal Insurance Company was underwriting. "Here they come."

"Who?" Daniel Mann, the head of museum security, had just finished his briefing and assigned positions to the additional guards hired for the special event. He wore a three-piece suit and tugged at a striped tie like it was a hangman's noose.

Ben used his chin to point at a limousine turning onto Stanford Drive. "The first of tonight's art thieves and criminals."

"And I thought I was paranoid." Called "Dan the Man" by those who knew him well, the head of security ran a finger between his neck and the stiff collar of his shirt.

"So far, the security systems have been focused on keeping people out." The bandage around Ben's ribs kept him from reaching high enough to swat at a mosquito drilling into his neck where the insect repellant had worn thin. "Now we're unlocking the doors and letting the professionals in—the same thieves you're used to guarding against."

"University students and art lovers? The only thieves around here are in administration."

"Not true. Otherwise, I'd be out of a job and the university wouldn't be paying premiums to Coastal Insurance Company." Ben watched a stretched Hummer with the oversized chrome wheels of a pimp's ride clip the curb and flatten the delicate white-and-yellow blossoms of a wild sage. There was something both ominous and familiar about the man getting out of the back seat. Ben elbowed Dan to get his attention. "See that guy right there? Getting out of the limo? That's one of the crooks I was talking about. The most dangerous one."

The man exiting the limousine had the deep-water tan of a wealthy Florida retiree with the perfect white teeth to match. An Armani suit and handmade Italian shoes whispered wealth. Bystanders automatically got out of his way.

"Thomas Benson." Ben uttered the man's name with the inflection normally reserved for profanity. "This is by invitation, only. Did you steal one?"

"No profit in it." He focused his gaze on the bandage covering most of Ben's forehead. "Still chasing parked cars?"

Ben had exposed enough crooks to trust his instincts. If Benson was nearby, larceny was inevitable. The ex-casino manager was slick, smart, and an accomplished thief. There was something off-putting about his soft hands, with fidgeting fingers that never stopped moving, touching the sides of his perfectly coiffed hair, straightening an already straight tie—Benson looked nervous and acted guilty. Ben suspected he was involved in the recent theft of Pendleton's Renoir: *Portrait of Señorita Santangel*.

Benson, however, knew enough about Ben to warrant the nervousness. Ben had earned his reputation as one of the most relentless insurance investigators in the business. A growing number of incarcerated felons could vouch for his persistence.

"Still laundering money?" Ben asked.

"Shopping for Renoirs." He smiled with the same show of teeth as a vampire approaching a fair maiden's neck. "I hear it's a growth market."

"What else have you heard?"

"Why should I tell you?" Benson licked his lips with the unconscious mannerism of a predator testing the air for a scent of its prey. "How's security?"

"Suspect, now that you're here."

"Excellent. I hope your fears are well-founded."

Ben watched him move to a nearby table. Benson grabbed a catalogue and crossed the foyer, his footsteps as silent as a lion on the prowl. He entered the outer gallery featuring Renoir's early works and was lost to view.

The brush strokes and complementary colors of Renoir's romanticized portrayal of *Oarsmen at Chatou* elevated the painting into a masterpiece reflecting the ethos of a bygone era. Elizabeth Moynihan tilted her head as if to examine the play of light against the canvas, while studying the motion detectors mounted in each corner of the ceiling. The sensors were brand new, installed within the last 24 hours, a smaller, updated model with a battery backup and an infrared anti-masking feature. A defensive mode allowed a higher threshold of movement. She circumspectly waved her hand and increased the tempo until the green light turned to yellow. Impressive. Anything much faster than walking speed—like a thief running through the gallery—would sound an alarm. She moved closer to the canvas. By tilting her head in the opposite direction, she could study the nearest window. Glass-breakage monitors had been attached to each pane and across the sill. Kevlar laminate across the glass made them impregnable to anything less than an armor-piercing anti-tank round. She noted newer, upgraded motion detectors installed in every corner. Multi-purpose sensors flush-mounted in the ceilings monitored glass-breakage or other un-natural vibrations. The museum had adopted cutting-edge technology to become a fortress lacking only a moat—Ben Abrams' doing, no doubt.

"*Oarsmen at Chatou*. Beautiful, isn't it?" A man wearing too much cologne tried to strike up a conversation.

She pretended not to hear him. By tilting her head, she could observe the play of light across the canvas and identify the motion sensors affixed to the wall behind the frame.

He moved upwind.

She shifted position. Temperature-sensitive receptors had been mounted in the corners—also new, and part of a significant upgrade in security. She used the two-foot ceiling tiles to calculate the angle of coverage.

"Ignoring a problem doesn't make it go away." Thomas Benson waved a manicured hand in front of her face, "and I'm currently your biggest problem."

"You're giving yourself too much credit."

He lowered his voice and leaned close enough for her to regret his musky cologne. "You going to jail and Ben Abrams asking questions about *Portrait of Señorita Santangel* are tied for second place."

"The wrong person could see us together," she hissed "What are you doing here?"

"Shopping. Same as you."

"Not now." She moved to a small canvas on the opposite side of the gallery, a distinctive pointillist landscape by Georges Seurat.

Tiny dots in dozens of unmodulated colors coalesced into a cohesive scene along the Seine when she took a couple of steps away from the canvas. She glanced at the flat disc flush-mounted in the center of the ceiling. When she snapped her fingers, the green LED light turned to yellow. Anything louder, such as the sharp crack of glass breaking or the high-pitched whine of a drill, and the light would turn red, triggering an alarm.

"You haven't seen my shopping list."

"Not interested." A long metallic strip mounted in the corner resembled Swiss cheese; lasers mounted in each opening sent a charged beam of light from one side of the room to the other to form a defensive perimeter inches in front of the canvases.

She edged closer and surreptitiously slid her toe toward the energized light, using the twelve-inch tiles to accurately measure the distance. She swung her elbow near the wall and interrupted the laser beams to judge reaction time.

The guard stationed in the corner put a finger to the transmitter nestled in his ear. Minimum wage buys minimum motivation. He looked up and scanned the room, but it was more of a cursory glance than determined vigilance. The woman working in the bookstore appeared to interest him more than the visitors in the gallery; Elizabeth assumed he would probably respond to a patron yanking a painting off the wall and making a run for it, however.

Benson followed her when she moved to the next gallery. She turned to confront him. "I prefer to work alone. Your threats aren't going to change that. You can't point a gun at me twenty-four hours a day."

"I've got something else to change your mind." He handed her a disposable phone. "*Beis Hei*. I'm certain you recognize the Santanagel coat of arms."

She studied the image, used her thumb and index finger to enlarge the detail. The grain, color of the wood, the frame looked familiar. "Where did you get this?"

"Not from the back of Pendleton's Renoir—which I *know* is what you were thinking. No need to run home and check the back of your stolen painting."

"Wha—" Elizabeth recoiled.

"There's a new game in town and you're looking at the dealer."

"Doesn't mean I'm working for him."

"Open the other image." He leaned close enough for her to feel his hot breath against her ear.

She swiped a finger across the screen. A corpse wearing a bright yellow bow tie came into focus.

"*D'Erve!*" She gasped.

"I'll be in touch—unless you want to be next."

W

ednesday, November 6, 6:15 p.m. Special Preview: The Impressionists and the Sea Exhibit

Chapter 14

Politicians, socialites, students, artists, and even the most jaded debutantes quieted after the studio technician flipped a switch to send power to the spotlights. Ben was standing close enough to the makeshift stage in the Lowe Museum's entryway to feel the heat radiating off the metal shields directing the intense beams. Elizabeth Moynihan's orange-tinted makeup transformed into normal flesh tones beneath the brilliant light. This was a special broadcast, so her signature audience meter with its damning red zone had been replaced with a clump of dignitaries anxious to claim a share of the credit for making the special exhibit possible. An offstage negotiation between the Governor's aides and Pendleton's personal assistant had left both prima donnas unhappy with their demotion from the number one spot on the appearance list.

"Renoir, Manet, Monet, Pissarro, Morisot, Signac, Caillebotte," Elizabeth began. Her sincere gaze into the camera lens slowly shifted focus as she tilted the microphone toward the museum curator and lobbed a softball question to her: "What prompted your idea to host an exhibition with a nautical theme?"

"The America's Cup Trials," the curator said. "The Impressionists were attracted to the play of light in nature. Nowhere is it more intense and varied than when combined with water."

No amount of poise or scholarly acumen could have compensated for the curator's ghostly pale image, compounded by the stark white background of the wall behind her. A black dress might have mitigated her washed-out appearance, but it had been Elizabeth's suggestion and subsequent demand that the curator exchange her original dark outfit for a pair of white pants with matching blouse. Elizabeth hadn't shared her access to a professional makeup artist, either, so despite outwardly sharing the stage, she remained the focal point of the shot.

Richard Pendleton III fared no better, upstaged by Elizabeth's demand to film the interview beside one of Renoir's most powerful works, probably his most famous painting and certainly one of his largest canvases.

The Boating Party was over four feet tall and nearly six feet wide. Pendleton was shorter than Elizabeth in her platform heels and equally dwarfed and upstaged by the imposing painting.

Ben watched Pendleton's face turn from pink to red to bright crimson. Serge, the personal assistant, consulted his clipboard after each of Elizabeth's questions; judging by the negative shake of his head and Pendleton's fumbled responses, the interview had taken an unexpected deviation from the prepared script. Elizabeth came across as an art expert, with the compassionate professionalism of someone accustomed to dealing with a person ill-equipped to carry on an intelligent conversation. Pendleton looked foolish and then angry. Serge looked like a man bracing himself to face a firing squad.

The next confrontation played to a much smaller audience and off-camera. Ben watched Elizabeth hand her microphone to the sound technician and exit stage left. Richard Pendleton elbowed his way through the throng to shadow her. Ben recognized the signs of an impending confrontation and charted an intercept course through the employees' breakroom.

Elizabeth Moynihan entered the one place Ben wouldn't—the women's bathroom. He changed his mind when Pendleton ignored social mores and followed her inside. Ben looked both ways to make certain nobody was watching before he eased the door open. He saw a couch and two comfortable-looking chairs in matching paisley print in a small antechamber. He could hear both of their voices as soon as he edged the inner door open far enough to eavesdrop without being seen.

"Gender issues?" Elizabeth didn't sound surprised to see Pendleton in the women's bathroom.

"*D'Erve* is dead."

"I just saw the picture. Not my problem."

"I don't want to be next." Pendleton said. "Do you?"

"Of course not. And again, not my problem. I don't want any part of your deal with Benson."

What deal? Ben wondered. Between Benson and Pendleton? And Elizabeth Moynihan? With Benson involved, it was guaranteed to be criminal.

"Like it or not," Pendleton pointed a condemning finger at her. "You're in this."

"Get out." Elizabeth raised her voice.

"I can't afford to."

"Out of the bathroom, you idiot." She pulled an iPhone from her bag.

"Who are you calling?"

"Security."

Pendleton scoffed. "I'll tell them we're having a creative meeting."

"Not if I yell rape."

"Don't insult me—or flatter yourself. Nobody would believe you."

"Let's find out." She tapped the screen and turned up the volume. Ben could hear it ringing despite standing in the next room.

"Kiss your collection goodbye when someone answers."

"What?"

"You heard me." Pendleton lowered his voice to deliver a counterthreat. "Gone. All your beautiful paintings."

"Nonsense," Elizabeth said. "What do you really want?"

"Money. Same thing as you. And the Santangel collection —what's left of it, anyway."

Elizabeth disconnected her call. "Have you seen them? With your own eyes?"

"My father had. I've just seen pictures."

Elizabeth returned the iPhone to her makeup bag and removed a different phone, a generic model sold at drugstores and on street corners. "Benson just gave me this. I didn't believe him when he said this was real."

Pendleton moved beside her. They stared at the screen.

Ben couldn't see what they were looking at. He could see their expressions, however. It wasn't good news.

"*Beis Hei,*" Pendleton muttered.

"*Baruch Hashem:* Thank God." Elizabeth translated. "I recognize the Santangel coat of arms."

Pendleton nodded. "No telling how many—" The sound of a toilet flushing interrupted him. He bent at the waist and peered beneath the stalls.

Elizabeth's reaction was more decisive. She put both hands on his shoulder and began pushing him out of the room.

Ben backtracked quickly into the hallway. To his right, a massive statue in the Antiquities Gallery—big enough to hide behind—but too far away to reach in time. To his left: nothing but open hallway. The decision was critical; the delay damning.

Pendleton opened the outer bathroom door.

There hadn't been enough time to take another step. Ben was still facing the door and standing on the threshold.

Pendleton jerked to a stop. Elizabeth's hands slipped off his shoulder and she bumped into him.

There was enough territorial guilt for everyone: Elizabeth and Pendleton were coming out of the women's bathroom; Ben was standing close enough to the door so it was obvious he had been eavesdropping.

"I didn't have you figured for a peeping Tom," Pendleton said.

"Nor you for a cross-dresser."

"Get out of the way."

"I'd rather you finish your conversation about the Santangel collection—what's left of it, anyway."

"So you were listening."

"I missed that part about the bargain with Benson, though."

"Move," Pendleton said. "I'm not telling you again."

Ben blocked the doorway. "You ought to know better than to get mixed up with Thomas Benson. Both of you. *D'Erve*'s dead and my boss is missing. You might be next."

Elizabeth removed a Taser from a cloth bag featuring a matte reproduction of a Renoir portrait. She flicked a switch to demonstrate what 50,000 volts looked like when jumping across the gap between two electrodes. The brief electrical sizzle left an acrid odor hanging in the air.

Ben stared at the distance between the two electrodes and remembered Lauren's comment about burn marks on *D'Erve's* neck. Elizabeth moved the Taser to eye level and sent another spark arcing between the electrodes. Painful yellow dots burned into Ben's retinas; he stepped aside.

Pendleton brushed past him into the hallway, Elizabeth following, still carrying the cheap disposable phone in her other hand.

Wednesday, November 6, 10:15 p.m., Key Largo

Chapter 15

Ben smelled something burning when he stepped onto the porch of his father's house. A grayish-blue smoke cloud drifted through the den; he followed the source to the kitchen. Alexi was making popcorn. A flurry of exploding kernels raised the lid above the pan; oil spilled down the sides and ignited when it met the burner. The smoke alarm sounded. Alexi detached the unit from the ceiling and put it on the floor where the air was still clear. He dumped the smoking batch into a bowl and brushed the burned pieces off with a knife. Alexi had learned to cook from their mother, whose solution for any cooking mishap was adding enough butter and garlic salt to make charred pieces palatable, or smothering critical mishaps with gravy.

Ben opened a window. He turned down the heat and made a fresh batch using olive oil.

"Sissy." Alexi wasn't impressed until Ben offered to share. The aroma reached the upper level of the house and was powerful enough to bring their father out of his office. When he made it as far as the top of the stairs and called down a request, Ben seized the opportunity. He made another batch and used it to bribe Alexi upstairs.

"Makes a nice change from ordering pizza." It qualified as high praise coming from Ben's father, and with a tailwind, might even be construed as a positive omen. Anything less than a complaint was a compliment. There wouldn't be a better time—or maybe even another opportunity to ask for help.

Ben brought Alexi and his father up to speed on the special premiere at the Lowe, and recounted the argument between Elizabeth Moynihan and Richard Pendleton without revealing his compromising location outside the women's bathroom. "What do you think?"

"Don't know him." His father kept his sentences short and his breaths long. "Seen her show a few times. It's not bad."

"I've heard it's a good idea to get cash up front if you're selling him artwork," Alexi said. "He's not interested in pottery, so I haven't had that particular money problem."

"Sounds like Elizabeth Moynihan does. I think he owes her for appraising his stolen painting. Makes sense. He owes everybody else."

"You buy yourself an enemy when you lend a man money." His father had an inexhaustible supply of Yiddish sayings that suited any occasion. "Imagine," it took an extra breath for him to complete the sentence, "a millionaire who won't pay his bills."

"Not *won't*," Ben said, "but *can't*. He's living on borrowed money."

Ben had spent hours trying to make sense of Pendleton's behavior and a possible motive had emerged. An insurance settlement for the theft of *Portrait of Señorita Santangel* solved his negative cash-flow, enabling him to make the next payment on a yacht he couldn't afford with enough left-over cash to take care of the builder's lien on his house. "The Renoir he had stolen is lacking provenance, so the theft keeps him out of trouble with the rightful heirs—if any survived—while solving his most pressing money problems."

"If you say so," his father took several deep breaths. "If the rich could hire someone to die for them, the poor would make a nice living."

"What painting?" Alexi asked.

"*Portrait of Señorita Santangel*. Where have you been?" Ben asked. "It's headline news. And what I've been working on since I got here."

"As opposed to sitting *Shiva*?" Alexi mimicked Ben's overly incredulous tone. He added sarcasm and a bad attitude to the timbre.

The crunch of angry men chewing popcorn grew unnaturally loud in the tense silence. Ben sorted through several possible retorts and didn't use any of them.

Alexi remarked that he hadn't been paying attention to current affairs, lately, and their father attempted an unfamiliar role as peacemaker when he realized both his grown sons were beginning to share his passion.

"*Ahem.*" Ben's father cleared his throat and pulled a spiral notebook from the middle of the tallest pile on his desk. It naturally fell open to an image of *Portrait of Señorita Santangel*. He turned on the desk lamp and adjusted the neck to illuminate the color photo pasted on the page.

The movement of light and shadow across the picture transformed the white dress she wore and turned the painted fabric into a delicate prism suitable for a rainbow. Subdued tones, blended with dramatic brushstrokes, heightened the colors while framing the subject against a lush background of simple tones. Classical forms, saturated colors, and a painstakingly accurate detail of the period fashion enshrined the subject in a timeless, yet fleeting moment. The elusive quality of a definitive masterpiece elevated the portrait of a young Isabella Santangel to a work of art.

"She looks like your mother." Their father opened the center drawer and removed his wedding photo.

"Who's the guy with the curly hair?" Alexi asked. "The one wearing a tuxedo and standing next to Mom."

"That's me." Their father had a comedian's sense of timing and a cloistered lifestyle free from political correctness. "A sad case, really." He slid his glasses down his nose and stared at Alexi with watery-blue eyes, "he had retarded sons."

"Clearly genetic," Alexi said.

Their father shifted the same damning gaze onto Ben.

"Probably hereditary," Ben said. "Good thing I'm adopted."

"*Oy gevalt.* I should be so lucky." Their father shook his head with mock sadness and placed his wedding picture beside the picture of *Portrait of Señorita Santangel*.

"It's like they're sisters," Alexi whistled through his teeth.

"A mirror image. They look like identical twins."

Ben wasn't the type to be rendered speechless. His mouth opened. No intelligible words came out, but he did better with the second attempt. "I'm not sure which is more surprising: the resemblance to our mother, or the fact that you have a color picture of a painting that no one else has. Not even the Art Loss Register has a photo of *Portrait of Señorita Santangel.*"

"Because they never owned it," his father said. He was enjoying the moment. "Clearly, we should have had daughters. Especially if they had looked like your mother."

"Or I should have been an only child," Alexi quipped.

Ben slid his parent's wedding picture next to the photograph of *Portrait of Señorita Santangel.* "I think Elizabeth Moynihan spent years of research to find an uncatalogued photo and has been covering it up ever since."

"Even a blind squirrel finds a nut now and then. Maybe she just got lucky."

"Or greedy," Ben said, an educated guess foretelling the future.

W
ednesday, November 6, Midnight

Chapter 16

Reflected in the pale, bluish-white illumination of the Miami skyline, a fingernail moon with the faint white of a well-formed cuticle ensured a dark night, perfect for breaking and entering. The interior of the Lowe Museum bristled with motion detectors, weight sensors, glass-breakage monitors, and laser-activated periphery defenses. But the most serious threat is always from within. Elizabeth Moynihan was a board member and valued consultant, with unrestricted access during normal business hours. She had modified her plan to allow for the recent upgrades in security and concluded the potential reward far exceeded the additional risk. She threaded a nylon rope through a series of pulleys and locking devices designed to rescue ice-climbers from glacial crevasses. The mountaineering hardware worked equally well for lowering an art thief into a museum.

She tightened the straps on her harness, braced herself, and raised the speargun to her shoulder. She pulled the trigger and sank the barb deep into a ventilation shaft that led to a six-way maze of aluminum tubes distributing air to the entire building. She could crawl to any gallery from this junction. She pulled a compass from a vest pocket, waited for the needle to find true north, and then crawled ten feet in the opposite direction until she was directly above the maintenance room shoehorned into the smallest room at the back of the museum. She used tinsnips to cut a hole in the bottom of the hollow shaft, removed the ceiling panel, and then lowered herself into the airspace above the floor. The keypad beckoned from across the room.

The red light on the pressure sensor flickered when the excess rope coiled atop a workbench and spilled onto the unfinished concrete. Fortunately, the weight sensor had been calibrated to detect humans, not sixty feet of excess nylon rope. This was the operations section of the museum—far removed from the valuable art at the opposite end of the building.

She began to twirl, suspended by the rope above the floor. She braced her feet against the wall and slowly let the rope play out until she was in a sitting position—an acceptable firing stance. The traction lock pulley functioned as promised. The tiny aluminum teeth resembled a dull saw blade, and the manufacturer guaranteed the ratchet would stop a climber falling off a mountain. Like an umbilical cord for thieves, the climbing rope and harness meant she could scramble back to the roof if she triggered the alarm. As far as the sensor was concerned, she was weightless.

The sound of shuffling cards was the Velcro straps releasing their hold on the gun and next spear. She waited. Her watch chimed the hour—time for campus security to make their hourly rounds. She gave them ten minutes to clear the building, then braced herself and pulled the trigger. The sudden whoosh of compressed air pinned her against the wall as the spear rocketed across the room . . . *thunk.*

She shined her light on the opposite wall. The coils of rope that had been below her now stretched across the room. She pulled against the rope until the barbs dug deeply into the far side of the wooden doorframe, much stronger than the flimsy drywall on either side of the door. She pulled the rope through the pulleys attached to her climbing harness and stretched it until the tension could have supported a tightrope walker. Not a skill she possessed, so she had a sling to support her feet. By sliding the carabiner attached to the front of her climbing harness along the rope, she pulled herself across the room a foot at a time, dangling beneath the makeshift tightrope spanning the room. Her arms started shaking. A painful cramp had lodged itself in her neck by the time she hung beside the door and within reach of the keypad.

She flexed her fingers. She knew the code.

She opened the door when the light on the keypad turned green. The motion sensors in the hallway were calibrated to detect rapid movement, so she performed her version of a slow-motion floor routine, with quarter-speed steps and the physical control of a gymnast. A faint glow coming from beneath the door of one of the adjoining rooms provided enough light to navigate by. The hallway floor was carpeted, so the padded soles of her shoes didn't make a sound; she left a faint trail of shoe-prints on the carpet from the dust she had knocked loose inside the ductwork. An employee breakroom on one side, administrative offices on the other, meeting rooms, a closet, a bathroom and a small kitchen, she softly approached the secure, middle section of the building where the galleries began.

The lighting in the central gallery was marginally better. She stopped at the outer edge of the parquet floor. Despite her cautious footsteps, a faint rustle from the fabric of the Velcro pockets attached to her tights traveled the length of the huge room. She shivered, studied the detectors mounted in each corner, and took note of the green lights glowing faintly beneath each one. No weight monitors in this room. She relaxed slightly. Prematurely. There was just enough light to cast faint shadows on the gallery floor and one of them was much too big to belong to Elizabeth.

Chapter 17

Disturbing dream images crept into Ben's uneasy sleep. *Trouble. A premonition. What had he missed? What could go wrong that he hadn't planned for? A flaw in the museum's security? Pendleton's alarm had been too good to beat—it had to be an inside job. Who was inside the Lowe Museum?*

Ben rolled onto his side and gasped when the movement sent a burning ache through his ribs. Lingering, half-remembered images from his nightmares coalesced into legitimate concerns with each additional minute he lay awake worrying. He picked up his phone—a habit. Unplugging it from the charger energized the screen. He noticed a recent text message from Lauren with an update on the floater's murder investigation: a judge had approved her subpoena for Harold Feinstein, a.k.a. *D'Erve's* phone and banking records. Lauren also repeated her original, unconditional offer to help, and a suggestion they meet for coffee.

Lauren was one of the few people Ben had trusted. Although they had drifted apart, she was a local, owned a boat, and had law-enforcement skills—an indication of core character traits reflecting honesty and trustworthiness—he hoped. Plus, he was curious about what had happened to her jealous, and recently ex, husband.

He responded to Lauren's text. *You awake? Still like puzzles?*

Lauren's response was so quick, she must have been holding the cellphone in her hand.

Yes 2 both.

She had been a night owl in high school and that hadn't changed. He tapped out a follow-up message. *Up for a quick boat ride to the Lowe?*

Seriously???!

Ben got seasick walking along a beach. He didn't swim. Fear of drowning was the result of hard-earned survival instincts passed down from a long line of ancestors, but living on an island meant losing the battle to avoid boats.

Yes. ASAP.

Checking with the babysitter . . .

Babysitter? An unexpected complication. Or was it? The unfamiliar ticking of Ben's biological clock rose another decibel but he was too preoccupied with his job to notice. His phone pinged.

Five minutes!

Lauren's text diverted his introspection. He hit the snooze button on his biological clock and walked out to the deck behind the house. He stopped to pick up a stick to clear a path through the spider webs, felt the darkness closing in on him, and thought about dead bodies floating near the dock. He went back inside for a flashlight. The smell of salt air, the gentle lap of waves against the pilings, the feel of the ocean breeze brushing against his skin—it was all familiar, as was the faint tinge of motion sickness. He detoured back inside for seasickness pills.

Lauren reversed the throttles and eased the passenger side of her boat close enough to the dock for Ben to gently step aboard. With a controlled burst of power to the starboard engine, they were underway before the side of the boat could brush against the pilings. "To the Lowe?"

"It's faster than driving. How close can you get?"

"At low tide?" Lauren took one hand off the wheel to point at the sliver of a New Moon. "Let's see. Biscayne Bay to Coral Gables Waterway . . . within 1000 feet if we stop at Triangle Park."

The intersection of Orduna Drive and Miller Road forms a lopsided triangle between Coral Gables Waterway and the University of Miami. The small park is a favorite among local dog walkers.

"Means crossing South Dixie Parkway and Ponce de Leon Boulevard on foot." Normally, Ben wouldn't cut across the well-fertilized park in a good pair of shoes or risk his life by attempting to cross two of Miami's busiest roads.

"You're wearing dark clothing. That'll help," Lauren added.

"Meaning I'll be less visible?"

"And a moving target."

He weighed the odds. "Fewer drivers, I might make it. How soon can we get there?"

"Let's find out." Lauren pushed the throttles forward until they reached the stops. "Hang on."

"Good advice." He tightened his grip and fought off motion sickness by keeping his gaze focused on the rapidly approaching Miami skyline instead of the wave crests flying by beneath the hull. He risked letting go with one hand and moved his left arm against his chest to stabilize his ribcage. Taking shallow breaths helped minimize the pain.

Lauren had to shout over the roar of the outboard engines. "Want to fill me in?"

"I was about to ask you the same thing." He was staring at her left hand where a wedding ring used to be. Her finger still had the tan line. "You have a kid?"

"A girl." Lauren smiled with the unbridled joy of unconditional love.

Ben noticed her left thumb curl beneath her hand and brush against her finger for a ring that was no longer there. "And the ex?"

"Gone," she said, and changed the subject. "What's so important that you'd voluntarily get on a boat?"

"Where do I start? With Elizabeth Moynihan and Richard Pendleton III, I guess."

"That's an odd pair."

"So is meeting in the women's bathroom at the Lowe. Add to that a stolen painting that belonged to my great-grandparents: *Portrait of Señorita Santangel.*

"Stolen from Pendleton?"

"That's the one. Elizabeth Moynihan is mixed up in the

theft somehow."

"Jeeze. I thought it was the floater, *D'Erve*." She moved the wheel a couple of degrees to avoid a dolphin pod feeding on herring. The silvery sides of the small fish glinted in the moonlight as the dolphins herded them into ever-smaller circles. "Or had you forgotten about him?"

"Not hardly. His name came up in that same bathroom conversation I overheard between Elizabeth Moynihan and Pendleton. She threatened me with a Taser when I started asking questions."

"*D'Erve* had Taser marks on his neck." Lauren watched Elizabeth's show for a change from classic black-and-white movies. "Explains why you called me. Not why we're in a boat headed for the Lowe."

"They say trouble comes in threes, and—"

"Oh brother. You and threes."

"Hear me out. Pendleton lied about not knowing Elizabeth Moynihan when I first met him. Clearly, they're a lot closer than he wanted me to realize. Thomas Benson was at the premier last night, and his name was mentioned in that same conversation I overheard in the bathroom."

"I know Benson is capable of murder." Lauren had crossed paths with Benson during a previous investigation. She suspected he was connected to her sister's murder but couldn't prove it.

"Add Thomas Benson in with that unlikely pair and it means stolen art. With *D'Erve* dead, Benson is positioning himself to become the premier middleman for stolen art. He's already got the cash-rich clients. Elizabeth gets him access to the art."

"Why Pendleton? He's already rich."

"Not really. He's cash poor and living like he's rich—unless . . ."

"Unless what?"

"Unless he's rich in black-market art work—the kind you can't sell through normal channels. It links Benson, Elizabeth, and Pendleton together. All three of them were at the Lowe and they were up to something. It's enough to give me a bad feeling about tonight."

Lauren throttled back the engines and eased the boat up to the public dock below the park. Ben had remembered to bring a flashlight, and Lauren, a gun. They cut across Triangle Park and dodged the traffic on South Dixie Parkway and Ponce de Leon Boulevard to reach the University of Miami campus. With all the perimeter floodlights blazing, the Lowe Museum was lit up like a movie theater at a Hollywood premiere.

"Over there," Lauren pointed to the figure moving toward the front door. "Police!" She held up her badge.

Ben shined the flashlight on the metal star so the guard could see it.

The man nodded at Lauren. "Hello? Is there a problem?"

"You tell me." She said.

"Sounds like it. Frank—the guy inside—isn't answering his radio. I'm glad you're here." He pulled a set of keys from his pocket and approached the front door.

Ben noticed a green light glowing from the keypad beside the entrance. "Looks like the perimeter alarm's off. Did you do that?"

"Nope. Set it before I started my rounds."

He didn't sound completely sure, however. Ben heard the scrape of metal against leather as Lauren pulled her gun out of its holster.

"Unlock the door. Stand back when you open it," she ordered.

The guard stepped out of the way.

"Clear," Lauren called, after entering.

Ben heard someone moan as they crossed the museum lobby. "Hello?"

He peeked around the corner, where the door hung open to the security office. There was nobody inside.

"Frank?" the security guard called. "Frank Perkins!"

Ben followed the carpeted hallway connecting the security office with the foyer. His shoes squeaked against the terrazzo flooring when he reached the entrance to the main gallery.

"A body," Lauren said, clasping her hand on his shoulder to stop him from entering the room.

"That's Frank!" The second security guard brushed past Ben and rushed to his partner's side.

"Turn on the main lights," Ben said. "Whoever did this might still be in here."

Lauren played the beam of her flashlight along the far wall of the gallery. Her flashlight stilled on a broken frame lying askew on the floor, directly beneath the wall where Renoir's painting of an idyllic boating scene was supposed to be hanging. "Pull the alarm."

T

he Lowe Museum: Thursday, November 7, 12:07 a.m.

Chapter 18

Elizabeth's fingers were mere inches from Renoir's *La Grenouillère*. She peered underneath the canvas to bypass the additional sensors, her nose close enough to smell a recent coat of paint on the wall and the aged oils on the canvas. The distinctive smell of centuries' old paint and lacquer formed a priceless, artistic aphrodisiac. The powerful allure of the Impressionists gripped her, even in the near-dark of the gallery. The urge to possess seized her—

Someone shouted. A man's voice. With a Cuban accent. In the hallway. She recoiled, spun from the painting. But she hadn't touched anything. She reached for the emergency pocket sewn onto the outside of her vest. *A guard? Inside! When did they hire additional security?*

She watched him reach for his radio instead of rushing across the gallery to grab her. A mistake. Or take his gun out of its holster and shoot her. Another mistake. She fumbled with a flap on her vest. The sharp ripping sound of a Velcro strip merged with a burst of static from the radio when the guard pressed the button to call his partner—he was out of chances.

Elizabeth sprinted across the lobby. She yanked a small metal box from her pocket, felt the textured steel case of a mini stun gun; she slid the safety switch forward to activate it, and discharged 50,000 volts into the man's nervous system. She maintained contact for three seconds and watched spasms ripple through his body, jerking his arms and legs like a disjointed puppet. The amperage was too low to cause permanent harm, but the voltage was strong enough to incapacitate him for ten minutes—maybe more if he had a weak heart. The handcuffs attached to his belt clacked against the parquet squares. His fingers tightened around the radio like he was having a seizure, but he couldn't speak—there was another brief burst of static followed by two seconds of silence before he dropped the radio and crumpled onto the floor. Not bad for an object small enough to attach to a woman's key ring, available in several colors and about twice the size of a disposable lighter. A residual twitch shuddered through his body. His eyelids fluttered, then closed with the gentle motion of a tired child fighting off sleep. He tried to raise his head but couldn't. Another small spasm, a low moan, and then he was still.

The adrenaline surge spurred her into action. Elizabeth had to look down at the floor to make certain her feet were touching. She took a deep breath to savor the freedom and feel the exhilaration.

The radio squawked. "Frank? You there? Come back."

Elizabeth swallowed a bitter aluminum aftertaste of spent adrenaline and backed away from the guard. She cleared her throat, cupped a hand behind her ear to listen, didn't hear an alarm, and quickly inspected her surroundings. She had worked too hard to get here, to be so close. And she was out of chances. These were her paintings; they belonged to her; she'd earned them—they were hers. She pulled a knife out of her vest pocket and unsheathed the blade. She returned to the Renoir and wedged the blade between the canvas and ornate frame. The impact triggered the motion sensor mounted on the wall behind the painting. A red light on the ceiling-mounted sensor began flashing. She knew the silent alarm was going out to the police department and campus security.

She considered cutting the canvas, weighed the time necessary to dismantle the ornate frame, and wedged the blade into the joint in the lower corner. She hammered on the butt of the knife until the wood splintered. She grabbed the knife with both hands and pried the canvas free, cutting along where the fabric attached to the wooden backing. She gently rolled the canvas into a tube until it was small enough to fit into the carrying case strapped to her back. She had room for another painting—the Degas . . . Monet . . . Pissarro. So many choices—upgraded security—not enough time.

She ducked into the next gallery. Now she was sprinting, footsteps quieting as she exited the gallery, dusty footprints marking her escape along the carpeted hallway. Past the kitchen and closet, approaching the employee breakroom when she heard shouts coming from the far gallery. All the lights came on and a different alarm blared. The Lowe Museum's motion detectors shrieked with a high-pitched note, penetrating her skull, eroding her concentration. She sprinted to the end of the hallway and ducked inside the maintenance room. She threaded the climbing rope through the traction-lock pulley. Frantically, hand-over-hand, she yanked the excess rope through the metal teeth until it pulled snug. She hauled herself off the floor and dropped a hand to pull the slack out of the rope beneath her. She repeated the process and moved twelve inches closer to the missing tile in the ceiling. Now she was suspended above the floor, beginning to twirl as the rope swayed from her exertions. She reached the duct and squirmed inside, crawled toward the ventilation shaft that led to the roof.

The muscles in her arms began cramping. Her training regimen hadn't allowed for the unexpected shock of a security guard stationed inside. One glove had snagged against the sharp edges of the duct and rope burns tortured her palm where the fabric was missing. Her arms were trembling by the time she reached the last stretch of vertical shaft, close enough to the roof for outside light to filter in. She wiggled up the last few feet of the narrow shaft until she could reach above her head with both arms and wrap her fingers over the edge of the flashing, pulled herself high enough to grasp the outer support brackets, and leveraged her body out of the tapered opening like a corkscrew uncorking a bottle of wine. The metal felt cold against her bare skin through a hole ripped in her tights.

Strobe lights from two converging police cars spun disjointed circles of kaleidoscopic red and blue light that bounced crazily off the walls beneath her. She crouched in the shadow of the roof-mounted air conditioner. High-intensity red and blue flashes bounced off the parking garage when the nearest cruiser slid onto Stanford drive and squealed to a bumpy stop on the cobblestone plaza. The bogus catering van, the rental car, the rusty work truck, Elizabeth abandoned the idea of using an automobile to escape and flung the rope over the northwest corner of the roof.

She released the climbing brake and rappelled into the shadows of the portico near the statue of the *Danaide*. The raft was near the Coral Gables Waterway, the powerboat was moored at the deep-water terminus of Mahi Waterway on the opposite side. The last 1200 feet of the Mahi Waterway was a densely forested outlet for the overflow from Lake Osceola. Elizabeth sprinted for cover along the neglected, shallow creek, choked with small trees and large bushes. She pushed aside a low-hanging branch with white blossoms and poisonous seeds and crept beneath the nearest tree large enough to offer cover. The northeastern side of the museum was less than 200 feet away but the bright spotlights couldn't penetrate the dense foliage. She waded into the center of the drainage and followed the tributary to a tunnel running beneath Ponce de Leon Boulevard. The boat was moored near the outlet mall on the other side of the street. She used the electric trolling motor to silently pull away until it was safe to start the outboard engines.

T hursday, November 7, 10:00 a.m.

Chapter 19

Ben used a secure connection to send electronic forms reporting the theft of an early Renoir from 1869: *La Grenouillère*. The current insured value had been set at seventy million dollars—a conservative value for insurance purposes that might double at a heated auction. He had the Coordination Center for Lost Cultural Assets bookmarked on his phone. *La Grenouillère* had been an anonymous donation to the Lowe Museum and the recent transfer date troubled him. The outwardly magnanimous gesture didn't make sense until he verified that the dates coincided with Richard Pendleton III's appointment to the museum board. The painting's dubious pedigree, with its undocumented ownership, was too much like the recent theft of *Portrait of Señorita Santangel* to be a coincidence.

"*Oy vey.*" The words didn't translate but nothing else came close to approximating the nightmare to come. If his boss ever surfaced, their next meeting was going to be acrimonious, and the overdue raise he had been promised looked like a longshot. He pushed his chair away from the table in the security office and stepped into the hallway. This view wasn't much better. Crime-scene tape had been stretched across the entrance to the gallery. He peeked around the corner.

"Don't even think of coming in here." The local FBI field agent was just finishing photo-documenting the crime scene.

"Find anything?"

"Since you asked me three minutes ago? Check back in an hour. Or better yet, wait for me to call." She turned her back on him and resumed dusting the splintered frame for prints.

His phone dinged with an incoming email. He checked the

subject line—still no answer from his boss. Instead, it was more bad news from Coastal Insurance Company's Legal Department. He groaned. More forms to fill out. He ducked beneath an additional strip of tape to reach the foyer and regretted bending at the waist. His ribs were still sore and staying awake all night wasn't helping them heal.

Portable bicycle racks formed a police barricade on the perimeter of the plaza. He avoided the gawkers by crossing the foot bridge spanning Lake Osceola. Another unwelcome email pinged his phone as he climbed the stairs to the Otto G. Richter Library on the University of Miami campus. Hardwood bookcases with glass-fronted displays lined the back wall. Searching through reams of documents and linear yards of shelved academic tomes predating the computer age was tedious, repetitive work—a perfect match for Ben's obsessive nature and highly attuned sensitivity to disorder—unless the item was missing.

Presumed **Missing**: the title of Elizabeth Moynihan's doctoral dissertation was intriguing and aptly named since nobody could find a copy. Equally intriguing was the image that Goldie had sent him, earlier.

"You got my message." Goldie waved him over to the reference desk and handed him a facsimile copy of the June 29th, 1939 catalogue from the Degenerate Art auction at the Theodor Fischer Gallery in Lucerne, Switzerland. "Did you just come from the museum?"

"Chased out, more like. By the FBI."

"It's been all over the news. No mention of what's been taken, though."

"It might surprise you. A canvas with incomplete provenance, but one that Elizabeth Moynihan authenticated."

"That narrows it down. Shall I guess?"

"Sure."

"Renoir?"

"Not much of a guess, given Elizabeth's fascination with Renoir. I'll even give you a hint," Ben said. "It's a recent addition to the museum's collection. With a problematic ownership chain missing a few links."

"*La Grenouillère*," she guessed. "Translates to *The Frog Pond*. One of many canvases Renoir gave to the restaurant proprietor, Monsieur Fournaise, because he didn't have the money to pay for his meals."

"I've heard the story. I didn't realize he gave him more than one canvas."

"Ah." Her grin opened a portal to what she must have looked like as a young woman. "*La Grenouillère* was also a French colloquial expression used during that time to refer to a class of young women . . . not exactly prostitutes, but not exactly amateurs, either."

"I didn't know that," he admitted. "Which is why I'm here to get your help."

"I love a challenge." When Mrs. Goldsmith promised, "the full cooperation of the library," her offer included every staff person from accounting to maintenance. It seemed they all owed her favors.

"Home-baked cookies," she revealed her secret, "and a daily planner marked with everyone's birthday."

Ben learned it was much more than simple kindness and baking when the head of maintenance dropped by with an update. "I've got my guys searching the History Department's archives," he said. "The best hiding place in a library is the bottom shelf. The bravest ones are searching the stacks—the miles of shelving where books go for eternal slumber." When Ben asked why the entire department had been mobilized, he recounted how Goldie still used her lunch hour to teach English as a Second Language classes. An undergraduate student from one of the classes joined the search for Elizabeth Moynihan's missing body of work, and as a member of the wireless generation, took the search global and emailed Ben links to all of Elizabeth Moynihan's published articles. He followed the most recent posting to an article she had written about Renoir's work in 1876.

The content had been withdrawn from publication—no reason given. Ben requested hard copies out of respect to the bibliophile surroundings. Goldie returned pushing a cart stacked with publications, unable to resist commenting on the issue sitting on top of the pile. "This one is strange. There's not even an article—just a preview." She handed him the library's advance copy.

"That's it? Just an abstract and a footnote?" He turned to the back of the advance copy and read the annotation about the lead isotopes in white paint. Elizabeth Moynihan matched the lead isotopes in the white paint Renoir used for three paintings that had been commissioned in 1876. She extrapolated her findings and authenticated *Portrait of Señorita Santangel* as one of Renoir's works despite the scarcity of provenance. It was impressive work. For someone who was so big on self-promotion, it seemed out of character for Elizabeth to forego the credit she was due.

"Probably Pendleton who made her withdraw the article," Ben guessed.

"The yacht fellow?"

"Richard Pendleton III. 'More trouble than versions I and II.'"

"So I've heard. He's on the museum board," Goldie said, "but I don't know him that well." Goldie rubbed her thumb against her fingers in the universal sign for money, lots of money.

"Yep. He bought his way onto the museum board with a sizeable donation: *La Grenouillère*, or 'The Frog Pond,' the other stolen Renoir with suspicious provenance that Elizabeth Moynihan and Pendleton have in common."

"Not a coincidence," Goldie said.

"No. Pendleton seems to be involved with stolen paintings in general. *Portrait of Señorita Santangel*, in particular, and *La Grenouillère*, indirectly." Ben returned to the cart stacked with Elizabeth Moynihan's publications and began to read everything she had written about Renoir.

Partway through his crash course on her collected writings, Ben sent Elizabeth a text suggesting they meet. When he didn't hear back from her within a few minutes, he followed up with an email. When that didn't generate a response, he called. When there was no answer, he left a message. Since Elizabeth wasn't responding, he moved a follow-up visit to Richard Pendleton III to next on his list.

◆ ◆ ◆

Gardenias grew like weeds in the flowerbed beside Richard Pendleton III's garage, scenting the air with the cloying fragrance of a dowager wearing too much cheap perfume. The atonal chorus from a large brood of cicadas clinging to Palmetto trees quieted when Ben approached the massive front doors. Once again, the brass knocker mounted in the center proved ornamental. This time it was Pendleton's butler who opened the door before Ben could knock. "Good afternoon, sir. And might I say, this is a pleasant surprise."

"Not as surprised as I am that Mr. Pendleton didn't have you meet me at the guard house—with a Taser to keep me off the grounds. Where's Serge? Out buying a vowel?"

"Looking for employment."

"And his previous employer?"

"Still waiting on a check from Coastal Insurance Company, sir."

"Which explains why he was willing to see me."

"Sir."

Although such a small word, the butler's command of etiquette turned the single syllable into a shared joke. He permitted the barest of grins to lift the edges of his normally staid expression and let his gaze rest on the stack of publications in Ben's hands. "Would you care to wait in the reading room? It appears you brought plenty of material."

"From the special collections at the University of Miami Library. I think Mr. Pendleton will be interested."

"I'm certain he will be, sir."

"Come to think of it . . ." Ben snapped his fingers to give the impression the thought had just occurred to him. "Maybe it would be better if I waited in the library."

"As you wish, sir. I'll announce your arrival."

Since Pendleton traditionally kept guests waiting five minutes, unwelcome guests should rate twice that—at least Ben hoped so. Pendleton had an impressive library, and Ben suspected there was a copy of Elizabeth Moynihan's doctoral dissertation in his personal collection.

He set the stack of her publications on top of a Shaker table and went to the "M" section of Pendleton's alphabetized library. Leather-bound, first edition copies of both her books rested on a polished oak shelf. There was a gap about the width of two fingers next to the copies, or the approximate size of the well-worn copy of her dissertation that he had noticed on the bookcase in her university office. It was circumstantial, at best, but the only gap in an otherwise tidy room full of carefully shelved books.

Ben removed *The Art of Appraisal* and turned to the flyleaf. Elizabeth had signed the copy, addressed Pendleton by his first name, and added a paragraph worth of appreciation for his "generous support and encouragement." He removed *Searching for Renoir* from the shelf. Elizabeth had signed this book and added a personal note that hinted at much more than just a simple exchange between an author and a loyal reader. *Yet Pendleton had pretended not to know her during his first visit.*

He checked the time on his phone—plenty of waiting-time remained in this round of one-upmanship. He stepped away from the shelves and moved to the center of the room where natural lighting offered a warm, inviting place to sit. Eight chairs had been arranged around a central table. Wear patterns on the red leather bottom of the chair at the head of the table hinted at this being Pendleton's favored seat. Since it was Pendleton's library, Ben needed to think like the crook who lived here. Replicating his vantage point was a good place to start. He sat on the worn chair at the head of the table and didn't hear Pendleton enter.

Pendleton wore soft-soled shoes and an angry expression. Ben didn't hear the footsteps but there was no mistaking the look of displeasure on Pendleton's face or the unwelcoming tone in his voice. "What do you want?"

"I found an article Elizabeth Moynihan wrote about the Theodor Fischer Gallery. She was working on her master's thesis at the time." Ben moved to the magazines he had left on the table and read aloud from the issue on top of the pile:

"A 'Degenerate Art' auction was held at the Theodor Fischer Gallery in Lucerne, Switzerland in 1939. Two paintings by Renoir were transferred from the state museum in Berlin, and they were just the tip of an iceberg. Over 7000 canvases had been removed from German museums prior to the Degenerate Art Exhibit of 1937. Ultimately, the number of canvases would exceed 70,000."

"What does this have to do with you finding my stolen Renoir?"

"I think the key to finding *Portrait of Señorita Santangel* is by following the flow of art from Vienna to Switzerland. Most of it passing through the Fischer gallery."

"Ridiculous."

"Elizabeth Moynihan doesn't seem to think so." *More trouble than versions I and II,* she had let slip during their clandestine meeting in the women's bathroom at the Lowe. Ben mentally thanked her for the tip and opened the next magazine to a bookmarked page and the second article in a series about *Entartete Kunst*—Degenerate Art. The evidence was damning. "Among the list of those in attendance at the auction was your father."

"I was having nothing to do with that," he said. His slipping command of the English language betrayed his nervousness.

Ben read from Elizabeth's article: "More than 16,000 works were confiscated, burned, or simply misplaced and presumed lost."

"Which has nothing to do with my Renoir, which you are supposed to be finding."

"I think it does." Ben was accustomed to dealing with the sociopaths who formed the criminal elite. Pendleton wasn't the first client without a conscience he had faced. Or was he an adversary? His evasiveness implied it.

"You are here to honor my claim—nothing else." He waved a hand in Ben's general direction with the same disdainful motion as a cow waving its tail at bothersome flies. "Leave before I call your boss to report your unprofessional behavior."

"Let me know if you reach him. I need to talk to him after you," Ben said, weakening Pendleton's leverage. "He still hasn't responded to my latest request for more information about your unusual policy or the questionable provenance of *Portrait of Señorita Santangel.*"

"Is that a threat?"

"A better one than yours. Go ahead and call my boss while I notify the *Koordinierungsstelle für Kulturgutverluste.* That's the Coordination Center for Lost Cultural Assets in Germany," Ben translated.

"I know what it is. You'll do no such thing." Pendleton placed his hands on the back of the chair.

Probably to keep them from shaking, Ben figured. Pendleton certainly looked nervous—a good time to apply a little more pressure.

"Your stolen Renoir probably passed through the back door of the Theodor Fischer Gallery in Lucerne, Switzerland."

Pendleton avoided eye contact.

Ben gathered the periodicals. Still discretely watching Pendleton, he stalled for time. He arranged the issues in ascending order by date, with the spines carefully centered.

There.

A flicker of awareness. Pendleton averted his gaze but not before Ben narrowed it to the stack of periodicals. Ben fanned the issues like a deck of cards spread across a gaming table. Pendleton gritted his teeth hard enough to form a bulge along his jawline that distorted his profile.

Ben ran his finger across the issues.

Pendleton relaxed his jaw.

Ben reopened the issue on top of the stack. Which one of Elizabeth Moynihan's articles had Pendleton so worried? Ben solved jigsaw puzzles as a hobby—good practice for unraveling a crime when so many pieces were involved . . .

He turned the issues upside down and spread them across the table—a strategy to counter Pendleton's effort at misdirection. Stolen art was only part of the crime. The answer wasn't just inside the magazines, it was also in the people connected to the theft of *Portrait of Señorita Santangel*.

Ben rested his finger on the issue that didn't fit—although it was a critical piece of the puzzle. He tapped his index finger on the library's advance copy. It was too thin. Elizabeth Moynihan's article was missing. It had been pulled from publication—but not the footnote. What was it about lead isotopes in the white paint that Renoir used in 1876 that had Pendleton so worried? Or was it something else? Something in the other missing document—her doctoral dissertation, maybe.

He drummed his fingers on the advance copy. His syncopated rhythm didn't have the expertise of Elizabeth Moynihan's nervous mannerism. The sound caused a heightened awareness in Pendleton, however. The change was subtle, an almost imperceptible turning of his head so his left ear pointed directly at Ben's clacking fingers.

"*Presumed Missing*," Ben said, hazarding an educated guess.

"What about it?"

It. . . . "*What about it?*" Pendleton knew what Ben was talking about—Elizabeth Moynihan's missing doctoral dissertation. Apparently missing from Pendleton's personal library, in addition to the University of Miami Library.

"*Presumed Missing,*" he stopped drumming his fingers. "It's a subtle change from her master's thesis, *Missing Masterpieces.* Don't you think?"

"I'm interested in one missing masterpiece—mine. *Portrait of Señorita Santangel,* the Renoir which you are supposed to be finding."

"Not the first time it's been stolen."

"Not my problem." He dismissed the fact with his customary indifferent wave.

"I was quoting Elizabeth Moynihan. 'Not the first time it's been stolen,' is her exact quote." His hand still rested on the library's advance copy. He slid the document to the edge of the table for effect.

Pendleton's gaze traveled across the room, along the shelves, up to the ceiling, and across every inch of the library except the table.

"Your father," Ben guessed, but turned his question into a statement and sounded confident saying it. He opened the copy to a single footnote about lead isotopes in the white paint Renoir used in 1876.

"What about him?"

"You inherited *Portrait of Señorita Santangel* from him. Was he the one who carried the stolen painting out the back door of the Fischer Gallery?"

He looked at Ben with the condescending stare a stepfather reserves for an illegitimate child.

"Not your father," Ben realized. "It's Elizabeth Moynihan you're worried about."

"Leave before I have you thrown out."

"Good idea. I remember the way; I'll show myself out." It was time to force a meeting with Elizabeth Moynihan. She was avoiding him; he was determined to find out why.

T hursday, November 7, 4:30 p.m.

Chapter 20

Ben stopped at an office supply store and printed a few old-fashioned color copies to prepare for his confrontation with Elizabeth Moynihan. It took three news helicopters to accurately report the scope of the massive traffic jam created by a parade in honor of the America's Cup Time Trials. Plenty of red lights, so Ben called, emailed, and sent follow-up texts to Elizabeth Moynihan as he navigated the congested streets between Pendleton's mansion on Key Biscayne and her gated fortress in the private housing development of Coral Gables Estates.

The decorative wrought-iron railing on Elizabeth Moynihan's security fence had started to rust where the thick black paint had chipped off. A yellow flyer fluttered from the lower right-hand corner of the gate, faded from the bright sun, tattered by wind and sand.

He pushed the intercom button to announce his arrival. No answer. He hit the button again and wrote a simple message in tiny, cursive letters—about the size of six-point font. He held the makeshift sign up to the surveillance camera beside the gate. It didn't take long—maybe a minute—until he heard the high-pitched whine of the camera lens when Elizabeth manually sharpened the focus to zoom in on his printed text: *Now that I have your attention . . .*

He turned the paper over and composed a different message, putting it on top of the fence along with a small rock to keep it from blowing away. It became a waiting game. Elizabeth would have to move the camera to read the message.

He watched a Monarch butterfly struggle to free itself from a clump of clasping milkweed growing in the watershed along the edge of the driveway. There was something about the way the waxy grains of pollen clung to the Monarch's feet that reminded him of Elizabeth's connection to stolen art. The camera pivoted with an audible, low-pitched whine. The letters were bigger, so the lens zoomed out with the familiar sound of tiny gears meshing. *If you want me to believe you're not home, don't move the camera.*

He leaned closer to the intercom and pushed the button to speak. "We need to talk. It's important."

"Stand back. I can hear you fine."

"What did you say?" He mumbled the question.

"You're so good with messages, write something."

"Too many unanswered questions to fit onto a single page." He left one of the color copies from the office supply store beneath the camera and walked toward his car.

"Wait. Pick that up," she ordered.

He pretended not to hear, didn't break stride or slow down.

"Wait," Elizabeth called.

He ignored her and opened the car door.

Thunk. The electronic lock on the side gate clicked open.

He returned to the entrance and picked up the picture of *Portrait of Señorita Santangel.* He followed the curving driveway and interrupted dinner for a doe with two fawns young enough to have spots. The deer scampered away from a late-blooming clump of lobelia while a few purple flowers remained. He stopped at the apex of the next curve when he heard the overhead camera rotate into position. He left a different color copy beside the mounting post: *Beis Hei* from the back of the frame.

Another curve, another camera, so he placed a color copy of a different Renoir painted in 1876, *La Grenouillère,* or 'The Frog Pond,' the second stolen Renoir with suspicious provenance that Elizabeth Moynihan and Richard Pendleton III had in common.

He cut across the last curve in the driveway. Nothing life-giving grew along the perimeter of Elizabeth's house. The deer had eaten the blossoms from an ornamental hydrangea growing along the watershed. The Monarch butterfly was somewhere deeper in the woods where native milkweed flourished in the marshy interior. Ben crossed the cobblestone plaza and followed a boardwalk covered with drifting sand that connected a detached garage with the front porch. There was no need to ring the doorbell, he turned to an overlooked footnote and held the advance copy from the library in front of the spyhole in the front door.

"What do you want?"

He glanced at the intercom mounted beside the door. The reverb in Elizabeth's voice reminded him of a guitar solo from the beach music of the 1960s. He returned the library's advance copy to the manila folder in his other hand and sorted through a growing collection of circumstantial evidence. He removed the facsimile June 29th, 1939 catalogue from the Degenerate Art auction at the Theodor Fischer Gallery and held it up to the door.

The catalogue triggered the unlocking and relocking of several deadbolts. It didn't make sense until he opened the door. Elizabeth stood behind an inner door with bullet-proof glass panes reinforced by metal bars with an elaborate deadbolt. She was barefoot. The nail polish on her toes matched the pink spaghetti straps resting against the tanned skin between her neck and shoulders. A loose sweatshirt and baggy denim jeans covered everything else. It didn't look like there would be any flirting today. She kept one hand hidden behind her back.

Ben assumed it was a gun she was hiding, unaware of the rope burns suffered during her break-in at the Lowe.

The wind rattled through the fake palm fronds attached to the porch above his head. A few grains of sand slid across the wood and crunched beneath his feet when he shifted his weight to the other foot. He returned the catalogue to the folder. "I'd like to borrow a copy of your Doctoral Dissertation: *Presumed Missing.*"

"What do you really want?"

"I'm serious. I can't find it, anywhere. I'd settle for a copy of your master's thesis, though, *Missing Masterpieces.* I can't find a copy of either one." Ben didn't care for affected mannerisms. He especially didn't like using air quotes which were rather high on his list of pet peeves, but nothing else quite captured the subtle differences implied in the titles of Elizabeth's dissertations. He used two fingers from each hand to punctuate the titles from her master's thesis and doctoral dissertations: "from '*Missing Masterpieces*' to '*Presumed Missing.*' It's a significant change in the titles of your research papers; I'd like to read both."

He watched her expression to see if she was flattered or annoyed. Her posture suggested impatience, so he stalled, taking his time riffling through the color copies in the manila folder. "From camera number one." He held up the copy of *Portrait of Señorita Santangel.*

Elizabeth crossed her arms.

He held up the photographic copy of *Beis Hei* from the back of the frame.

She leaned forward close enough to the screen door for her breath to form a small plume of condensation against the thick glass inserts.

Progress. He held up a picture of the Renoir stolen from the Lowe Museum, also painted in 1876: *La Grenouillère,* "The Frog Pond."

"I remember what you told me the first time we met at your office," he said, "or rather what you *didn't* tell me—about professional secrets. You authenticated *Portrait of Señorita Santangel* by matching the lead isotopes from the white paint Renoir used in 1876. I'm impressed, but what bothered me was that you didn't take credit for it. You tried to, you even wrote an article about your research, but Pendleton found some way to get it pulled."

"I don't know what you're talking about."

"Sure you do. I didn't know it the first time we talked. I do now because of your snide comment in the bathroom. 'Richard Pendleton III, more trouble than versions I and II.' I didn't make the connection until I saw your autographed books in his library and read about his father, 'version II' being at the Degenerate Art auction on June 29th, 1939 at the Fischer Gallery. I'm holding a copy of the sales catalogue. There are some real bargains in here."

"Surely you didn't go to this much trouble to tell me something I already know."

"I think you know a whole lot more—about *Entartete Kunst*. About canvases that have been unaccounted for since 1933 when the Nazis pulled 16,000 pieces from German museums. I can't prove it—yet, but that's how Richard Pendleton got his Renoir—or at least had it until it was stolen on Halloween."

"Speaking of which," she said. "Shouldn't you be out there looking for *Portrait of Señorita Santangel?*"

"Among others." Casually, Ben asked. "Didn't you appraise *Madeleine Leaning on Her Elbow with Flowers in Her Hair* in 2011? For the same Houston couple, it was stolen from?"

Elizabeth didn't reply. She looked pale, but it could have been the thick glass between them, or a lack of makeup. Maybe she wasn't feeling well.

He waited. He didn't think her capable of speechlessness, so it was either bad manners or guilt. Maybe both since she turned on her heel and began to walk away. Her footsteps quieted when she reached the carpeted hallway. She turned the corner and moved out of sight.

The setting sun used overcast skies as an artist's palette. The prelude to a spectacular sunset peeked over the horizon and blended basic hues into pastel shades with gossamer strands of dissipating clouds. Ben figured if he hurried, he could make it back to Key Largo before dark. It was going to be close. He remained optimistic until he was on the causeway and a yellow light prompted him to glance at the fuel gauge. He slowed to optimize miles-per-gallon and hoped there were enough fumes to coast the rest of the way to the Quik Stop and the nearest pump. Getting home before dark moved into second place behind running out of gas.

The Police Cruiser parked beneath the awning at the Quik Stop had a bicycle rack attached to it. Lauren was inside, helmet in hand and looking very much like a modern, bike-mounted law enforcement officer.

"Hey," she called out. "I just heard the news."

"About Elizabeth Moynihan's apparent complicity? My missing boss or his reckless insurance policies? Maybe something to do with the dead body floating near my father's house, stolen Renoirs painted in the same year, a yacht racer I'm beginning to suspect of war profiteering, an art thief still on the loose . . ." Ben was still adding to the list when Lauren interrupted his litany of problems.

"About Coastal Insurance Company filing for bankruptcy." She pointed at the company credit card in his hand. "You think that's gonna work?"

"If it doesn't, I might need a ride. Or a job."

"The sun's down. Don't you ever stop working?"

"Not lately—too many cases. Although I don't have a whole lot else going on, or anybody waiting at home for me." The words slipped out as a confession. Maybe he was too tired to put up a front. Or it could be that he had known Lauren for long enough to let down some of his customary defenses. The momentary tenderness from their last meeting remained promising.

"That sounded borderline honest—and kind of sad."

"You're still in uniform. I could ask you the same thing."

"In my defense," she said, "I was headed home to watch an old movie."

"Will there be popcorn?"

"Gourmet."

"Want some company?" Ben asked.

"It has to be PG."

"The show, perhaps. Afterward, however . . .?"

"And the night. I have Brenda."

"Your daughter?"

"Of the same name."

"Sounds like a date," Ben said.

"Maybe."

T

hursday, November 7, 8:30 p.m., Key Largo

Chapter 21

Ben heard Lauren's fingers scrape against the bottom of the wooden bowl. Her daughter sat in the middle with the popcorn bowl in her lap. When Ben reached over to sort through the kernels in hopes of rounding up a few stragglers, Lauren playfully slapped his hand away from her own determined prospecting.

She hasn't changed that much, he thought. *Except for the kid. And a jealous ex-husband licensed to carry a firearm.*

"Sure makes a change from watching old black-and-white movies." Lauren pressed "Record" when the opening theme music for Elizabeth Moynihan's show began playing. "And that crack I made about you always working. It was supposed to be a joke."

"You said I could choose," Ben reminded her. "And Brenda said it was okay as long as we watched a cartoon first."

"She's easy." Lauren put her arm around her daughter.

Brenda was destined to be easy and loving for her entire life. She might learn a skill and lead a productive life, perhaps reach a certain level of self-sufficiency by living in a group home. An additional chromosome was responsible for the slight upward slant of her eyes and broad, slightly flattened facial characteristics, along with her developmental delays.

"She was a happy baby," Lauren explained. "That hasn't changed much. Probably never will, entirely. I wanted to raise a loving child, and that's what I'll always have."

Ben listened and learned. Maybe Brenda liked puzzles. Chess was out but checkers might be fun. They already shared an affinity for popcorn and were in consensus about the need for another bowlful—after Elizabeth's show, of course.

The opening shot of Elizabeth Moynihan's broadcast was an aerial view of the Lowe Museum that tightened focus, moving inside to the largest and most famous of Renoir's paintings on display: *The Boating Party*. The camera panned across the figures in the painting before narrowing its focus onto Elizabeth Moynihan and Richard Pendleton III.

"That's a pretty picture," Brenda said. "It sure is big!"

"It sure is, sweetie. And those are big shoes," Lauren drew Ben's attention to Elizabeth's footwear. "Four-inch heels. Makes my feet hurt just to look at them. She usually wears dress flats."

"They make her taller than Pendleton. Goes with the dominating canvas and the unexpected questions she's about to ask him."

"I like the hats. I want a hat like that, mommy." Apparently, Brenda liked wearing hats. Her current choice was a beanie with mouse ears. "Can I get a hat like the one in the picture?"

"Maybe later, sweetie."

"About those hats," Ben began. "Those are straw boaters and—"

"—Enough about the 'H.' 'A.' 'T.' 'S.'" Lauren locked eyes with Ben before glancing at Brenda. "She's got a closet-full already," she whispered.

"Okay, but she gets credit for mentioning them. Elizabeth Moynihan didn't hold the interview in front of this painting to make Pendleton look small, well maybe partly, but mostly she did it because of who's in it—specifically who's wearing the two ha— 'H.' 'A.' 'T.' 'S.' Alphonse Fournaise, Jr., and Alphonsine Fournaise, the son and daughter of Monsieur Fournaise who owned the restaurant where this scene is painted. Renoir gave Monsieur Fournaise several paintings, among them "*La Grenouillère*, or 'The Frog Pond.' Which also happens to be the painting that Pendleton donated to the museum to buy his way onto the board."

"The one that was just stolen." Lauren added, "and I know how you feel about coincidences. That's entirely too many."

"There's more. See the way Elizabeth unconsciously raised

her hand to her chin? She did the same thing at her university office when we were discussing another stolen Renoir: *"Madeleine Leaning on Her Elbow with Flowers in Her Hair.* I checked. She did the appraisal for that one, too."

"Good thing we're taping this." Lauren settled back against the couch. "I know how we can resolve a few of those 'coincidences.' I'll log onto the Police data base after bedtime."

"Brenda's or ours?" Ben asked.

"Brenda's." Her smile suggested it wasn't the worst idea he'd had.

Lauren had learned to type on a manual typewriter. Her fingers pounded on the keyboard with the rapid clack of castanets. She hit the *Enter* key hard enough to give the message a running start and tilted the screen a few degrees to offer Ben a better view.

He had been using his phone to check his email—still no answer from his boss. "Can you file a missing persons' report?"

"Sure. On who?"

"My boss. He's been missing for five days."

"Not long enough."

"Six if we stay up till midnight."

"Wouldn't matter if it was a week. Your boss is an adult. Technically, he's not missing. Could be something as simple as an unplanned vacation."

"He's not the type. Besides, there's half-a-billion-dollars' worth of stolen art to go along with his unexplained disappearance. Which coincides with all the questionable policies he just started writing on equally suspicious paintings lacking provenance." Ben continued the list he had started at the Quik Stop. "There's still the matter of the floater at my father's dock, *D'Erve*—who deals in stolen art, along with two recently stolen Renoirs. Thomas Benson is a money-laundering gangster taking an unhealthy interest in masterpiece art . . ." Ben held up four fingers and curled down his thumb. "There's more. Let me change hands." He counted on a different set of fingers. "That strange scene with Elizabeth Moynihan and Pendleton—first at the museum when they were taping that segment for her show, and then immediately afterward in the women's bathroom at the Lowe." Ben folded down two more fingers. *"Portrait of Señorita Santangel* and *Madeleine Leaning on Her Elbow with Flowers in Her Hair*—Elizabeth's appraisal of two Renoirs that were subsequently stolen, her article about the lead isotopes in white paint from 1876 that I suspect Pendleton had pulled from print . . . there's more but I'd have to take off my shoes and use my toes. What would it take?"

She cocked her head to the side and reconsidered. "Hard to say."

"Try English."

She smiled despite the seriousness of the matter, and there it was—that slight narrowing of her right eye and a fleeting smile reserved for a hard-won closeness between two people that meant more than just physical pleasures, that emotional connection that had launched thousands of greeting cards and inspired the delivery of millions of red, long-stemmed roses.

Ben noticed how the light glinted off Lauren's light-brown hair. Elizabeth Moynihan was blonde and a bombshell—and probably a crook. Not that her apparent larceny somehow made her any less exciting and desirable. Lauren, however, was smart, independent, trustworthy, and had access to law enforcement databases. "Let's start at the beginning: the floater. You said you had a subpoena to check *D'Erve's* bank and phone records."

She wiggled the mouse and clicked through to a different screen. "Here are his phone records for the last month."

"That's Elizabeth Moynihan's number. Fourth from the top."

"You sure?"

Ben pulled up the call log on his phone to check. "Yep. Same one. I wonder if he had better luck getting her to answer."

"Looks like it. I count five conversations. None of them shorter than two minutes."

Ben scooted his chair forward. Another of the numbers drew his attention. "That one's familiar, too. The one with a 212-area code. That's Manhattan."

"Yeah?"

"My boss's number. I didn't recognize it at first because it's programmed into my phone. I'm used to tapping an icon instead of keying in the numbers."

"Why would *D'Erve* be calling your boss?"

"For the same reason he's missing: suspicious insurance policies on equally suspicious stolen Renoirs lacking complete provenance."

Lauren highlighted the common phone numbers with a click of the mouse. "Might also explain why *D'Erve* was calling Elizabeth Moynihan."

"Pretty observant. They teach you that in Detective School?"

"Police Academy." She put her finger on the screen beside the highlighted numbers. "You're the one who likes jigsaw puzzles. What do you make of this?"

"Proximity is a good technique. My boss and *D'Erve* were neighbors. Richard Pendleton and Elizabeth Moynihan are closer than they want people to know. All four of them are connected by phone calls."

Lauren clicked through to the FBI's Art Loss Register. "Let's see what else they have in common."

Ben already had a pretty good idea—from the subtle change between the title of Elizabeth Moynihan's master's thesis: *Missing Masterpieces*—and from the focus of her doctoral dissertation: *Presumed Missing*. The title was ironic and appropriate. He leaned back in his chair. Midway through the backward arc, he realized that someone else must have found a copy of Elizabeth's dissertation and made a connection to the art that had been missing since 1933, during a time when the Nazis were pulling 16,000 pieces of degenerate art from German museums.

Nothing else explained the missing Renoirs: *Portrait of Señorita Santangel* and *La Grenouillère*, both of which further linked Pendleton to Elizabeth Moynihan and the information buried in her doctoral research.

"Maybe I need to change my strategy," Ben said, "and approach this from a different angle."

"What do you mean?"

"I've been chasing the art and you've been trying to catch the crooks. Let's switch. With your access, you can follow up on these phone calls and look at their banking records. I'll start working from the other end, tracking the thieves. I'm adding my boss to that list, but I'll start with Thomas Benson—a known crook and easier to find."

F riday, November 8, 6:00 a.m., Miami

Chapter 22

The evening winds relinquished control of the heavens; the clouds dissipated and a pale gray dawn turned the skies an aquamarine shade of blue. Rather than try and hack into their records or breech the Miami Biltmore Hotel's security, Ben used the lobby phone and called room service to order an early breakfast for Thomas Benson. He waited until a waiter emerged carrying a tray, and then followed the apron-clad man who emerged from the kitchen to the bank of elevators.

"Let me get that," Ben said, and stretched out his arm to hold the door open while the waiter settled the tray on his shoulder and picked up the tray stand. "What floor?"

"Six, sir."

"How about that? Same as me." He tempted fate and pushed the button. Poor quality control at the factory, manufacturing defects, hydraulic leaks, or metal fatigue, elevators were locked cages one drop away from death. He took deep breaths to control his understanding of gravity.

He watched the brief encounter between the waiter and Thomas Benson from the alcove housing the ice machine. The waiter was polite but puzzled and returned to the kitchen where the mix-up would be blamed on the front desk.

Ben knocked on the same door, having planned for a better response.

Benson acted surprised to see him, but there had been no light coming through the spyglass—he had verified Ben's identity before opening the door.

"Not hungry?"

"That was you?" Benson narrowed his gaze. "Reasonably

clever. How did you find me?"

"The limo driver. It's amazing how much information twenty bucks will buy."

"What do you want?"

"To borrow your copy of *Presumed Missing*."

"Go to the library."

"Already stolen."

"Then ask Elizabeth Moynihan," Benson suggested. "She wrote it."

"Knowledge you would have, only if you've read it. Or stole it." Ben noticed how Benson's grip tightened on the door. It was subtle, but the skin covering his knuckles turned white from increased pressure. "You remember Elizabeth Moynihan, right? I saw you standing in the autograph line at her show."

Ben watched the pronounced vein in Benson's temple. If he was nervous, it wasn't affecting his pulse. The hand wrapped around the door was equally uninformative. The blood had drained out of Benson's fingertips, his nails were white instead of pink, but that could be attributed to gravity. Benson laundered money for drug dealers, so he was cool under pressure and certainly capable of committing murder.

Benson met Ben's gaze with an indeterminate nod, without implying understanding or admitting complicity. He didn't blink. The fingers he had wrapped around the edge of the door remained steady, but the door inched a few degrees closer to his body.

Ben didn't play poker but knew when someone was bluffing. "I've been reading *D'Erve's* phone records. You probably know him as *The Fence*. I found him floating beneath a dock."

"Probably a case of mistaken identity. I believe you share a resemblance."

"Passing." It was enough of a veiled threat to elevate Ben's pulse. He and *D'Erve* looked enough alike for Lauren to misidentify the corpse. He felt the rush of blood to his head and resisted the urge to unbutton his collar.

"*Portrait of Señorita Santangel*," Ben countered the subtle threat with circumstantial evidence.

Benson edged the door closed a fraction of an inch.

"*La Grenouillère,* another stolen Renoir, this one from the Lowe via Richard Pendleton III's collection."

Tightening his grip on the door drained more blood from Benson's knuckles.

"*D'Erve* is dead. Coastal Insurance Company is out of the 'ten percent recovery fee and no questions asked business.'" Ben counted the beats distending the prominent vein showing on Benson's forehead and established a baseline for his anxiety level.

"Yesterday's news." Benson shrugged off the accusation.

"*D'Erve's* timely death. Coastal Insurance Company's business reversal. Now there's a glut of undocumented paintings: a chain of events you engineered to become the heir apparent in the stolen art business."

"You're giving me too much credit. It's a clever theory, however."

"It's more of a business model. Your cash-rich, drug-dealing, money-laundering customers are investing in masterpiece art. Pendleton is a likely source and Elizabeth Moynihan has the connections you need. You stand to benefit more than anyone else."

Ben watched the vein on Benson's forehead. His increased pulse meant he wasn't as calm as he looked.

"Why are you telling me all this?" Benson kept his tone matter-of-fact, although his rigid stance and tense posture belied the outward illusion of calm.

"Three reasons."

"I've heard about you and threes. Go on."

"First: 16,000 missing paintings from *Entartete Kunst.*"

Benson shrugged—an affected mannerism. Vampires and poisonous snakes could learn some pointers from the evil intent behind his calculating smile.

"Second: two stolen Renoirs with the same suspicious lack of provenance."

"I'm sensing a trend." Benson's tone was mocking. His pulse belied the façade, however.

Ben noticed Benson's posture shift, slightly. He began leaning toward the door instead of away from it—a clear indication of interest.

"That *trend* includes murder."

"I wouldn't know anything about that." The serpent-like grin reappeared.

"Which one? Trend or murder?"

"Both." Benson was too good of a criminal for a confession. He moved closer to the door, however, a definite sign of curiosity bordering on guilt. Enough of a reaction for Ben to apply more pressure.

"*D'Erve's* murder, remember?"

"All I know is what I've seen online."

Since stolen paintings appeared to raise his blood pressure, Ben stayed on topic. "After nearly eighty years, two paintings from the Santangel collection are back in circulation. What if there are more?"

"You'll need to ask Doctor Moynihan about that." He wrapped his hand around the knob and slammed the door in Ben's face.

Ben raised his fist to pound on the door but didn't make it past the backswing. Benson was through talking. The only people liable to answer were hotel security guards.

"'You'll need to ask Doctor Moynihan about that,'" Ben muttered, weighing the significance. It was good advice except he'd already tried that. Where could he find a copy of her Masters and Doctoral research? The harder he looked, the more he was certain that *Missing Masterpieces*, and *Presumed Missing* were akin to a treasure map.

Richard Pendleton III fired Serge after the interview fiasco at the Lowe Museum. Unemployment meant revocation of his temporary work visa; deportation meant two years of mandatory armed service in his war-torn homeland. Few survived conscription. Serge was desperate.

Thomas Benson had a lucrative sideline in taking advantage of desperate people, however, and offered Serge a job—with a two-part catch. The first part was easy: share all the insider information on Pendleton that a nosy servant could collect. Serge had the dirt on his ex-boss and was glad to spill it. The true test, however, was exposing Elizabeth Moynihan. Benson had a plan and Serge was the scapegoat—a desperate scapegoat who rationalized the need to stay alive versus the risk of breaking into Elizabeth Moynihan's office. Serge removed the white linen garments of servitude and changed into modern clothing suitable for infiltrating the University of Miami. He slung a backpack casually over one shoulder and adjusted the strap so the crowbar wouldn't dig into his back.

The campus was sparsely populated on early Friday mornings; he waited in the shadows directly opposite the ivory tower that housed Elizabeth Moynihan's office. He hid beside some kind of holly until no one was watching. Serge was better at breaking and entering than plant identification. A four-foot lever opens a two-inch lock; he used a stainless-steel bar to pry the metal security door away from the frame. He taped the door shut from inside to give the impression it was still securely locked and figured no one would notice one more mark on a heavily-used portal. Early morning sunlight filtered through the windows, casting dappled shadows on a glossy tile floor. He took the stairs and left a set of muddy footprints that led from the edge of the lobby to Elizabeth Moynihan's office.

Serge broke the lock on the office door in less time than it normally took Elizabeth Moynihan to open it with her key. The filing cabinets were just as easy. *Madeleine Leaning on Her Elbow with Flowers in Her Hair* was the first item on Benson's larcenous list. Elizabeth made stealing easy, she had carefully labeled and alphabetized a folder for every painting she had appraised. Benson had used capital letters for the next item and had nearly torn the paper with his pen when he had underlined it: the Theodore Fischer Gallery in Lucerne, Switzerland. Serge checked all the drawers in the filing cabinets—nothing about the gallery until he opened an unmarked folder tucked away at the very back of the bottom drawer.

"Aha." Serge had been employed long enough to know about Pendleton's Renoir bearing the distinctive Santangel coat of arms. *"Beis Hei,* indeed." *Baruch Hashem:* Thank God for stolen art. Serge understood enough archaic Yiddish to recognize the symbols representing billions in missing art—make that temporarily missing, judging by the amount of research contained in the folder.

Missing Masterpieces, Presumed Missing, and *La Grenouillère* —The Frog Pond, Serge stuffed each file folder into his backpack and drew a line through the last incriminating item on Benson's list. He checked his watch and decided there was still plenty of time for some personal shopping.

The file folders in the top drawers were unusually thin, suspiciously thin when compared to the unlabeled companion files in the bottom drawer. Serge satisfied his curiosity by pulling the folder entitled: *Portrait of Señorita Santangel.* Although there were only two sheets of paper inside, he possessed enough inside knowledge for the scant information to be explosive. Lucrative.

He stuffed the folders marked "Richard Pendleton III, and "Degenerate Art" into the backpack. Anything he could use to discredit his ex-employer was a bonus. He moved to the bookcase and grabbed the well-worn leather-bound edition of *Presumed Missing,* Elizabeth Moynihan's personal copy of her doctoral dissertation as he left her office.

F riday, November 8, 8:30 a.m., Key Largo

Chapter 23

Ben rehearsed his lines until he could deliver them with a compelling blend of corporate need and personal concern; he needed to justify a security breach to a business that profited from preventing them: Coastal Insurance Company. He picked up the phone. The main office in Manhattan was a madhouse on a normal business day, and on Friday mornings, the patients were in control. He contacted the ultimate authority—Joyce, the Office Manager.

"Hello?" Joyce was smart enough not to go down with the ship, in this case the metaphorically sinking Coastal Insurance Company ship. Ben listened to her current dilemma. "Nobody can find him. Our boss is still missing. Along with the unusual policy he issued to Richard Pendleton III."

The subsequent theft of *La Grenouillère* from the Lowe —another ill-advised policy on a Renoir lacking provenance— added an additional level of worry bordering on panic. She was more concerned with keeping her job than keeping secrets.

"If we can't find the man," Ben paused for effect. "How about we find the next best thing? His phone."

"What good will that do?"

"It's a start."

"Not much of one."

"Not yet, anyway." Ben remembered what it was like to work at the main office, however. The opportunity for a small victory, a single measure of success in a bleak situation, typically appeared as a godsend in a chaotic atmosphere. "Keep in mind, he's never far away from his phone, so I'd like to know his approximate location. Within a particular zip code counts as progress. My goal for today is to get at least one positive result in this investigation."

"You're an optimist. My goal is to keep my job."

"Here's your chance. I'm betting you know where he keeps the password for his computer."

"On a piece of paper taped to the bottom of his keyboard."

"I was afraid it was in his wallet."

"He loses that, too."

"If we can find his phone, the location will tell us where he is."

"Or was," she didn't sound optimistic.

"Still qualifies as progress." He walked her through the steps. By logging onto his boss's personal email account, she was able to pinpoint the location of his cell phone. The chances were good that he would be nearby—even if he refused to answer. The device manager on his boss's email account synched with his phone and gave the location—south of Miami, on a small island in international waters.

"Never heard of it," she said. "Probably need a boat to get there."

"No thanks," he said, until he consulted a better map and identified the owner of the remote island—Richard Pendleton III.

"A plane would be faster."

"And deadlier."

"Not necessarily. Want me to arrange a charter?"

"No."

"Are you sure?" She asked.

"Yes. But go ahead and do it, anyway. I know a local pilot who's still alive—so far."

Lauren Welles learned to fly before she could drive a car. Ben crossed his fingers for luck when the airport clerk ran the company credit card to pay for the charter. It didn't help. The charge went through and there was no way to manfully back out of taking the flight. He understood enough Newtonian Physics to calculate the acceleration of a falling object due to gravity. If a plane went up, it inevitably came down—faster by the second. He remembered acceleration as being thirty-two-feet per second, squared, although he would be flat after impact. He tightened his already tight grip when Lauren banked the airplane to circle Pendleton's island.

She made a big show of tapping each of the mechanical gauges with the tip of her finger. The needles didn't quiver; they remained steadfastly within what passed for normal operating range.

Lauren patted his knee to reassure him. "Don't panic. Re —"

"Too late."

"Remember, mechanical trouble is just a cover story. There's nothing wrong with the plane. We need an excuse to make an emergency stop—strictly a reason to pay an uninvited visit." Lauren switched the radio to "transmit" and broadcast her concern about the flight-worthiness of the plane, announcing her intention to make a forced landing.

"Aren't they all?" Ben asked. "Forced landings?" Claiming potential engine trouble gave them an excuse to make an unscheduled landing on Pendleton's private island but flying—especially landing—was risky enough without tempting fate.

Lauren reduced airspeed. "Once we're on the ground we can take a look around, but remember, I don't have any jurisdiction here."

"And I don't have any business being here. Tracing my boss's phone is already borderline shady."

"Wow." Lauren lowered the flaps and throttled back. "This is a short runway."

Ben closed his eyes and braced for impact. The only prayer he could remember was the *Kiddush*, a Seder blessing for wine when the Passover began on a Friday. He was scared, not thirsty, and there wasn't enough time remaining in his life to get drunk in preparation for a violent death. He felt the impact before he smelled it, pictured the motionless wheels on the plane's under-carriage as they quickly spun to 120 miles-per-hour. The outer layer of tortured rubber ignited from the sudden friction and melted off.

The padding in the seat cushion compressed beneath the force of the impact until he could feel the unyielding metal frame beneath his thighs. Every joint in the plane's frame rattled at the weakest point, where bolts and rivets joined components predisposed to failure. The vibrations intensified when Lauren applied the brakes and the plane furthered the inevitable process of shaking apart. A crosswind buffeted the fuselage and further stressed the decaying metal. The plane yawed with an unnatural sideways motion as she corrected their course.

Who's going to say Kaddish or El Maleh Rachamim for my departed soul? Facing death improved Ben's memory and a litany of prayers resurfaced. While he braced for the inevitable crash, the prayer for his mother's soul tumbled from his lips. *"Eil malei rachamim, shochayn bam'romim,"* he chanted. When that didn't appear to be slowing the plane fast enough, he hedged his bet by switching religions and searched his memory for the words to the Rosary in case God was Catholic.

Lauren applied the brakes with enough force to bury the shock absorber on the nose wheel against the limit of travel. The violent deceleration shook dust loose from nooks and crannies in the interior, vibrated the microphone off its hook, and sent all the loose items in the cockpit onto the floor or into the narrow shelf where the dash and windshield came together.

Ben opened his eyes to a cockpit in disarray. Most of the loose objects had gathered on the floor by his feet. A map yellowed by age and neglect had vibrated loose from the visor and fallen onto his lap. He leaned forward and shoved a flight log away from the windshield. Seven, maybe eight feet of pavement remained before the runway ended abruptly at the wet sand along the narrow beach. "Never thought I'd hear myself saying these words, but—nice landing."

"Thanks. In fact, I may get out and join you in your standard ritual of kissing the ground after every flight." She glanced at Ben. "I can almost hear the abacus beads in your mind clicking together. Are you already figuring the odds of surviving the return flight?"

He nodded. "It's not promising."

Lauren released the brake on one wheel to rotate the plane in the allowable space and taxied to the opposite end of the runway. "Strange. Looks like the hangar doors are open."

"Looks like an invitation to go inside to me."

"Nope. Looks suspicious. It's easier to use the side door. When the main doors are only open a little bit, it usually means there's a problem." She brought the plane to a gentle halt in front of massive doors that should have been all the way open or completely shut.

Ben unfastened his seatbelt and opened the door while Lauren was still following the checklist to properly shut down the plane.

"Hang on." She reached out to rest a hand on his thigh. "I'm armed. Let me go first."

A steady procession of flies buzzed in and out of the open hangar doors, bodies glinting bright green in the sunlight. The air inside the hangar smelled rancid—like rotting flesh—once smelled never forgotten.

"I see what you mean about the doors. It smells like *D'Erve* did when he was decomposing beneath the dock." Ben tried calling his boss's phone. Didn't hear a ring tone.

Lauren had her holster unsnapped. Her right hand rested on the butt of her pistol. "This is the police," she yelled. "Hello? Anybody here?"

They waited. No response.

"How many times does it usually take for someone to answer?"

"Depends on their reasons for hiding. Once usually does

it." She drew her gun. "You armed?"

"No. Having second thoughts about it, though."

"Stay behind me, then. I'm going to check that plane inside the hangar."

The cockpit was empty. The small passenger compartment held four leather captain's chairs but no people. A folding table that attached to the wall was propped open.

"See anything?" From his vantage point on the hangar floor, Ben could see inside the cabin but the table surface was above eye level.

"Just a courier envelope."

"What's in it?"

She removed a pen from her pocket and used it to open the flap. "A cellphone. News articles. Copies of . . . looks like an old-fashioned receipt, back when they were using carbon-paper."

"Dated August 2, 1938?"

"How'd you know?"

"There's something about that date . . . Ben quoted from memory. "If it says, 'Sold: *Portrait of Señorita Santangel*, painted by Auguste Renoir in 1876,' grab it. Elizabeth Moynihan had the same copy. The next receipt should say, 'Paid in full, November 11, 1939.' A lot can happen in a year and a half and there's something off about those dates."

"What if it's evidence?"

"We'll return it."

"This may be a crime scene."

"I'd bet on it. Probably insurance fraud—especially if that's my boss's phone." Ben pressed redial and didn't hear it ring. "The battery is probably dead. Grab it anyway."

"Looks like a burner. Prepaid and disposable." She used the pen to gather the papers and slide them into the envelope, hesitated, and used a napkin to avoid leaving fingerprints when she picked up the envelope. "Let's check that freezer in the corner. Looks like the only place left to hide."

"Smells like it, too."

They crossed the empty hangar, periodic squeaks from

their shoes echoing off prefab walls and sounding hollow against the sealed concrete floor. Lauren veered left to avoid the birds nesting in the rafters and the discolored floor immediately below. The detour brought them to an examination table with portable fans set along the perimeter.

"This looked like a makeshift emergency room from the entrance." Ben put his hands behind his back as a safeguard against sullying the crime scene. The combination of heat and humidity inside the hangar had plastered his shirt to his skin. "Now I think it's a portable lab for authenticating original canvases."

"Is that an x-ray machine?" Lauren pointed at an expensive-looking device connected to a computer monitor.

"Sort of. It's a synchrotron-based scanning x-ray fluorescence microscope."

"Sorry I asked. Let's check the freezer." Lauren reached into a vest pocket and removed a latex glove. "Here. Put this on to open the door." She moved into a firing stance on the opposite side of the freezer door.

"Other hand," she ordered.

Ben looked at the door, worked out the safest place to stand, and nodded. He turned his back to the freezer. By using his left hand to grasp the handle, he was as far away as possible from the line of fire. Opening the door would give him additional protection. "Shouldn't you have a bulletproof vest?"

"Shouldn't you?" She shrugged and moved into position on the opposite side of the door. "Open up," she yelled, and pounded on the side of the freezer.

Seconds became hours. An eternity passed between the last impact of Lauren's fist against the freezer and her second warning.

"Open up! Come out with your hands above your head."

In the lengthening agony of expectancy, Ben's repertoire of remembered prayers grew exponentially.

"On my sign," Lauren moved away from the side of the freezer for a clear shot.

She moved directly into the line of fire, from Ben's perspective.

She nodded.

He unlatched the handle. Yanked open the door.

F

riday, November 8, 2:30 p.m.

Chapter 24

Moisture-laden air rushed out of the freezer and carried the rancid odor of decomposing flesh. Ben watched as Lauren used her gun to scan the small room. A few degrees left, then right, she steadied her aim and finished with the barrel pointing at the floor in the center of the room.

"Clear." She took her finger off the trigger. Engaged the safety.

"Empty?" Ben stepped away from the door.

"Not exactly." She placed two fingers against the carotid artery of a man who was sprawled across the floor of the walk-in freezer. "He's dead."

"Jesus!"

"Wrong century." Lauren had seen enough bodies to develop a detached sense of humor. "Besides, no sandals or robe. Just an expensive suit with a tan to match."

"One I've seen before," Ben said. "On the guy who used to own *Portrait of Señorita Santangel.*"

"The yacht guy? Richard Pendleton III?"

"Not anymore." He used the flashlight on his phone to illuminate the interior of the freezer. Professional mounting hardware with specialized security features hung from the walls. "I wonder what was in here."

"Not who killed him?"

"That too. And how he died. I don't see any blood."

Lauren pulled on a pair of latex gloves and used her phone to photo-document the crime scene before shifting the body. "He's been moved. Looks like he was shot, too. Hang on." She bent down once again to examine the body. Pendleton's skin color was mottled, otherwise he looked like he was sleeping.

Lauren had a distasteful look on her face as she slid a gloved hand into the front pockets of Pendleton's pants to check the contents. She examined his neck, carefully rolling his head from ear to ear. "No taser marks."

"No art, either." Ben scanned the interior walls. "I count two complete sets of cables, so the same number of canvases are missing."

"How's that help?"

"It's a pattern. Each picture is hung with two wires. Those are professional mounting brackets with built-in security features, so it means two extremely valuable canvases were hanging side by side."

"They're still empty and he's still dead."

"It's the twos—two paintings . . . hung the same way. We've got two missing Renoirs: *Portrait of Señorita Santangel,* and *La Grenouillère.* Both of them worthy of extreme care. Like being housed in a highly controlled environment, for instance."

"Still not getting the connection." Lauren finished searching Pendleton's pockets—they were empty—and stepped out of the freezer.

"It might be quicker to show you. The scanning microscope should have stored images."

"Great, but we're dealing with a murder. I need to call this in first." She checked her phone. "No signal. I'll have to use the radio on the plane."

"We're in international waters. Who you gonna call?"

"The FBI. That's probably Pendleton's plane," she pointed at the King Air in the hangar. "It's got a N-number on the tail. Means it's registered in the U.S."

Ben crossed the hangar. A magnifying glass and a jeweler's loupe sat on the examination table beside a surgical scalpel. A portable microscope held a slide with a sample, so he bent over and peered through the lens at a tiny scrap of paint smaller than the period at the end of a sentence. The paint looked old enough to have come from an original canvas painted by Renoir.

"Whatcha looking at?" Lauren asked.

Ben flinched.

"Sorry. Didn't mean to sneak up on you."

"An old paint chip." He stepped aside so she could see.

"Okay." She switched eyes. "What am I looking for?"

"It takes a long time for some of the oil paints that artists use to completely cure—months, sometimes years. Look at the edges."

"You mean where it's yellow?"

"Varnish ages with varying discolorations of yellow or green depending on the chemistry and the quality of paint manufacturing of the era. Dating the paint or varnish is one of the best ways to authenticate a canvas." He took a pen out of his pocket. "Unless we have a synchrotron-based scanning x-ray fluorescence microscope."

"Sounds expensive."

"Because it is." He used his pen to push the power button on the control panel. "Let's take a look."

The machine hummed as it powered up. The monitor flickered and turned blue before displaying a spectral image.

"Why is that guy upside down?"

A pale black-and-white image of a young man with a beard appeared in the center of a scanned painting. In addition to looking like a cross between a ghost and a Castilian Spanish dandy, a solid black square of impenetrable paint concealed his hair and everything but his forehead, cheeks, and neck.

"It's the original image. Renoir reused the canvas by painting over the original work with black paint. Just the flesh tones show through." Ben used his pen to forward the machine to the next scan.

"I can't see the guy with the beard anymore, but I recognize the elongated lines in the face of the lady painted over him. That's your missing Renoir, right?"

"One of them. The first one: *Portrait of Señorita Santangel*. I wish my Father was here to see it. The guy with the beard who's underneath her, that's got to be Isaac Santangel—who sat for the original portrait. Isaac's father wasn't happy with the results and refused to pay, so Renoir reused the canvas and painted a picture of Isaac's sister, instead."

"That's a nice backstory."

"More than that, it means the legends are true; it's authentic and apparently it belongs to our family. Plus, it's worth a fortune. The last Renoir that sold at auction brought 78 million bucks and that was twenty years ago. If it was auctioned today, it'd bring at least double, maybe triple that."

"Worth killing over." Lauren's resigned tone hinted at having seen too many people killed for less.

"Especially if *La Grenouillère* was hanging next to it. Let's see." Ben used his phone to take a picture of the screen before pushing the button to call up the next image. Want to bet this next image is the other missing Renoir, stolen from the Lowe?"

Lauren waited until Ben forwarded the image. "No."

Professional courtesy between fellow law enforcement officers allowed Lauren to cut through most of the federal and international red tape wrapped around a murder investigation. But not all of it. Ben was a civilian and automatically suspect because of chartering a plane that had made an unscheduled landing at a homicide scene. It was dark by the time they were finally cleared for take-off, and skeptical eyebrows raised a notch higher at the miraculous self-healing nature of their plane's mechanical woes. The senior agent nearly revoked their permission to leave while Lauren was going through the preflight checklist. She talked the agent out of forcing them to stay by promising to return—if needed.

"Never thought I'd be so happy to be taking off in an airplane." Ben looked for something to hang on to.

"We're not airborne yet," Lauren taxied into position for takeoff.

"Just don't slow down. It might give them enough time to change their minds about letting us leave." Ben checked his seatbelt and tugged at his door to make certain it was securely closed.

Lauren pulled the throttle out until the engine stabilized at 2,000 rpm, double-checked that all the gauges showed normal operating conditions, released the brakes, and started the small plane rolling.

It was a slow plane and a short runway. For a man like Ben who equated being born without feathers as a reason to avoid flight, this was a homemade recipe for worry with a dash of panic. "This thing go any faster? The ocean keeps getting closer."

"Reaching fifty-five knots on the airspeed indicator. Hang on," Lauren gently pulled back on the controls.

Ben took her literally and tightened his grip.

She lined up the cowling with the visible horizon and climbed at seventy-five knots, maintaining the runway heading until reaching safe altitude. "You can open your eyes, now."

"I'd rather not."

"We're airborne."

"An even better reason to keep them closed. How about telling me something else to take my mind off this unnatural act?"

"You got a good look at Pendleton when they moved his body, right?"

"That's not helping."

"No blood. He'd been moved after he was killed."

"Definitely not helping. I think the stench from his decomposing body has lodged inside my nose."

"The odor from rotting flesh permeates the fabric. Soak your clothes in tomato juice before you wash them. Works for skunks, too." She trimmed the flaps. The engine note changed from labored strain to loud clatter.

"What's wrong?"

"Nothing. That was a climate-controlled room. I checked the thermostat; it was fine. Somebody was sending a message by leaving the body there and then turning off the A/C."

"I meant with the plane."

"Nothing's wrong."

"It sounds different."

"It's supposed to. Forget about the plane. Worry about why someone killed Pendleton and moved his body, instead."

Like most good advice, it came as a surprise. "No taser marks on Pendleton's neck. The taser used on D'Erve had a star pattern in the center of the electrodes."

"More than that," Lauren said. "The security guard at the museum? The two little marks on his neck were round and looked like burns; they didn't break the skin."

"The same kind of taser Elizabeth Moynihan threatened me with at the museum."

"Doesn't make her a killer. If anything, it helps clear her." Lauren spoke from experience. "Most murderers don't change their technique."

"Key word being *most*, but I never really had Elizabeth pegged as a killer. That's Benson's style. Pendleton's death is more about sending a message about art—make that *missing* art. Whoever killed Pendleton left his body where his art used to be."

"It's about money; it always is. Half-a-billion dollars is missing. One of the best motives for murder that I've ever seen."

"Not just money: *lack* of money. Pendleton was broke and living like a billionaire on quickly-drying-up credit. Those two paintings were high-dollar assets, but they were war crimes assets he inherited from his father and couldn't sell. Insurance fraud neatly side-steps that problem and would've given him enough cash to satisfy his debts and keep living like a king."

"That's your area," Lauren said. She trimmed the flaps to counteract the weight loss of spent fuel. The engine note returned to its previous pitch.

Ben didn't distract her; he recreated the crime scene on Pendleton's island, instead. Tenacity made Ben an exceptional investigator. Coupled with his ability to interpret patterns and predict outcomes, it meant he had an uncanny ability to recreate crime scenes. His compulsive need for order forced him to make sense of conflicting information or lose sleep and a corresponding degree of sanity. To make sense of the apparent disorder, he tried thinking like a thief. With Pendleton dead, Elizabeth Moynihan emerged as the front-runner among thieves. With *D'Erve* dead, Benson was firmly in place as the number-one dealer in stolen paintings. Ben imagined himself in his boss's position: his Manhattan neighbor, *D'Erve*, was dead; his client with the questionable art collection, Pendleton, was dead, too. Insurance fraud must have started looking like a bad choice to his boss after the second murder—no wonder he left Pendleton's island. Ben reached for the headset and toggled the microphone switch to share his theory with Lauren. He gave her the condensed version.

"You think your boss helped?"

"Sure looks that way. We've traced his phone to Pendleton's island which implies that he was there recently. There's also the missing provenance that he found a way to circumvent. Pendleton needed money and had an art collection he couldn't sell. When Elizabeth Moynihan figured out a way to document *"Portrait of Señorita Santangel,* Pendleton had all he needed to arrange the theft and file an insurance claim. I think my boss made their fraud possible by issuing the policy."

"Mostly circumstantial. Doesn't mean you're wrong, just that you need proof." Lauren took the plane off autopilot and prepared for a landing approach. Ben was too busy designing a trap to notice the added turbulence.

The weather on Key Largo was good enough for visual flight rules. Ben dared to hope for a landing he could walk away from and Lauren didn't disappoint him. She taxied the plane to the Ocean Reef Flying Club's hangar and turned the engine off. Ben waited until she had completed the last step on the post-flight checklist and took off her headset.

"You still have the courier envelope from Pendleton's plane, right?"

"You noticed?"

"I noticed the big-city attitude of the FBI agent. You looked like you were going to shoot him."

"Until I remembered it was a punishable offense." Lauren took the key out of the ignition. "I was going to turn it over until he called me 'honey,' and started mansplaining." She leaned forward and wrapped her thumb and index finger in her shirttail. She eased the courier envelope from beneath her shirt where it had been tucked into her waistband.

"Here," she handed him a pair of disposable gloves. "Look inside. If you don't leave any fingerprints, then I can avoid a tampering with evidence charge if I need to return it."

Ben pulled on the gloves and opened the Winged Sandal Courier Service envelope. A disassembled, disposable cell phone and two pieces of generic printer paper were stuffed inside. He tilted the envelope to let the items slide onto his lap. The top sheet had five potential meeting sites, along with corresponding dates and times.

"Who's it from?" Lauren asked.

"Doesn't say. All five dates and times are from earlier this week—a pretty slick way to contact someone and remain anonymous."

The second sheet had printing on both sides—copies of newspaper articles.

"Two of my old cases," Ben said. "Probably my best work." *The Garden of Monet's House in Argenteuil* (1874) by Claude Monet, and *Shepherdess Bringing in Sheep*, by Camille Pissarro, confiscated during World War II, had been returned to their rightfull owners. Since the theft of the paintings had been war crimes, everyone involved had lost millions on the deal.

He reassembled the phone. A number had been programmed into the memory. Only the last digit was different—probably to a companion phone with the same area code and prefix. He pushed "send" and engaged the speaker phone function.

"You really think that's going to work?"

"It's got three bars." The phone rang four times and went to voice mail. Ben ended the call, waited, and then pressed redial.

"What do you want?"

Ben disconnected.

"Why did you hang up?" Lauren asked.

"Because trouble answered."

"Sounded like a woman."

"Indeed, it sounded like Elizabeth Moynihan."

"We just watched her show."

"She's also an academic who's devoted considerable time and effort researching missing or stolen art. I already knew she was mixed up in the theft of Pendleton's Renoir. Now I suspect she's involved with the theft of *La Grenouillère* from the Lowe Museum, too."

"That raises some questions about the phone conversations between Pendleton and *D'Erve*." Lauren opened the door.

"Add Elizabeth Moynihan to the list. She called *D'Erve* at least five times—that we know of. She called Pendleton, too. It had to be business; I can't imagine Pendleton having any friends. I've got some questions I'd like to ask his enemies, but there may too many for me to get to in this lifetime."

"Start with his staff," Lauren suggested. "Chances are they knew him best, means they saw him at his worst."

F

riday, November 8, 5:30 p.m., Miami

Chapter 25

Serge paid cash to sublet a furnished apartment and shed the last vestige of servitude when he pulled the file folders stolen from Elizabeth Moynihan's university office out of his backpack. He could purchase citizenship in any number of countries with these documents. *Portrait of Señorita Santangel*, Theodore Fischer Gallery, Degenerate Art, Richard Pendleton III, these folders he stacked to one side of the faded Formica table. Elizabeth had filled the entire bottom drawer of one of her filing cabinets with information about the Santangel family. Wrinkled tabs and battered edges spoke to recent and repeated use. There had to be a profitable reason she had devoted so much effort into researching their history. Serge opened the thickest folder because it had pictures.

The Santangel heirs had been forward-thinking collectors who took the precaution of marking their acquisitions with an image of the family crest that their patriarch, Luis de Santangel, adopted to honor Christopher Columbus. Serge had eavesdropped on Pendleton's conversations about two Renoirs in his collection; Pendleton became nervous and then flew into a rage when the art appraiser and then the insurance investigator had started asking questions about 'Baruch Hashem' the Yiddish characters on the back of both frames: ה ׳׳ ד. Serge didn't read Yiddish, although the phonetic spelling made more sense than the English he was struggling to master. He put this folder aside and reached for the one labeled *Portrait of Señorita Santangel.*

A week ago, Richard Pendleton III had a Renoir hanging in his library entitled *Portrait of Señorita Santangel.* Serge had seen the same foreign symbols inscribed on the back of the frame. He removed a photograph of the painting to add to his growing collection of snapshots sitting on the table and reached for the next folder.

La Grenouillère, the painting by Renoir that Pendleton used to buy his way onto the Lowe Museum board—after he had the canvas reframed. Had the same Yiddish symbols been inscribed on the back of the old wood? And there was that name again: Santangel.

Serge reached into his backpack for Benson's larcenous shopping list. He ran his index finger down the items. Number four looked promising: a Renoir, *Madeleine Leaning on Her Elbow with Flowers in Her Hair*, stolen from the Houston couple who paid Elizabeth Moynihan for the appraisal. Richard Pendleton III paid Elizabeth Moynihan for the same service on his stolen Renoir, *Portrait of Señorita Santangel*.

"Hmm . . ." He leaned back in the lumpy kitchen chair. The paintings made sense when he began to limit the number of thieves. He arranged snapshots of *La Grenouillère, Madeleine Leaning on Her Elbow with Flowers in Her Hair*, and *Portrait of Señorita Santangel* into a line that covered the worn spot in the center of the table. He delved into all the folders and covered the table with pictures. When every folder was emptied, when every flat surface in the kitchen, and the entire floor in the small apartment was covered with photographs and documents, a pattern emerged. When read from the kitchen to the living room, right to left, the phonetic Yiddish characters on the back of the paintings formed the same image as the symbol in the corner of Christopher Columbus's letters to his son, Diego: *Beis Hei*.

Baruch Hashem, Thank God. Serge was surrounded by pictures of stolen art. Although Elizabeth's research was incomplete, Serge had the foresight to steal corroborating evidence from Richard Pendleton III. Everyone who watched her show knew she loved Renoir above all other artists, but now Serge could prove she loved owning *stolen* Renoirs above all else. This was the type of secret that translated to money; blackmail was a universal language.

F

riday, November 8, 6:30 p.m., Key Largo

Chapter 26

Waiting for Alexi to cook an evening meal meant choosing between fast food or burnt food, so Ben made breakfast for dinner. The refrigerator held enough left-over vegetables to combine with pan-fried potatoes. Eggs on toast was easy.

"What's for supper?" Alexi wandered into the kitchen at the squeak of porcelain plates rubbing together. He had an uncanny knack for making an appearance at mealtime, a trait inherited from his father.

"Nothing wrong with your timing." Ben handed him three plates and a preview of the menu: toad in the hole with bubble and squeak.

"Smells better than it sounds."

"It's common enough in England. We'll see if it translates, here. I figure the old man will make it downstairs in twenty seconds."

"That's on the low side. Takes at least a half-minute to set the table." Alexi slid open the silverware drawer. No dinner bell ever rang so true as the sound of knives and forks being readied for a meal.

Both brothers listened for the uneven tromp of their father's footsteps on the stairs. A home-cooked meal always lured him from his lair. He called from the head of the stairs while Ben was still folding the first napkin. "I saw a strange car drive up, but I didn't hear the pizza guy knock."

Alexi checked his watch. "Ten seconds."

"I don't smell any smoke . . ." A loud thump and a soft curse came from the bottom of the stairs.

"His walker," Alexi said.

"He's gotten older."

"A *lot* older. And slower." Alexi cocked his arm. "We're already at forty-three seconds."

Ben followed the sweep of the second hand on Alexi's old-fashioned watch.

"Well," Ben's father pretended to be shocked. The surprised act bought him enough time for an extra hit off the oxygen machine. "The table," he paused to inhale, "is already set."

Ben watched his father struggle for oxygen. He used the same shallow breathing technique that Ben had adopted because of his cracked ribs. Did it hurt his father to breathe, or was he that weak?

Click, the machine delivered another dosage. "What are..." *Click*, "we having?"

"Better you don't ask," Alexi said.

"It's not burned." Another greedy breath from the machine, "so I wouldn't recognize it, anyway." He swept his gaze over the formal table setting, lingering on the cloth napkins beneath a full set of silverware. "No TV trays?" He caught his breath. "What's the catch?"

"I've got some questions about the Santangels," Ben said.

Alexi's eyes grew wide at the scope of the topic. To ask their father about family lore was to risk exposure to an information dump of gargantuan proportions.

"Specifically, about a painting with lumpy texture in the lower left-hand corner of the canvas and a scratch on the frame." Ben scrolled through the photo gallery on his phone until he reached a pale black-and-white image of a young man with a beard. A solid black square of impenetrable paint concealed his hair and shoulders.

"Isaac Santangel." There was no hesitation or doubt in his father's voice. "Where's the painting?"

"No telling. This is what it looks like now," Ben called up the photo of *Portrait of Señorita Santangel*.

"I knew it! The stories are true." His father grabbed a napkin and drew a monogram in cursive script.

"That's a cloth napkin you just ruined," Alexi pointed out.

"*Meh.*" It gave him enough time to catch his breath and form a follow-up question. He handed the napkin to Ben. "Was this on the back of the frame?"

"Exactly. Also matches the picture the floater had hidden in his money belt," Ben said. "*D'Erve*, the dealer in stolen art work until recently when death ended his career."

"No coincidence," his father said. "It's the monogram Christopher Columbus used." He held up his hand to signal there was more to come after he caught his breath. "On the thirteen letters he wrote to his son, Diego."

"Let me see that." Alexi reached across the table and spun the napkin 180 degrees. "*Beis, Hei.* Why would Columbus use the Yiddish initials for *Baruch Hashem*?"

"To honor Luis de Santangel," his father said, waiting for the oxygen machine. "Santangel financed his journey to the New World . . ." The machine clicked. ". . . in exchange for their protection from the Spanish Inquisition."

"You said, 'their.' More than one?" Alexi asked.

"All of them . . . all the descendants of the Santangel family." Another deep breath, "this we know for certain." Another pause. "We suspect the same is true for the families of Christopher Columbus . . . as well as the other backers of his voyage." It took him a while to gather enough oxygen to finish. "All of them Jewish: Gabriel Sanchez, Alonzo Pinzon—who also sent three of his sons, and Rabbi Isaac Abravanel—"

"Hang on," Ben interrupted. "That was our last name before it was Americanized to Abrams."

"Of course. Common practice for immigrants passing through Ellis Island." A shallow breath. "At least that's the story," his father said.

"Some story," Alexi said. "Any proof?"

"On the back of every piece of art belonging to the Santangels." Ben scrolled through the photo gallery for additional pictures. His phone beeped to announce a high-priority message and ended his search but provided an escape.

Alexi and his father had perfected the ability to show up when a meal was about to be served, but nobody was better than Ben at orchestrating a sudden departure before it was time to wash dishes. He filled his plate and held up his phone as proof. "Looks important. I'll step outside and return this call while I eat. Don't wait on me. No telling how long I'll be gone."

Saturday, November 9, 10:00 a.m., Coral Gables

Chapter 27

The crash of waves breaking against the shore, a hum from the refrigerator as the compressor cycled on, the clatter of ice cubes dropping from the icemaker, these small noises normally relegated to the background, now sounded unnaturally loud in Elizabeth Moynihan's kitchen. She doodled when she felt nervous. It was easier on her teeth and she was vain about her nails. The bottom of a nearby tissue box served as a convenient sketch pad. Dollar signs drawn with blue ink morphed into question marks after she read Richard Pendleton III's obituary—all that lovely stolen art still missing from *Entartete Kunst*. 16,000 canvases! Who was guarding it, and how many paintings had Pendleton's father carried out the back door of the Fischer Gallery? Like smoke follows fire, where there were two stolen Renoirs, there were also canvases by Picasso, Degas, Monet, Cezanne, Klimt, Modigliani, and so many more . . .. The next heist could satisfy her goal of becoming the world's first billionaire art thief.

Elizabeth got a bigger piece of paper and plotted strategy. The geometric progression of symbols reflected her thoughts as a trapezoidal doodle morphed into an unfinished propeller blade. Thomas Benson, with his float plane and bad habit of pointing handguns at her, was too dangerous as a partner. A filled-in question mark sprouted a triangular hyphen to become a symbolic "D." Harold Feinstein—*D'Erve*—her trusted broker for stolen property was dead. She filled in the blanks to form a capital "C." Coastal Insurance Company was out of the "ten percent reward and no questions asked" business. Ben Abrams rated a stick-figure skull and crossbones doodle as a threat

She was more comfortable in the previous century, when

a researcher equipped with hindsight could find masterpiece paintings at bargain prices. *Beis Hei.* Thank God for Luis de Santangel, who purchased his family's freedom from the Spanish Inquisition and had enough money left over for his heirs to purchase masterpiece paintings by Renoir. She drew a line across the entire page and added thicker gloves to her breaking and entering list.

The antique grandfather clock in the den rang five bells: 10:30 a.m. Elizabeth checked the time on her phone. Slow. Her grandparents had filled the house with their antique clock collection and none of them kept accurate time. She couldn't bear to part with a single clock, however. Every Saturday she honored her grandparents' memory by winding the timepieces, so the passing of each hour took a few extra minutes one day a week. There was a comforting sense of continuity amid a previous century's worth of mechanical chimes, a nostalgic connection to time and timelessness . . . until an electronic buzzer intruded, a modern device bringing ancient trouble. The intercom transmitted a burst of static, followed by a man shouting.

"Hello? Hello? Winged Sandal Couriers, ma'am. I've got a delivery from Luis de Santangel."

Elizabeth pressed the intercom button. "Who?"

"Luis de Santangel, ma'am—I think I'm saying that right. It's for Christopher Columbus, only at your address."

"I beg your pardon?" Elizabeth tightened the focus on the camera mounted above her front gate.

"And there's some message in Yiddish," the courier said. "I can't read it, but the guy who paid me swore it wasn't a joke." He held the envelope up to the camera so she could see the characters: *Beis Hei,* forming the distinctive coat of arms that matched a stolen canvas hanging in her vault.

Elizabeth Moynihan acted, instead of reacted, to the courier letter from "Christopher Columbus." She lifted a bicycle out of her boat and pedaled to the parking area of the Coco Plum Yacht Club. Bicycles are innocent, underrated escape vehicles, able to navigate trails too narrow for police cars or unidentified persons sending veiled threats via courier. She had a switch vehicle parked in a nearby cul-de-sac. With a burst of furious pedaling, less than a minute—tops—she could throw the bicycle in the back of the rusty work truck, cover it with a tarp, and be on her way. Wearing biking attire gave her an excuse to wear gloves and hide the gauze bandage on her palm. The cut was swollen and the rope burns had formed unsightly blisters. Any number of contagious diseases could have been lurking in the Lowe Museum's ventilation system.

She used binoculars to watch "Christopher Columbus" park an economy car beneath a palm tree offering shade. Elizabeth recognized him as one of Pendleton's servants but hadn't bothered to learn his name. He must be working for Thomas Benson, now, which explained the delivery of a disposable phone and a list of meeting locations delivered via courier. She wrapped her finger around the trigger of the gun in her pocket and scanned the parking lot. All the other cars looked empty—nobody lurking on a stakeout. The parking valet hadn't moved other than to turn the page of the text book he was studying. The street was clear. She slid off the seat but didn't get off the bike. The ocean sighed. A gust of wind fluttered the brim of her hat. Palm tree fronds clacked above her head and sounded like a gunshot. She flinched and felt a cold spot on her chest where a high-powered rifle scope focused. She looked down: it wasn't a laser scope—no red dot. The cold spot became an iceberg when she reinserted the SIM card into the disposable phone this lowly servant had dared send her. She tapped the icon for the only number stored in the phone's memory, clenched the brakes and rested her weight on the pedal until the bike strained against the front hub like a greyhound pulling at its leash.

"Why haven't you been answering?" He was mad enough for his voice to be audible over Elizabeth's phone. He spun around at the sound. "This is you? On a bicycle?"

Elizabeth disconnected the call. "Walk to the edge of the dock," she said, in a normal voice.

"You are joking with me?" He looked flustered and was still speaking into the phone.

"Just do it." Elizabeth was close enough to hear her own voice repeated in the phone, a confounding form of stereo.

"You expect me to sit on the handlebars?"

"I have a boat." Elizabeth cocked her head in the direction of the bay and kept her left hand in her pocket. She carried an M9 Beretta loaded with fifteen rounds. "Who are you and what do you want?"

"What you already have. Money and a Renoir: the one you are stealing from Richard Pendleton III."

"He's dead."

"I am not."

"Yet." She pressed the gun against the stretch fabric of the front pocket in her biking top. The outline of an automatic was unmistakable.

"You are not shooting me. I left a letter in case I am not returning."

"You're an amateur. Anyone even *remotely* connected to Pendleton makes me want to pull the trigger."

"I have files. On you," he added.

She stepped off her bicycle and began to push it toward the dock.

He hesitated.

"There must be something you want," Elizabeth called over her shoulder. "Which makes this a negotiation." She lifted the bicycle onto the boat. "Get in or get left out."

Serge reached for a life jacket as soon as he stumbled aboard. He sat in the center and held on with both hands, scowled at the water on either side of the boat, and shirked from the spray kicked up from the prow once they were underway. The further from shore they traveled, the more he acted like a man who couldn't swim, especially when the hull skipped across the wake from a passing boat.

Elizabeth noticed his discomfort and altered course to take advantage of rougher water. A school of Spanish mackerel followed the tide, the dark green stripe running along their spines matched the turbid water in the channel. A careless fish swam too close to the surface and exposed its bright silvery sides toward the sun when Elizabeth guided the boat between the red buoys marking the channel. An osprey soared atop the updrafts rising from the bridge spanning the mainland and Coral Gables Waterway. She noticed the bird's shadow as it passed overhead, witnessed the silhouette change when the osprey spread its talons and dove to snatch another meal from the ocean. The osprey metamorphosed into a feathered missile as it swooped from the sky to pluck the unsuspecting fish from the surface with the deadly screech of a hunter's cry.

Elizabeth watched the osprey's massive wings cast ripples on the surface as it struggled for altitude with the heavy fish writhing below. Pendleton's servant was in much the same position. "How have you managed to live this long without getting plucked from your comfortable little home like that fish?"

"You are the fish," Serge waved off the insult.

"It's a miracle you haven't been caught already." She cut the engines and dropped anchor once the boat drifted to a stop in deep water.

"You are the one with worry. I know about American prisons." Serge was better with pictures. He removed the photograph of *Portrait of Señorita Santangel*. He added a picture of *Madeleine Leaning on Her Elbow with Flowers in Her Hair*. "These are stolen by you. After the, uh . . . looking—no, seeing on the paintings."

"Appraisals?" Elizabeth suggested.

"It is the stealing afterwards I am most interested in."

"Coincidence. I appraise art," Elizabeth spoke slowly, and

with exaggerated elocution. "The *thefts* afterwards were simply random occurrences—flukes if you will, unremarkable coincidences, statistical anomalies."

Serge looked like a man in need of a dictionary and a thesaurus. He couldn't translate Elizabeth's college-level vocabulary, but he certainly understood her obsequious tone. "You will give me money or go to prison with other American thieves."

Elizabeth watched the osprey circle below its perch, unwilling to let go of the fish, unable to climb high enough to consume its catch. She wouldn't make the same mistake, not when presented with the gift of a disposable man sitting in her boat. He might prove useful as a temporary partner until someone better came along—or if she needed a sacrificial lamb to extricate herself from Benson's grasp. "You are the one who should worry."

"Nonsense." He stood and shook his finger at her. "You listen to me now—"

Elizabeth wrapped her fingers around the gun and pulled it out of her pocket. "Can you swim?"

"What?"

"Care to go for a swim?" She embellished her patently false politeness with a threat. "I hear the water is fine. The sharks certainly like it."

He tightened his grip on the railing.

"I didn't think so. You can't go to the police, either." In a matter-of-fact tone, she played a hunch—but an educated one. "Where are the rest of the paintings in Pendleton's dirty little collection?"

"Why?"

"Wrong question," Elizabeth said. "Don't you mean, *what paintings*?"

He dismissed her love of semantics with the belittling flick of his fingers he had learned from his ex-employer.

Elizabeth lowered the gun and ventured a conspiratorial smile. "Coastal Insurance Company is out of the 'ten percent reward and no questions asked' business. That means it's a stealer's market." She smiled at her own pun. "That's where you come in."

Saturday, November 9, Noon, Key Largo

Chapter 28

Ben's phone dinged with a text bearing bad news. The U.S. Department of Homeland Security notified Coastal Insurance that his boss had requested asylum in Majorca. Instead of a raise, Ben had been burdened with more responsibility. Worse, the temporary promotion entailed significant plane travel, and flying between London, Miami, and New York City was a death threat to someone who understood gravity. One phone call turned his burden into a blessing when he countered with an incentive. He gained an immediate ally when he promised Joyce, the Manhattan Office Manager, a performance-based raise for every week she helped him avoid the unnatural act of commuting by plane.

"Are you kidding? Where do I sign?" She shouted.

Ben moved the phone away from his ear.

"I've been worried about keeping my job and being charged as an accessory to insurance fraud. Why else do you think I'm here on a Saturday?" Joyce sung in the church choir; her powerful voice kept backsliders in the balcony awake. "Now you're talking about a raise? What do you need?"

"Everything you can find out about *Portrait of Señorita Santangel.* It's a Renoir that was stolen from Richard Pendleton III."

"Consider it done. What do you think I've been working on all week?"

"Okay, add *La Grenouillère* to your list."

"Another Renoir," she said, "stolen from the Lowe Museum. I started working on that as soon as it went missing. Give me a challenge."

"Locate Elizabeth Moynihan's two-part magazine article

about the lead isotopes in the white paint Renoir used in 1876. Pendleton got the article pulled from publication. I want to know why. Especially since he's the one who donated *La Grenouillère* to the Lowe Museum before it was stolen."

"Pendleton—the yacht guy?"

"Not anymore. I don't guess his obituary made much of a splash in New York. It's a big deal in Miami, though."

"Guess I'm not the only one having a bad week. What else you need?"

"Copies of Pendleton's insurance policies, well—anything —and everything, you or the boss had on him."

"Hang on . . ."

Ben heard the rustle of clothing brushing against an office chair, footsteps, and then the clack of a keyboard as Joyce moved to the adjoining office—a high-rise cellblock he hoped to avoid.

"Would you settle for the policy on *La Grenouillère?*"

"It's a good start. Can you send it as an attachment?"

"Consider it done. And . . . I can do better than that," she said, and followed her promise with a furious burst of arpeggio typing. "I'm getting you set up for remote access to his computer. Technically, it's yours now. If he's extradited, he won't be coming back here."

Ben opened the attachment containing a facsimile of a suspicious insurance policy issued on an equally suspicious work: *La Grenouillère*, 'The Frog Pond.' The policy was incomplete. He followed Joyce's instructions to log onto his boss's computer via a secure connection. He typed "P" for Pendleton in the search field, and when that didn't produce any results, tried "S" for Santangel, looking for hidden files lurking in the electronic maze of myriad folders—digital needles hidden in a haystack of data. Nothing.

Ben's expatriate boss got his start with the company as an actuary, so on a hunch, he searched for files with numbers instead of names. June 29, 1939 popped up. An infamous date that should appeal to a larcenous actuary, specifically the day when paintings stolen from the Santangel collection were presented for auction at the Theodore Fischer Art Gallery.

The only thing Ben liked better than the hunt was the discovery. He double-clicked the mouse to open the secret folder and started reading his boss's confidential files.

The Santangels predated the concept of "old money." The family estate had been parceled into small countries before modern surveying methods created the concept of real estate. The connection became personal when Ben followed their holdings to several purchases made at an art gallery on *Donaukanal* in Vienna—the one his great-grandparents had owned.

According to the stored images on his boss's computer, Ben could trace the provenance by the Santangel coat of arms burned into the frame on the back of Pendleton's stolen Renoir. He recognized the Yiddish characters *Beis Hei*. His boss had listed Christopher Columbus's letters to his son Diego as corroborating documents. Ben read the footnote, first.

Columbus had originally intended to sail on August 2, 1492, a day that happened to coincide with the Jewish holiday of *Tisha B'Av*, marking the destruction of the First and Second Holy Temples of Jerusalem. Columbus postponed his departure by one day to avoid embarking on the holiday, which would have been considered by Jews to be an unlucky day to set sail. Ben remained skeptical, although the date seemed familiar: August 2. What was it about August 2—why did it keep cropping up? It had to be more than just a religious holiday.

He closed his eyes; Ben possessed a photogenic memory— not perfect or photographic, yet far above average. His ability to form connections was a signature strength; his ability to spot patterns and link outwardly dissimilar events solved cases. The second day of August had personal, spiritual, and job-related significance. He felt the connection before he checked the next footnote to confirm it.

It was no coincidence that the Jewish holiday of *Tisha B'Av*, August, 2, coincided with the forced sale of *Portrait of Señorita Santangel*. He reread the footnote to be certain, although he had recognized the name of a Gentile maid employed by the Santangel family, a woman who hid a scared little girl inside a shipping crate designed to protect masterpiece paintings. The innocuous crate ultimately reached the Theodore Fischer Gallery in the neutral country of Switzerland, which is how *Grossmutter* survived and why Ben Abrams was alive.

His company phone beeped with a high-priority message. Joyce had sent him an email with a digital copy attached. He glanced at the subject line: *Season Two, Episode Six of Elizabeth Moynihan's show*. He downloaded the file.

"Check out the mystery artist," Joyce had added in the body of the email.

Ben opened the file and clicked on the arrow superimposed on top of the screen. He recognized the Public Broadcasting logo and the call letters from the local television station. The familiar theme music from Elizabeth Moynihan's show began to play. The stage was familiar, too. The lights mounted above the simple set dimmed. Shadowy figures dressed in black pushed the props to the wings. A baby spotlight illuminated her face as she began to narrate the early life of an artist who saw his father replaced by a machine and suffered the same fate, himself.

"Rheumatoid arthritis caused his fingers to curl into claws in the 1890s," Elizabeth lowered her voice to heighten the reveal. "He strapped a paintbrush to his wrist and painted through the pain."

The back wall of the set was a giant screen. It flickered to life. The outlines of a faint image coalesced as the screen warmed up. A pale black-and-white image formed, revealing a young man with a beard. In addition to looking like a cross between a ghost and a Parisian dandy, a solid black square of impenetrable paint concealed his hair and everything but his forehead, cheeks, and neck.

"Why is he upside down?" Elizabeth posed a hypothetical question to prepare the audience for her answer. "It's the original image. The artist reused the canvas by painting over the original work with black paint. Just the flesh tones show through."

The next image was a grainy black and white picture taken in Paris with the Eiffel Tower in the background. An older man with his son stood outside an art gallery. The power of computer-generated images combined the face of the young man in the photograph and the shadowy image from the canvas and revealed them to be the same man.

Ben had seen the same image stored in the synchrotron-based scanning x-ray fluorescence on Pendleton's island. He watched the video until the credits started rolling and hit "Pause" when the permission rights appeared onscreen. The photograph of the two men standing in front of the art gallery had been used with permission from a personal collection. No name, no additional credit given. From Elizabeth Moynihan's research, perhaps? He searched through the video for another look at the scene: the gallery in the background looked familiar.

A video shot of a black and white photograph is a pixilated approximation, designed to fool the eye at twenty-four frames per second to give the illusion of motion. Additional detail emerged when Ben enlarged the image—not as much definition as he had hoped for, but enough to identify the older man: Solomon Santangel, the same man who had sold a Renoir on August 2, 1938, *Portrait of Señorita Santangel*. Why had he waited fifteen months to issue such a terse-worded receipt? "Sold: *Portrait of Señorita Santangel*, painted by Auguste Renoir in 1876. Paid in full, November 11, 1939," without listing any information about the seller, the buyer, or the purchase price?

Elizabeth Moynihan knew the answer and had refused to share it during their first meeting. Someone had sent Richard Pendleton the same information in a courier envelope that had been aboard his plane. The Santangel coat of arms, the anniversary of the destruction of the second temple with its connection to Christopher Columbus, Ben wondered if Solomon Santangel had been sending a message with the only means at his disposal —via the receipt for a painting he didn't want to sell?

A lot had happened in the year after *Kristallnacht*, more than he could imagine. If only *Grossmutter* was still alive. She would know; she would join him at the kitchen table with the oven door propped open, the wonderful aromas of freshly baked cinnamon, and brown sugar scenting the room, a magical alchemy of ingredients creating babka, crème-filled *sufganiyot*, or that first bite of *Rugelach*: chocolate, hazelnuts, and apricot jam, encased in tender cream-cheese dough. A secret ingredient in each of her recipes transformed the combined elements into a taste sensation that superseded the summation of the individual items. For *Grossmutter*, it had been kosher salt.

"To atone for Lot's wife, who withheld salt in her meals to the needy to discourage the generous ways of her husband." She would smile and share a joke that Ben had been too young to understand. "When one visits Sodom and Gomorrah, it's wise to throw a little extra salt over your shoulder—just in case."

Grossmutter, Ben, and their common ancestors had been trapped by their past; they were enmeshed in a spiderweb of secrecy that ruined the weak, like his brother Alexi, and haunted the stronger ones, like his father. Ben resolved to find the truth, to break free, rather than risk remaining as sick as their secrets.

He printed reference copies directly from the screen before exiting the program; he needed to send an email to a dead man.

"You need to do what?" Dan the Man, head of security for the Lowe Museum, looked like a man ready to hang up in the middle of a prank call.

Except Ben was standing in Dan's office because it's much harder to say "no" in person.

"Have you lost your mind?"

"A long time ago. I hardly miss it."

"Okay. Well . . ."

"You have access to the group email for the museum board members," Ben said.

"So?"

"In order for the message to look legit, I need you to send a group email through official channels. Richard Pendleton III is the dead board member."

"You're thinking another board member killed him?"

"Or whoever killed him is reading his email. One or the other—could be both. I'm not sure," Ben admitted.

"And this is going to do what for me? Besides make trouble."

"Locate a missing Renoir."

"Which one?"

"Good question. Either one, I guess."

Portrait of Señorita Santangel, or *La Grenouillère,* Coastal Insurance Company benefitted from the recovery of either one. Ben had a personal connection to the Santangel family that wasn't entirely obvious. It was increasingly clear that he owned the Santangels a debt of gratitude for somehow being instrumental in helping *Grossmutter* survive, however.

Dan wiggled the mouse to wake up his computer. "If you think this will do it, I'll change the meeting schedule to build in ten minutes so you can address the members. Besides," he deadpanned. "They've been wanting to talk to you about paying extra for security on the night the museum was robbed."

"On second thought—"

"Just kidding. Hell, you're liable to be the guest of honor."

"No way."

"Because you haven't read the agenda." Dan changed screens. "There's a special election to name a replacement for Pendleton as the Honorary Chairman of the Board."

"Before his body cools?" Filling Pendleton's vacant position on the museum board so soon after his death seemed to be in unusually poor taste—until Ben learned that Pendleton had left his considerable art collection to the museum if they built a new wing to house it and put his name on the outside of the building. "Aren't they worried about reparations?"

"Not yet." Dan rolled his eyes. "They're still arguing about architectural plans and Pendleton's stipulation that his name appear in neon lettering and the size of the font."

"Hence the emergency, although it's going to seem minor compared to the fallout from everything in his collection being tainted by war crimes." Ben noted the perplexed look on Dan's face and clarified. "His father, Richard Pendleton version two, was a World War II munitions profiteer. He stole and/or bought his collection from the Nazis who were looting Europe."

"Means the museum will need to buy ink by the gallon just to print admission tickets," Dan said. "Now, about this group email—what am I getting myself into?"

"The half-billion-dollar question. I'm not sure. Except..."

Dan motioned for him to continue.

"I've been reading footnotes—that's the *why*," Ben said. "Someone else has been reading Pendleton's emails—that's the *how*. This is what I need you to say..."

"Let's hear it." He clicked through to his email. "I'll make up my mind about pressing *send* when I've got the whole thing in front of me."

"*Koordinierungsstelle für Kulturgutverluste*, the Coordination Center for Lost Cultural Assets in Germany has announced —"

"—Hang on." Dan held up two heavily scarred hands with only seven fingers and offered to switch chairs. "Maybe you'd better type."

> *Research into previously missing records from the Theodore Fischer Gallery in Lucerne, Switzerland have raised concerns about ownership rights to three Renoirs painted in 1876. A spokesperson for the FBI rapid deployment team from the art loss section refused comment.*

"Really?" Dan asked.

"Precisely the question I want the thief, the fence, or the

killer asking," Ben said, and pressed *send* without waiting for permission.

S unday, November 10, 8:30 a.m.

Chapter 29

Stacks of books covered every flat surface in his father's house except one side of the kitchen table. Ben wiped off the dust and emptied the contents of the courier envelope found aboard Pendleton's plane. More from habit than for hope, he pressed redial on the disposable phone. The call went directly to the generic voicemail feature. He didn't bother to leave a message. If Elizabeth Moynihan was no longer answering, then the companion phone was probably at the bottom of the ocean or broken into small pieces. He followed the only remaining unknown and called Winged Sandal Courier Service. Ben played a hunch and requested delivery service. It was warm enough to wait on the front porch.

The courier had a plastic billboard with an illuminated flying shoe attached to the roof of his car. A bluish plume of smoke wafted from the tailpipe. Ben recognized the driver, having attended the same small island school where class size was measured with single digits. He subtracted a few years, added a few extra pounds, and dredged his memory for his classmate's name—he knew there were two of them.

"Been a long time, Donny Ray."

His grin meant Ben's memory was still intact. Donny Ray raced the engine, burning a few extra drops of oil before shifting into neutral, where the car settled into a lumpy idle.

"I want you to look at some pictures and let me know if any of them have been recent customers." Ben tapped his phone to retrieve an image. "What about this guy?"

"Not so sure I ought'a tell you. Pretty sure I signed something about not telling nobody nothing."

Ben pulled a twenty from his wallet.

"Then again, taking an oath don't pay the bills." Donny Ray turned off his car and took the money. "Sure. I've seen him. Too smooth and too much tan. The kind of guy that could smile while driving a knife through your ribs. I'd recognize him anywhere."

Ben provided a name. "Thomas Benson."

"Done a couple of deliveries for him. I know he's staying at the Biltmore, 'cause they call up to his room and he meets me in the lobby. All very hush-hush."

"I know the routine. When was the first delivery?"

"Couple weeks ago. Why?"

"Wondering about the floater who washed ashore beneath my father's dock. Just checking to see if Benson had been in town long enough to put him there." Ben scrolled through the images. "How about him?"

"The Yacht Guy?" Donny Ray asked.

"Richard Pendleton III."

"He's dead. Saw it online."

"We found a Winged Sandal Courier envelope on his plane. Parked in the same hangar where we found his body."

"I didn't do it."

"But have you been to his house?"

"Well . . ."

Ben reached for another twenty.

"Now that you mention it." Donny Ray put the bill in his pocket before continuing. "I dropped off something at the guard shack."

"For Pendleton?"

"Some other guy. Wouldn't leave a name. Talked like a Russian—hard and fast—like he was mad at the alphabet. Didn't seem to know all the letters."

"Pale, skinny fellow? Looked like a Scottish waif in need of a vowel and a sandwich?"

"That's him. Cheap bastard had exact change. No tip." Like

all service workers, Donny Ray remembered the cheapskates.

"I'll make up for it." Ben reached for his wallet. Holding out another twenty for motivation, he scrolled to an image of Elizabeth Moynihan. "How about her?"

"Been to her place, too."

"Remember who sent you?"

"Both of them. Tan guy and cheapskate."

"Interesting. Enlightening, even." Ben reached back into his wallet and removed his last two twenties. "What else can you tell me? No detail is too small."

"There's an ATM a couple of miles from here." Donny Ray eyed the potential bribe with the cautious greed of a Florida politician. He got out of the car and leaned against the fender. "Ain't going to jail for forty bucks."

"No law against paying for information." This time Ben reached into his billfold and removed his Coastal Insurance Company credit card. "Plenty more where that came from."

"You ain't gonna like the answer. Cause this last one was just plain weird."

"Try me."

"The cheapskate sent that same lady another envelope, only he said it was from Christopher Columbus. The other name was probably made-up, too. Some Spanish guy I never heard of."

"Santangel?"

"How'd you know?"

"Long story. With a lot of stolen paintings. Call me the next time Elizabeth Moynihan or Thomas Benson has a delivery and I'll save you the trip."

"Reckon that's stretching things past the breaking point. Ain't gonna visit you in jail, neither."

"Fair enough. We'll go to the police station first. Lauren can get a subpoena and keep us both out of trouble."

"Ain't going nowhere near the Po-lice. Parking tickets," Donny Ray explained. "Occupational hazard."

"Then let's leave the police out of this. I'll just pay for a special kind of courier service."

"Oh yeah? Just how high is the credit limit on that card?"

"High enough. Come back in an hour and I'll have a delivery for you."

The courier envelope bulged with as many historically incriminating resources as Ben could fit into the package and still leave enough room to include a disposable phone. Homing devices hidden inside the seams of envelopes only worked in movies. Which is why he opened a generic email account and synced it to the preprogrammed phone inside the envelope—an effective tracking device. Ordering Elizabeth Moynihan to carry the disposable phone ensured he could triangulate her location. He added a copy of Richard Pendleton III's obituary, and photographs of *Portrait of Señorita Santangel* and *La Grenouillère*. A facsimile copy of the June 1939 auction catalogue from the Theodor Fischer Gallery went into the eclectic mix, along with her unpublished magazine article about the isotopes in Renoir's white paint. He figured the promise of locating a painting by Renoir would provide enough motivation to expose Elizabeth's unknown machinations. He knew she was guilty, he just needed to narrow down the crimes.

Ben parked in a wooded cul-de-sac offering shade and a view of Elizabeth's security gate. He watched Donny Ray yell into the speaker, saw the gate open, and watched as he drove along Elizabeth's curved driveway and pass out of sight. He figured by the time Elizabeth finished sifting through all the potentially incriminating material, she was bound to act.

He didn't have long to wait.

Elizabeth drove a bright red Mercedes-Benz sports car through the security gates. Ben called Lauren to let her know they were moving and followed at a discreet distance, still driving an innocuous rental that appeared identical to every SUV on the planet. Elizabeth drove to the Coco Plum Yacht Club and pulled into a visitor parking spot offering an unobstructed view of the docks. She remained in her car and raised a pair of binoculars to reconnoiter her surroundings.

Ben drove past her and parked in front of the general store. He called Lauren with an update about his location and went inside the store to purchase an ice chest, a straw hat, and a fishing pole for cover. He sat in the shade at the end of the dock, keeping his face hidden beneath the garish hat.

Pendleton's yacht was too big to fit in a normal-sized mooring and was anchored at the end of the pier, arranged in a semi-circle among the other boats that had outgrown the marina. Elizabeth carried the courier envelope and approached the yacht with the caution of someone being forced to walk the plank aboard a pirate ship. She scanned the area one final time before she stepped aboard and rang the doorbell. Ben was close enough to hear the chimes and the sound of her knuckles striking the teak door when nobody answered.

He laid the fishing pole aside. There was no bait on the hook since Elizabeth was already carrying it in the courier envelope. He grabbed the ice chest and approached the yacht when she turned to leave. "This is Pendleton's yacht. Are you looking for some more of that missing art from the Fischer Gallery?"

"What are you doing here?" Elizabeth avoided his question by asking one of her own.

"Putting together buyers and thieves. Recognize the quote? That's the same question Pendleton asked you in the lady's room at the museum."

"I was called here for an appraisal." Elizabeth avoided the next question by lying about the previous one.

"Not by Pendleton. He's dead."

"Explains why nobody answered."

"Harold Feinstein—*D'Erve* is dead, too." Ben watched her hands.

She used her left thumb to pick at a nail that didn't quite match the others, probably a fake attached to a previously gnawed finger. Bright red nail polish disguised the damage, although Ben counted three potential repairs.

"My boss has requested asylum and Coastal Insurance Company is out of the 'ten percent, no questions asked business.' Means you're about out of partners. Are you sure it's a good idea to do business with Thomas Benson?"

"I don't know what you're talking about." Elizabeth played dumb. Her pained expression showed how much it hurt.

"Where's your bike?" Ben asked, mainly to keep her off balance.

"I beg your pardon?"

"Your bike," he pointed to the fingerless gloves she was wearing without realizing it was a clever way to hide the gauze bandage applied over her rope burns from breaking into the Lowe Museum. "If you don't want to leave fingerprints, you need to get some gloves with longer fingers."

"It's a fashion accessory. I'd explain but it would take too much time."

"There's plenty of time. How about some light reading while we wait for the local police to bring a search warrant? It won't take long; I've already called them."

"Why?"

"Because you just led me to the biggest source of stolen artwork."

"You can't prove that."

"Interesting response. Usually people claim innocence." He opened the ice chest and removed a facsimile from the library's advance copy. "This was impressive research into the isotopes in the paint Renoir used in 1876."

"We've already had this discussion—during your last uninvited visit."

"Then let's pick up where we left off: the subtle, intriguing difference in titles between your masters' thesis, *Missing Masterpieces*, and your doctoral dissertation, *Presumed Missing*.

"Still part of the same boring discussion. You need some new material."

"Let's try Yiddish, then. *Beis Hei*, featured on the Santangel coat of arms and inscribed on the back of every painting from their collection—including the pieces still missing since World War II."

Elizabeth unconsciously raised a finger to her mouth. She caught the nervous mannerism with a grimace and laced her fingers together to forestall a repeat.

Ben suspected a coating of cayenne pepper from her pursed lips and the way her cheeks and tongue recoiled. He reached into the ice chest and removed a copy of the June 1939 auction catalogue from the Fischer Gallery. Just how many of these pieces did you authenticate for Pendleton?"

"He's dead. Remember?"

Ben recognized the haughty air of superiority and the same self-satisfied smirk she had been wearing while humiliating Pendleton during their interview at the museum.

"I've seen your phone records. You've been talking with Harold Feinstein—your go-to guy for stolen art, a.k.a. *D'Erve*. I counted five conversations. None of them shorter than two minutes. And those are just the ones I know about. You were also on much better terms with Pendleton than you wanted people to know about."

"Nobody was on 'good terms' with that man."

"Not according to what you wrote to him on the flyleaf in autographed copies of both of your books—first editions, no less. The only thing D'Erve and Pendleton have in common is stolen art. Oh, and they're both dead, and were ex-partners with Thomas Benson. Are you sure you want to be next?"

"Sounds like you're the one who should be worried."

"I'm trying to *find* stolen art, not buy, sell, or steal it."

"With a billion dollars at stake, even innocent bystanders get killed. And you're anything *but* innocent."

"That's where you're wrong."

"Rarely."

"You may have underestimated me—"

"Easy to do."

"Not this time. You haven't made many mistakes, but that's one of them. My father is a fanatic when it comes to Renoir and has every book in which he's mentioned. I was practically raised on his art work."

"Oh? And here I was, thinking you'd been raised by wolves."

"Here's where it gets personal. My father's grandparents owned an art gallery in Vienna. The Santangels were their best customers. My boss at Coastal Insurance Company used the Santangel coat of arms, the intertwined Yiddish characters of *Beis Hei*, that were stamped on all their works as proof of authenticity for Pendleton's Renoir when he wrote the policy."

"That's mildly interesting." She used her palm to cover an exaggerated fake yawn. "Barely."

"So is your show, *barely*. I watched the rerun of a much earlier episode where Renoir was the mystery artist. Thanks for the incriminating evidence about how the canvas was reused. It ties you directly to *Portrait of Señorita Santangel*." Ben waved his arms in the prearranged signal and watched for Lauren's approach. "Now that you're here, we have grounds to execute a search warrant for Pendleton's yacht. Stick around, I think we're going to find some of the paintings you've been looking for."

Freelance cameramen have a better response time than the FBI. An audio technician drove up in a communications van to establish a satellite uplink. Elizabeth Moynihan turned complicity into publicity before the search warrant arrived.

She stepped in front of the camera and spun her version of events. Ben was on the phone with the investigating FBI agent assigned to the case and overheard Elizabeth avoid being charged as an accomplice by serving up Pendleton as a suspect.

"Insurance fraud!" She proclaimed, wide-eyed with enough disbelief to sell the lie.

She adopted an innocent act for the camera. "A Renoir, *Portrait of Señorita Santangel*, that was recently stolen has been linked to a suspicious pre-war sale involving a war profiteer and Nazi collaborator—his own father, Richard Pendleton the second."

The cameraman changed position to feature Elizabeth in front of Pendleton's yacht. It was a dramatic shot—guilt by association. Anyone rich enough to afford such an outlandish boat was certainly capable of insurance fraud.

Elizabeth's voice carried over the water when she described the Santangel coat of arms on the back of the frames. She adopted the academic air of a lecturing professor as she explained how the intertwined Yiddish characters proved authenticity. In a dramatic stage whisper loud enough for customers in the bait shop to overhear, she linked the mysterious death of Harold Feinstein—a convicted felon with a history of dealing in stolen art—to Pendleton's unsolved murder.

Ben couldn't stop her lies—unless he was willing to be caught on camera violating her freedom of speech. "You don't really believe that, do you? Elizabeth's story?" Ben asked the FBI agent who was in charge. "How could Pendleton steal his own art after he's dead?"

"It's not like he's gonna argue," the agent said. "Besides, it counts as a major victory and lets us off the hook for the theft of *Portrait of Señorita Santangel*."

"It's still missing."

The FBI agent lowered her voice so nobody would overhear. "Take the gift," she advised, "and Coastal Insurance Company won't have to pay. We both get to keep our jobs."

W ednesday, November 13, 6:30 p.m.
Chapter 30

Elizabeth Moynihan's damning account of Pendleton and his blood-stained art collection shocked enough viewers to build a massive audience. His murder and precarious finances ignited the scandal. Rarely has a fall from grace been so steep or well-reported. Every sordid detail was run at the top of the hour on cable news and rebroadcast on national television. Elizabeth's video went viral. The publicity generated by her video spun out of control when she aired a follow-up broadcast about the terms of Pendleton's Will leaving his art collection to the Lowe Museum. The President of the University of Miami spent Tuesday dreaming of dollar signs and convinced the museum to raise ticket prices on Wednesday morning.

Irate board members demanded an emergency meeting to distance themselves from Pendleton and the fallout from offering him a position on the board. The board members were worried about being associated with war crimes and years of contentious litigation. A discussion about contesting Pendleton's Will was added to the agenda to discuss his replacement as the honorary chairman of the museum board. Richard Pendleton III was finally getting the attention he craved, but he was dead and it was all bad.

The Florida chapter of Aryan Nation paid the city of Miami's fifty-dollar filing fee for a demonstration permit and were exercising their First Amendment right to free speech with megaphones. Skinheads dressed in black Neo-Nazi uniforms gathered opposite the Lowe Museum Plaza and carried signs demanding the return of *Entartete Kunst* paintings to German museums. A few of the signs called the Holocaust a Jewish conspiracy to hide wealth.

The Southern Poverty Law Center had secured their own permit and occupied the high ground on the opposite side of the street near the museum entrance. Most of these members also wore black, but with enough cloth to form three-piece suits or yarmulkes with rabbinical vestments.

Elizabeth Moynihan arrived half-an-hour before the board meeting started. Her scowl matched the black dress she wore when she noticed Ben in the lobby.

"Hello Eliza—"

"That's Doctor Moynihan to you." She stressed "Doctor" with enough force to draw spit and preempted Ben's civil greeting with a dismissive wave of her hand. "I'm not interested in anything you have to say."

"You will be."

"Is that a threat?"

"No, an agenda. For the board meeting." He handed her a copy of the revised itinerary.

Elizabeth appeared to have an agenda of her own and stuffed the paper into her purse without looking at it. The sharp retort from her heels echoed off the marble tiles as she crossed the lobby. With her black skirt and white blouse, she reminded Ben of an angry penguin, until she paused in front of a new exhibit: an image of a pale young man with a beard. A solid black square of paint concealed his hair and everything but his forehead and cheeks. High-resolution photographs of the distinctive Santangel coat of arms flanked the ghostly images.

Still missing: *Portrait of Señorita Santangel* and *La Grenouillère*. Ben's caseload guaranteed his employment into the next century. The prospects for Coastal Insurance Company emerging from bankruptcy had improved dramatically by denying Pendleton's claim for the theft of *Portrait of Señorita Santangel*, although lawyers representing Pendleton's estate had filed motions contesting the loophole. Meanwhile, Ben's expense account was weathering his increased expenses. Custom Caterers once again provided food for museum board members. The mojitos featured top-shelf rum, and the antique buffet in the meeting room held enough food to satisfy every finicky board member and ensure leftovers.

◆ ◆ ◆

Serge rented an unmarked, white van: the universal vehicle of the service industry. He filled the cargo space with enough pans and assorted food serving paraphernalia from a thrift store to complete the façade. He wore a generic catering company uniform, purchased from the used clothing section at the same place he bought the pots and pans. A turban covered his head, transforming him into a Middle Eastern man of strict religious beliefs, and making him completely unrecognizable. He carried three large serving pans on his shoulder and used them as a screen to hide his face.

Ben overheard one of the protestors ask a catering employee if he had a camel. A skinhead with a swastika tattoo on his forehead called the man a terrorist and asked about his connection to *Al-Qaeda*. The police interceded; two of the museum guards volunteered to escort the man past the demonstrators. A phalanx of police and security guards formed an additional line of defense behind the line of bike racks serving as a barrier. The man passed directly in front of Ben, who didn't recognize him in the outlandish disguise.

Serge entered the museum amid a deafening upswell in the skin-head protest. He ducked into the bathroom and hid in the handicapped stall while the unruly crowd threatened to storm the building. The guards were too busy with the protestors to notice his suspicious behavior.

Serge waited until 7:10 p.m. to give the board members enough time to fully assemble and for the meeting to be underway. Smoke bombs and tear gas rested beneath the layers of cookies and wax paper in a generic metal serving tray identical to the ones being used by the catering company. He slipped a gas mask over his face and sent tear gas canisters and smoke grenades rolling into the hallway, waited for the smoke to obscure his movements, and then opened the door to the boardroom and lobbed the rest of the grenades and canisters inside.

The board meeting had just been called to order when the attack began. Ben saw Elizabeth grab her purse and push her chair away from the table as smoke and tear gas turned the room into a "no-see" zone. He heard Elizabeth's heels clacking against the parquet floor with sharp pops that sounded like automatic rifle fire. She screamed. Her footsteps came to an abrupt halt. It was too dark to be certain, but a loud thump sounded like her body collapsing on the floor.

The alarm sounded with a shrill, ear-splitting tone. A cellular backup automatically notified the police of an emergency, although the blaring siren could be heard for a radius of ten blocks and it seemed like half of the police force was already outside.

Ben grabbed his phone and activated the flashlight. Black and gray smoke swirled in a dense, choking haze. His eyes burned and filled with water. Blinking made the pain worse. Pulling his shirt above his nose and mouth didn't help. He heard more footsteps, recognized the heavy trod of work boots belonging to the security guards. A woman gasped, cried out. Ben heard shouts from outside. A loud bang came from the hallway —maybe the sound of the outer door slamming shut.

More footsteps—a similar heavy tread, and one of the guards ran into an unseen obstacle with a heavy thud and the *whoof* of suddenly expelled breath. Then came the expensive sound of splintering wood, perhaps an antique picture frame or a Chippendale table. Someone crashed into the hors d'oeuvres tray and porcelain plates splintered against the floor. Ben kept his arms in front of his body to feel for obstacles and banged his shins against an overturned chair. He took smaller steps until he reached the edge of the gallery. He opened both doors; smoke clouds and tear gas billowed out of the room and mixed with the same concoction filling the hallway.

Through his tears, he recognized Daniel Mann, head of museum security, running toward him. A dozen security guards and policemen followed him and an equal number of people rushed past them to escape the smoke.

"Are you okay?" Dan shined a powerful flashlight into the room.

"It's tear gas." Ben wiped his face with a sleeve. "You'd better call for backup. It's like World War I in here."

Serge removed his gas mask and turban; he joined the confused mass of people exiting the building. Elizabeth Moynihan's purse rested inside the empty trays he carried on his shoulder.

Serge pressed the middle button. A multiband transmitter disguised as a garage door opener had been clipped to the sun visor of Elizabeth Moynihan's bright red Mercedes-Benz sports car. The scrambled frequency opened the security gate at the entrance to her private driveway. Serge left the car beside the front porch instead of parking in the detached garage. The locks on the front door were easy because he had her keys. The alarm began flashing when he entered the house. He ignored the keypad and figured he had had sixty seconds before the alarm sounded. Plenty of time to snatch a few valuable items and give him some leverage.

A marble bust from ancient Greece or Rome sat on a pedestal in the entrance. It looked valuable, so he grabbed it. Same with the blue vase from some Chinese dynasty; he wrapped this piece in a towel. He recognized a bronze ballerina in a tutu by Degas, so he stuffed this in the same bag. He used the only copy of a special key to unlock the door to the master bedroom and felt his feet sink into the plush carpet as he crossed the room and stepped into a walk-in closet. Serge pointed the key fob at a mirrored display of designer shoes and pressed the button with the image of an open trunk. Elizabeth shouldn't have kept such detailed records and receipts in her university office. The entire back wall opened like a clamshell to reveal a full-sized vault—secured by a steel door and a combination lock.

"*Rotzak.*" He couldn't get past the door without dynamite or the combination, so he turned and looked for something valuable and easier to steal. The picture above her dresser looked promising. It had an old frame with the gilt flaking off the edges. The wood at the bottom of the frame was scratched and water stained. He peered at the lower right-hand corner where the artist had signed his name: Gustave Caillebotte. Worth stealing.

The mounting hangers required a special tool. He upgraded from pliers to vise grips when the teeth kept slipping off the heads of the bolts. The threads crossed on one particularly difficult bolt and it wouldn't budge. He used a hammer. The head sheared off and he smacked his knuckles against the jagged metal edge hard enough to draw blood

"*Ratzooi.*"

His watch beeped: one minute had passed. A phone call was going out to the alarm company and the police. He changed tools and strategies, using a crowbar and a knife to remove the inner canvas and left the ugly wooden frame hanging on the wall. A drop of blood splattered against the painting. The edges were getting smeared, too. He looked around for a protective covering. The throw rug beneath his feet would work—it looked clean enough. He pulled on the edge of the rug. It wouldn't budge. He set the painting on top of an elongated dresser and used both hands. Still nothing. He tried to slide the piece of furniture off the rug and nearly pulled a muscle.

"Hmmm..."

He considered the surroundings and examined the cabinet with a fresh perspective. Solid oak and deceptively wide, containing two locking drawers of considerable depth: a custom filing cabinet, perhaps? The folders in Elizabeth's university office had been especially helpful.

The gap between the drawer and the frame was too small for the blunt edge of the crowbar. The hardwood resisted the intrusion until he used a hammer to drive the claw into the wood. The wood splintered but the lock held. He wedged the crowbar into the widening gap, climbed on top of the cabinet and jumped onto the bar with both feet until the lock broke.

Some of the titles on the hanging tabs looked familiar when he yanked open the drawer: *Entartete Kunst*, Theodor Fischer Gallery, Hungarian Gold Train, *Jeu de Paume*, running alphabetically all the way to Renoir and Van Gogh in the bottom drawer. Worth an extra trip. He stowed the files in the passenger compartment of Elizabeth's car when he ran out of room in the trunk.

Serge stashed the distinctive sports car in a parking lot near the public beach where it would serve as another dead end for the police to investigate. He switched to a less conspicuous sedan. The dented car had been parked near the ocean long enough to resemble a lumpy sugar cookie. He transferred the stolen goods from Elizabeth's car to the trunk of the decrepit sedan.

The car started but wouldn't idle. Ocean mist and sand had turned the windshield opaque, with the marbled texture of a bathroom window. The wipers worked but not the washers. Twin smears of intersecting arcs compromised the view from behind the wheel. He rolled down the window and cleared as much of the windshield as he could reach with his sleeve, keeping his foot on the gas pedal while shifting into second gear so the car wouldn't stall. With a slight grind of the gears and a puff of smoke, he headed for the anonymous repository of a self-storage rental unit. Incriminating evidence had just elevated him to Elizabeth Moynihan's equal partner.

T hursday, November 14, 10:00 a.m., Miami

Chapter 31

Ben pulled beside a police car blocking the entrance to Elizabeth Moynihan's private driveway. It seemed like overkill with a reinforced security gate already preventing access. It wasn't until the police officer verified his ID that he learned Elizabeth's purse had been stolen, along with her car and the remote that opened the gate. Another police car was parked in front of the house. He showed a different officer the same ID and rang the doorbell.

"Are you the *only* person working for Coastal Insurance?"

"The only one within 1000 miles," he said, instead of: If this trend keeps up, we'll be opening a regional office. "I'm truly sorry for your loss. I promise I will do everything I can to help."

"Well," she briefly made eye contact. "Okay. I have some documents that will help."

"Thank you. I'll look around first. Meanwhile, is there anything you need?" Like a new fence, or more trustworthy business partners? Of course, he didn't say this aloud because of her loss and vulnerable condition, but he couldn't help thinking she was reaping some of the discord she had sowed.

"We'll see." She turned and walked through the kitchen. A door slammed somewhere on the other side of the house.

"Whew." He took a moment to collect his thoughts. A sisal mat holding a pair of designer flats blocked the entryway, sending a powerful message of voluntary compliance. White carpet, pretentious but appropriate for the surroundings, explained the ban on footwear. He took off his shoes out of respect. Robbery victims had already suffered enough trauma and feeling violated was a common response; he didn't want to raise Elizabeth's pain threshold.

An empty pedestal in the entryway looked forlorn without something valuable resting on top. The chandelier above his head was a bit much. His feet were cold and the marble tile looked like it had been taken from a European church. The ceiling trim was hand-carved and dated from early in the previous century when craftsmen used hardwood. He moved to the hallway.

Something was off. He stopped, looked, and listened, turned 360 degrees to get a better sense of his surroundings. He committed the image to memory: the faint smell of Elizabeth's perfume mixed with carpet-freshener, the feel of the soft carpet beneath his feet, the slant of sunlight from the skylight in the entryway. He didn't move until he could identify what was troubling him.

The spacing between the pedestals in the hallway was inconsistent. He knelt on the carpet a fourth of the way further down the hallway. This section of the rug showed signs of recent vacuuming. He got down on his hands and knees and ran his fingertips along the carpet to feel for flat spots in the underlayment pad. A circular depression the approximate size of the other two pedestal bases bore the imprint of something heavy. A matching pedestal once sat here. What had it held and why had Elizabeth moved it? Contraband art, maybe? Moved to avoid self-incrimination, perhaps?

Probably. He dusted off his pants and continued down the hallway. He paused outside the door to her bedroom. Elizabeth's grief had looked and sounded real enough, but Ben had investigated false claims filed by worse actresses. The special lock on her bedroom door wasn't scratched, supporting her "stolen keys" story. Less believable was the location where her keys had been taken. Something was off about the incident at the museum board meeting, although his eyes still hurt, so the tear gas and smoke grenades had been convincing enough. His wiggled his toes in the plush bedroom carpet and stepped on a sand burr.

"Ouch." The multi-barbed clump of pain left a sticker embedded in the tender skin below the arch of his foot when he pried it loose. He took off his sock and turned it inside-out to remove the tiny thorn. Evidently the intruder hadn't bothered to take off their shoes—further supporting Elizabeth's alibi.

Splintered wood on both drawers of an empty filing cabinet testified to the thief's determination, and the quality of the locks meant something valuable had been secured inside. He rested his knee on the floor. His flashlight revealed a trace of the fine, white dust shed by old paper. The drawers had been full of aged documents that shed microscopic pieces of brittle parchment. The unique powder lining both sides and the back of each drawer reminded Ben of sandy footsteps tracked in from a beach. Elizabeth Moynihan's masters and doctoral research had located two Renoir's that had been missing since the start of WWII. What might these files have revealed?

And what had been inside the splintered frame hanging from the wall? Museum-grade mounting hardware required special tools and was designed to be difficult and time-consuming to remove. The more valuable the artwork, the harder it was for a thief to dismount. Most thieves stole the painted canvas and left the frame. It looked like this thief was an amateur, large chunks of plaster were missing from the wall where the mounting hardware had been. Something else was off about the room —the excessive damage was only part of the incongruity. A meticulous sense of order permeated Elizabeth's entire house, other than the uneven spaces between the pedestals in the hallway. Whatever imbalance he was feeling, it was uniquely related to Elizabeth's meticulous personal sense of order.

He moved to the center of the room and repeated the same process as in the hallway. An errant brush stroke, a minute discoloration caused by improper layering of paint, even the thickness of the artist's typical underlayment coat of paint was enough to unsettle Ben's sense of order and consistency. He pressed his cheek against the wall. Something was off about the dimensions of the room, and it didn't make sense until he noticed the unusual thickness of the dividing wall between the closet and the bedroom. A vault, maybe? Only someone with a touch of obsessive-compulsiveness would notice the incongruity. It made him an effective investigator who regularly put criminals in prison. Maybe Elizabeth would be next. Two missing Renoirs was no coincidence and the missing pedestal in the hallway bothered him. For a suspicious-natured guy, however, Ben could be diplomatic. He was here to investigate a theft, not blame her for a prior one.

Elizabeth offered to make coffee after he had completed his inspection. He joined her in the kitchen and expressed genuine sorrow for her loss. "It doesn't seem like it now, but I've investigated enough claims to know that your pain will eventually fade."

"I can't bear to go in there," Elizabeth said. Two frown lines formed parentheses on her forehead directly above the bridge of her nose. A clumsy dentist would recognize her expression—the sharp pain from puncturing an exposed nerve ending. "I feel violated."

"I hear that, too. The insurance check helps. Unfortunately, the theft still leaves a scar." Ben could commiserate with her loss while remaining suspicious. *That's because your policy doesn't cover stolen artwork. What was on that missing pedestal?*

"You're right. It's not helping." Elizabeth sipped her coffee. The nails on the fingers she wrapped around her cup were still intact.

"What was in that frame?"

She slid a folder across the table and let the contents answer his question.

"Wow. Your grandparents bought a landscape by Gustave Caillebotte. That was a good move. I think the last painting of his that came to market sold for 1.4 million."

"One million, four-hundred-and-twelve thousand, five-hundred and eighty dollars, to be exact."

"It's shaping up to be a bad month for Coastal Insurance Company. Fortunately, in cases like yours, and with an umbrella clause in your policy to allow for additions too recent for inclusion in the accounting for your annual renewal, some exceptions allow an amended claim."

"In English?"

"Recent acquisitions that aren't listed on your policy may be eligible for coverage. If anything else was stolen, it may be automatically covered. You could get a check for replacement value."

Elizabeth let go of the cup. "Go on."

"You need proof. Receipts, copies of appraisals, but you already know all this. The good news is if anything else was stolen —like whatever was on that pedestal in the hallway or anything else . . . it might be covered by your policy." Since her hands were below the table, he watched her eyes and body language. Her spine stiffened; her eyebrows dipped; a slight grimace wrinkled the tender skin along her temples.

"Is something else missing? Something valuable but too new to be listed?" *Stolen art, perhaps?*

"Unfortunately, all my receipts were in the file cabinet."

"In your bedroom?"

She nodded.

Liar. Ben knew she was too smart for such an amateur mistake. Elizabeth was a professional art appraiser. Part of her service was to ensure that documentation existed for her clients —always at multiple, secure locations.

"There had to be some sort of surveillance. What about video?"

"Stolen along with everything else."

Another lie. An alarm this good would have multiple forms of back up—probably a streaming service with a real-time feed to an offsite recorder and a link to a remote server with cloud storage. "A safety-deposit box, perhaps?"

"Refill your cup?" Elizabeth walked to the counter and poured a few drops into her nearly-full cup.

"No thanks." *I'm not giving you any more time to come up with a better lie, either.* "You mentioned a prior break-in at your university office? Could it have been in preparation for last night's theft? A copy of the police report might help."

"I didn't call the police about that break-in. Nothing worth reporting was stolen."

"Nothing valuable?"

"I didn't say that." Elizabeth was too prideful to diminish the importance of her research. She returned the coffee pot to the burner and approached the table, resting a hand on the back of the chair.

"I'm assuming it was research papers?"

"Let's just say there wasn't anything covered by the umbrella policy you mentioned."

"Too bad. What about . . ." He took a sip of coffee. Waited. Watched her fingers on the back of the chair. "What about the missing pedestal that was in your hallway?"

Click, click . . . clickity-thump. Only three fingernails remained intact on her other hand.

Ben left his car in Elizabeth Moynihan's reserved parking spot on the University of Miami campus. There was nowhere else to park within walking distance of the Otto G. Richter Library. Every reference item that Elizabeth Moynihan had requested since her undergraduate days filled three tables—compliments of Goldie's research assistants. Ben treated the tables as multiple jigsaw puzzles. The possible combinations defied order until he applied known limits: *Portrait of Señorita Santangel* and *La Grenouillère*.

As the outer pieces of a jigsaw puzzle have distinctive straight edges, so do the frames of masterpiece art. The Santangel coat of arms, with the Yiddish characters of *Beis Hei*, were as recognizable as the rounded shape of a corner piece in a puzzle. This strategy moved him a step closer to a solution.

He walked around each table as he would walk around a pile of puzzle pieces dumped onto the floor. Color, size, and shape, all the books and pieces formed patterns. It had been his unexpected discovery of a black-and-white photograph of *Por-*

trait of Señorita Santangel that provided an early breakthrough in the investigation, so he sorted the materials printed in black-and-white like he would normally arrange puzzle pieces according to color.

He stepped away from the table to think like a thief. If he was going to steal a painting, he wouldn't take the frame, especially if it was damaged. Elizabeth's research was impressive and he had been reading nothing else for the last week. The water stains on the bottom of *Portrait of Señorita Santangel's* frame were the result of it having been hidden inside a hastily erected brick wall in the back of a servant's closet. The frame around the painting in Elizabeth's bedroom bore similar water stains. Had her grandparents been war profiteers? It certainly explained the mansion in Coral Gables. Or were her records forgeries and the painting somehow connected to Pendleton's collection?

One of Goldie's ESL students volunteered to send out group emails bearing digital images. Despite the uncirculated nature of the painting, someone was likely to recognize such a distinctive frame—a solid lead and one often overlooked. Who goes to a museum to stare at frames?

"What's this about the frame?" Goldie returned, pushing a cart laden with DVD copies of Elizabeth's recent shows.

"*Beis Hei:* the entwined characters featured on the Santangel coat of arms. This is a close-up of the seal from Pendleton's stolen Renoir."

"*Baruch Hasem.* Not a day goes by that I don't thank God. I'll forward the image to some people I know. There's a support group for survivors."

Interesting, had *Grossmutter* been a member? Ben looked up from flipping through pages of the Theodore Fisher Gallery's auction catalogue. "Then maybe you can help unravel this mystery." He grabbed a different book and pointed to a puzzling photo. "This looks like tape. And it's on most of the buildings in the background of these pictures."

"It's white tape—the universal sign for landmines during World War II. The Allies put white tape around art galleries and all the buildings where there was cached art." She noticed his puzzled look. "It was the only way to prevent looting. I'll get my students to look through photos of confiscated art."

"Start with *Jeu du Paume*," Ben suggested. "Elizabeth Moynihan did extensive research into the museum."

"No wonder. The Nazis turned it into a clearinghouse for stolen art," Goldie said. "They shipped the art out of Paris by train, there was so much of it."

"Now that we know where to look and what we're looking for," he said. "It should make it easier to find."

Goldie's ESL connections extended to the digital media lab, the digital production and scanning facilities, and the conservation laboratory. The university's print, multimedia, and networked information resources mobilized when her name was mentioned. A phone call to the land line on her desk from a member of her survivor's group further narrowed the search to occupied Paris and provided an approximate confiscation date. Which led to an archival collection of black-and-white photos that documented the stacks of Degenerate Art that had passed through the *Galerie Nationale du Jeu de Paume* in occupied France.

"Look at this!" Ben forgot to whisper when he studied the photo. "Look at all of these Post Modernists. It's like a Who's Who of *Entartete Kunst*."

"The Nazis made a bonfire outside *Jeu de Paume* and burned 600 canvases: Picasso, Miró, Klee, too many to catalogue. A tragedy," Goldie said, "but not what we're looking for."

"Not entirely. Look at the frame sticking out from behind the stack on the floor. It's bigger than the others." He held a magnifying glass above the photo. "There's a distinctive scar on the bottom left corner of the frame. Made by an errant dreidel according to my *Grossmutter*."

"May her memory be a blessing: *zikhronal livrakha*," Goldie said. "A cherished member of our survivor's group."

"I'd like to hear more about that. My father won't talk about it."

"A difficult man."

"You don't know the half of it."

"And yet he is proud of you in his own way."

"News to me," Ben admitted.

"Because you haven't heard him bragging about you in temple. Maybe you should ask him for help."

T

hursday, November 14, 6:00 p.m., Key Largo

Chapter 32

Ben hadn't asked his father for *anything* in twenty years. The ancestors were tired of waiting; they overcame Ben's reluctance to ask for help with a hybrid solution: a proverb and baked goods. The proverb was easy since it was one of his father's favorites: *A good friend is often better than a brother.* He called Lauren for backup in case he needed a moderator or things got so out of control a professional law and order officer was needed. Baking meant going to the grocery store and cleaning the cobwebs out of the pantry.

Ben followed *Grossmutter's* recipe and baked *Rugelach.* Chocolate, hazelnuts, and apricot jam, encased in tender cream-cheese dough, improved the odds of gaining access to his father's study. Lauren arrived early and appointed herself to the "official taste-tester" position. Alexi heard the unusual squeak of the oven door opening and joined them in the kitchen. The rest was up to the ancestors.

"I recognized the aromas." Ben's father greeted them at the head of the stairs and invited them into his study. "This calls for a blessing before we eat," he said, and surprised everyone but the spirit of *Grossmutter,* who had been attracted to the same aromas wafting from the kitchen. Ben's grandmother was tired of waiting on the men of the family. Being hidden inside a shipping crate motivates even the most patient of spirits. As the only member of her family to survive the holocaust of World War II, *Grossmutter* had been entrusted with the key that still unlocked the family's ancestral estate in Spain—the key to a legacy. It was one of the few cherished possessions to survive when her ancestors fled to Vienna in 1492. She also knew every grain, knot, and splinter of the wooden box that had enabled her to survive the latest diaspora to befall her family: *Kristallnacht*—the Night of Broken Glass. It was a fitting tribute that she had made the frame honoring the family's one remaining artifact from the most valuable wood on the planet—the shipping crate that had delivered her to safety.

Past, present, and future: *Grossmutter* gave Ben the courage to ask his father for help, and then she stuck around to intervene as needed.

Ben placed a black and white photo taken from inside the *Galerie Nationale du Jeu de Paume* on top of his father's desk. "Take a closer look at the corner of that frame that's mostly obscured behind the stack of paintings. Please." He put his finger on the painting in the background. "If there are any surviving heirs, I'd like to see it's returned to them."

"Looks like the stack of post-Modernist paintings that was burned behind *Jeu de Paume*," his father said.

"Wait until you look at it with a magnifying glass." His father had a collection of magnifying glasses that cycled between misplaced and currently in use. Ben selected an available model with powerful magnification and a light incorporated into the lens.

"What about catching the thief?" Lauren's police training framed the obvious question.

"Which thief? Elizabeth Moynihan? She stole a stolen painting from Richard Pendleton III. I can't prove it, yet, and I'm not sure I want to since she lost money on the deal by having a few pieces from her personal collection stolen—at least four —one for each empty pedestal. I'm betting everything she had stolen is tainted by war crimes, turned up during her research into art that was looted during World War II. She didn't file an insurance claim on anything except the painting her grandparents bought legitimately. I'm suspicious about that one, too, after seeing water stains on the frame."

"Sounds like poetic justice," Lauren said.

"What about *Portrait of Señorita Santangel*?" Alexi asked.

"It's still missing, right?"

"For now. I think Elizabeth had help beating Pendleton's alarm—it's too good—that's what made me suspicious in the first place. I think she conspired with Richard Pendleton III, a different kind of thief, the kind who stole millions with a pen. Unfortunately, he couldn't steal enough to keep up with his opulent lifestyle and turned to insurance fraud."

"He had help from his father," Alexi said. "According to the news feeds I've been watching."

"Certainly looks that way." Ben added a codicil. "Pendleton came by evil naturally, he inherited it from his war-profiteering father, who was at the Theodore Fischer Gallery's auction of *Entartete Kunst* paintings in 1939. Richard Pendleton III had a lifestyle he couldn't afford and an inheritance he couldn't sell. The black-market artwork from his father's personal collection lacked provenance, so he needed an expert with an impeccable reputation for accuracy and a weakness for stolen portraits by Renoir: namely, Elizabeth Moynihan."

"Don't do favors for evildoers and no evil will befall you." Ben's father had a Yiddish proverb for every occasion. "A sad business for all concerned. And the man under my dock? He was a thief, too?"

"A professional thief, with a history of dealing in stolen paintings. I think he was the middle man who set up the theft of *Portrait of Señorita Santangel*. Thomas Benson has a reputation for killing competitors and *D'Erve* got in his way."

"No shortage of thieves," his father took a deep breath to underscore the irony. "Sounds like job security. So many thieves . . ." He let the oxygen machine catch up. "Seems like you ought to be able to catch some of them."

"That's where I've made some progress," Ben said, "and I've got you to thank for the idea. Do you remember the photograph in *D'Erve*'s money belt?"

"Of course," his father said, "just like I recognized the wood and what was inscribed on it, *Beis Hei*: the Santangel coat of arms."

Ben placed a copy of the photo retrieved from *D'Erve's* money belt on his father's desk. "This helped me formulate a slightly different approach: looking for frames. Most people focus on the painting." Ben gave credit to the library staff and described the search for *Portrait of Señorita Santangel,* and *La Grenouillère.* "We concentrated on finding photos of distinctive, water-stained frames. That's what turned up this picture from *Galerie Nationale du Jeu de Paume."* He pointed to the picture from *Jeu de Paume* resting beside the picture found in *D'Erve's* money belt.

"You found someone else's painting?" Alexi asked. "What about our Renoir? The one with the dreidel scratch? I'd like to see that hanging in our hallway."

"I was thinking the same thing," Lauren admitted.

"*Meh.* I'll find it." His father sounded as unimpressed as Goldie had in the library. "I just need to do a little more research."

Ben looked around at the clutter—stacks of books and boxes of documents representing fifty years of his father's research without a conclusive result. He bit back a retort. No argument could change the past. Only Ben and his father could change the future.

"This painting," Ben called his father's attention to the picture from *Jeu de Paume,* "was documented by Rose Valland. Which means there's a verifiable record. So, I'm with you, Alexi," Ben said, enjoying the inside joke. "I'd like to see it returned to its rightful owners. Us. And if anyone can identify it, it's our father." The compliment tasted strange coming from his mouth. Ben ignored his discomfort despite wanting to issue a retraction.

His father glanced at him—probably to check for signs of sincerity.

They would always have their differences, but something good should come from his father's sacrifice. "It's true," Ben said, two heartfelt words worth more than a lifetime of compliments when compared to a past littered with estrangement and devoid of personal emotion.

"I'll take a look, then," his father said. "Where's this picture?"

"It's right there. On your desk." Ben pointed out the obvious.

"Again? We've already been through this." His father gave him a look that could undo a generation of amends.

"Not quite. Humor me." Ben took the first slice of *Rugelach* before it had cooled enough to serve—better to risk burning his tongue than hurl the harmful words gathering in his mouth toward his father. Alexi knew better than to hazard a guess. Lauren raised an eyebrow in question. All three of them waited on the oxygen machine when no one volunteered an answer.

"They're the same frame! Look at the wood. This is the frame around *Portrait of Señorita Santangel.*" His father's hands shook. "See the grain? The missing gilt edging? The pattern, the spacing is the same."

"And the scratch?"

"Identical."

"Let me see." Alexi borrowed the magnifying glass and stared at both pictures long enough for Lauren to get antsy about waiting her turn.

"An exact match," she said.

"That's what I thought. It means I can prove Pendleton was trying to raise money on stolen paintings by filing fraudulent claims. *D'Erve's* phone records document his conversations with Pendleton and Elizabeth Moynihan. I know he had both their help arranging the theft—it's the only way she could have beat his alarm, although I can't prove it."

"What *can* you prove?" Lauren asked the penultimate question.

The ancestors held their collective breath. Ben helped himself to another slice of *Rugelach* and *Grossmutter* gently guided his eyes to the framed key hanging on the wall of his father's study. He crossed the room and took the artifact down from the wall and ran his fingers along the rough, unfinished wood that had once formed a packing crate for the painting about to be discussed.

The ancestors gently reminded Ben of how Solomon Santangel had hidden the keystone clue in the receipt for *Portrait of Señorita Santangel.* The wooden frame around the family key was the connection. Generations of men who shared the middle name of Isaac guided Ben to the hidden connection.

"*Portrait of Señorita Santangel* was almost certainly sold under duress. The first receipt was dated August 2, 1938.'"

"*Tisha B'Av,*" Alexi said, "marking the destruction of the First and Second Holy Temples of Jerusalem. The only reason I remember is because it also happens to be my birthday."

"There's that," his father allowed. "It also happens to be the date Christopher Columbus set sail for the New World, fleeing the Spanish Diaspora. Which seems appropriate, since it's also the anniversary *Grossmutter* honored to celebrate her survival." He glanced at Ben before helping himself to a slice. "You making *Rugelach* reminds me of her."

"I don't think it's a coincidence." Ben propped the frame holding their key against a stack of books on his father's desk. "I know one of the Santangel's Gentile maids shipped *Portrait of Señorita Santangel* to the Theodore Fischer Gallery with *Grossmutter* hidden inside the crate. Solomon Santangel must have known someone at the gallery who was expecting the shipment. I think he was sending a message of her expected delivery the only way he knew how, by using *Tisha B'Av.* It explains the date and the fifteen months between the time of the sale and the shipment. It must have taken that long to figure out a way to smuggle *Grossmutter* to safety."

"In that case I will do my best to help you," his father promised. "In her memory. And your mother's, of course. She was proud of you, too."

F

riday, November 15, 9:00 a.m., Key Largo

Chapter 33

His bait worked so well the first time; Ben decided to use Winged Sandal Courier Service to set another trap. The poetic justice of using a technique pioneered by a thief, Thomas Benson, to expose a trio of thieves had a powerful, personal appeal. Thomas Benson and Elizabeth Moynihan were his primary suspects and Serge was the wildcard. Ben knew all three were involved. He couldn't predict how they would react, but he had enough leverage to expose them. Lauren had assured him there was enough circumstantial evidence for an arrest.

He knew Benson had a room at the Biltmore; Elizabeth Moynihan lived in her grandparent's house in Coral Gables, and one, or both-of-them, knew how to contact Serge. He decided to let Elizabeth or Benson do the footwork. The daily limit on his Coastal Insurance Company credit card reset at midnight. He withdrew the maximum cash advance and ordered four sets of copies. He dropped by the general store and bought five prepaid phones before calling Donny Ray for extra envelopes.

Four envelopes: four sets of photos from *Jeu de Paume* showing the distinctive scratch on the corner of the frame that had been around *Portrait of Señorita Santangel,* photos of *Beis Hei* taken of the back of the same frame and found in *D'Erve's* money belt, and copies of the sales catalogue from the *Entartete Kunst* auction at the Theodor Fisher Gallery. He added copies of the suspicious receipts from August 2, 1938, and November 11, 1939. The theft of *La Grenouillère* from The Lowe Museum was connected somehow, so he included a photo of this canvas, as well. He synched all four prepaid phones to his computer and put one in each folder so he could track their locations. He addressed two envelopes to Serge; Thomas Benson or Elizabeth Moynihan would know where to forward them, and he gave Donny Ray a big tip for the delivery.

Elizabeth Moynihan made the first phone call. Within two hours, all three of the conspirators were engaged in conversations. Ben listened while they made plans, compliments of Lauren and a subpoena from a sympathetic judge who loved the Impressionists.

◆ ◆ ◆

Warm, moist air over the Atlantic Ocean began to rise when a cold front sank beneath the prevailing winds. Massive clouds produced thunderstorms. Gusts of wind approached hurricane velocity and displaced Elizabeth Moynihan's television personality hairdo. She used a clump of tissues to clean a spot on the driver's door before leaning against the rusty sedan. She had a flashlight in one pocket and an M9 Beretta loaded with fifteen rounds in the other. She wasn't a killer, although shooting someone—Serge especially—came to mind. He couldn't sell the art stolen from her because it was linked to war crimes and subject to reparations. The police still had her Mercedes, although Serge had worn gloves and drenched the interior with bleach to avoid implicating himself. She had video of Serge while he was inside her house, but couldn't use it without incriminating herself because he was stealing stolen art. Thomas Benson was a solid number two on her people-needing-to-be-shot list. She might make an exception for Ben Abrams; however, who she blamed for her predicament.

Elizabeth heard the roar from Benson's amphibious plane before it was visible on approach. He emerged from the cockpit after the propeller stopped spinning and used the pontoon as a ladder to reach the ground. She watched him raise both hands to his face and slowly scan the perimeter. His eyes were hidden—probably by night-vision goggles. She waited until he was looking directly at her before switching on a police-issue flashlight big enough to double as a truncheon. Maybe the light would blind him.

"The car stalled," she yelled, and directed the beam along rusty doors and salt-encrusted glass.

Benson produced a flashlight of his own and illuminated Elizabeth, the car, and the surrounding area. "What happened to the Mercedes?"

"Stolen. Like this painting. Come see for yourself." She unlocked the trunk. When the open lid shielded her from view, she flashed two short bursts of light out to sea. The faint hum of a battery-operated trolling motor returned her message.

Benson crept into pointblank range with an odd mixture of confidence and wariness, as a predator hunting dangerous prey might carefully weigh the potential outcome in a fight for survival.

"Where's my money?"

"In the plane. Where it's safe," Benson said. "I like to see what I'm buying before I pay."

"Then look under the blanket." Elizabeth gestured to the trunk and stepped aside for a much better shooting angle.

Benson directed the flashlight beam onto *La Grenouillère*—the Frog Pond. "I can't believe you're actually letting this one go."

"For enough money to fund my search for ten more just like it. Besides, Ben Abrams is getting too close; I have too much to lose." She drew Benson's attention to the gun in her other hand. "So do you," she reminded him.

"Of course," he said, with the vampire smile she remembered from the museum. He snapped his fingers as if a thought had just occurred to him. The façade was as carefully orchestrated as the manicured fingers he used to playact the farce. The next words out of Benson's mouth would be lies.

Elizabeth gently slid the safety off the automatic. A man like Benson only thought he could play with fire; she could incinerate him if it meant getting what she wanted. She'd done it before—she could do it again.

"I can sell *Portrait of Señorita Santangel* for twice what this is worth."

"One stolen painting at a time. I'll have others for you to sell. That is . . ." she swept the beam of her flashlight across the painting secreted in the trunk, across his face, and then to his plane, "if you brought the cash."

"I said I would."

"Prove it." Elizabeth said

"Certainly." He reached into the trunk. I'll just get *La Grenouillère* and save both of us a trip."

"Not so fast. I want my deposit, first." She mocked his patently false tone. "Eight-million dollars. More of a down payment, really, for a Renoir worth somewhere between eighty and 170 million dollars."

"Some partnership," Benson said. "Based on mutual distrust."

"Aren't they all?" She used the gun as a pointer. "Put the painting back in the trunk. It stays there until I get my cash."

"You aren't going to shoot me. I don't even think you can pull the trigger. But just in case . . ." He raised the canvas to his chin and covered his torso. "You're not going to put a bullet through a Renoir."

"True." She aimed the flashlight behind him. "Which is why someone with a grudge and not enough money is standing behind you with a spear gun."

Serge's pants and shoes were wet. An inflatable raft glistened on the shore behind him. Pendleton's ex-aide gestured with a spear gun. "Put it back."

"Money first," Elizabeth said. "All three of us are going to walk over to your plane and count the money."

Benson didn't let go of the painting. He looked over his shoulder where Serge was standing. "Sure you can trust his aim?" He asked Elizabeth.

"Want to find out?" Serge moved close enough to poke him in the back with the barb.

"I hear Montenegro is nice," Elizabeth said, with cloying

sweetness. "What do you think, Serge?"

"No extradition treaty." He prodded Benson with the tip of the spear. "Walk."

Elizabeth pointed the pistol at Benson's ankles. "Micronesia is warm. The Marshall Islands are nearby. None of these countries have extradition treaties, and you've got a float plane loaded with cash. Or do you?"

"Come see for yourself," Benson said. He reached for his pocket.

"Keep both hands on the painting." This time Serge prodded him hard enough to draw blood.

Elizabeth's watch chimed. The alarm kept ringing until she pressed the button to turn it off. "Thirty seconds. Remember your little countdown? The one you gave me at the dock? Not even a minute. Quit playing games. Where's my money?"

"In my plane. Not of all it, but you already knew that."

"Tick, tick, tick," Elizabeth said. "If you're not airborne in the next few minutes we're liable to have some unwanted company. The FBI has helicopters, and their response is going to be much faster this time."

"But they can't land on a private airstrip in South America and refuel . . . after meeting with the cash buyer for *La Grenouillère.*"

"A drug dealer?" Elizabeth scoffed. "This is your idea of a haven? He'll probably charge you for fuel and then shoot you."

"She," Benson said. "*Viuda Negra*: a widow, also an art lover who's far more dangerous than the husband she killed to take over the cartel."

"Refueling is good," Serge said. "Maybe I hold off shooting you until we land."

"I'm not taking you with me," Benson said. "She doesn't deal with strangers; she shoots them."

Serge looked to Elizabeth for a decision.

"Cash first" she said, and aimed the gun at Benson's foot.

"Tick. Tick. Tick. I have a plane," Benson reminded them. "You two can stick around and get arrested. I'm ready to leave."

Benson gripped the painting hard enough to drain the blood from his knuckles. Lucifer could have picked up a few pointers from his evil smirk.

"First we split the cash." Elizabeth called his bluff and fired a warning shot close enough to his foot to get dust on his shoe. "Tick, tick, tick."

◆ ◆ ◆

Elizabeth Moynihan and Thomas Benson had enough criminal experience to leave their phones behind. Serge was an amateur and had the prepaid phone in his pocket. When Ben triangulated his location to within a few feet, Lauren called the FBI rapid deployment art crime team. Their response was hampered by a tropical storm brewing off the coast of Cuba that had grounded their helicopters. Two of the crooks got away and were smart enough to not have stolen artwork in their possession.

The FBI had jets that flew above inclement weather, however, and were much faster than Benson's propeller-driven float plane. *La Grenouillère* never reached South America; Thomas Benson committed the deadly mistake of losing eight-million dollars of *Viuda Negra's* drug money and made her an enemy for the rest of his brief, endangered life. She got in line to exact her revenge, because the FBI recovered *La Grenouillère* and locked Benson in jail at an undisclosed location.

Elizabeth Moynihan kept the cash. Serge demanded half before he would return her files and stolen art work. She alerted the immigration office when he insisted on keeping the Degas statue. Elizabeth had done the research, now she had the capital to become the world's first billionaire art thief. Approximately 500 of Pablo Picasso's paintings were still missing from the looting of Europe and she had solid leads on enough of his work to assure she met her goal. A collection of Degenerate Art in Argentina looked promising. Ben Abrams remained a problem, so she moved *Portrait of Señorita Santangel* to a safe location.

One Month Later

Chapter 34

Repeated at the closing of every Passover Seder since the Middle Ages: *L'Shana Haba'ah B'Yerushalayim*: "Next Year in Jerusalem." *El Al* operated daily flights from Miami to Tel Aviv, but for security purposes, Coastal Insurance Company chartered a private jet and hired an armed contingent to accompany Ben when he returned a Renoir entitled *La Grenouillère* —The Frog Pond, to its rightful owners. Of the estimated six million European Jewish men, women, and children who were systematically stripped of their possessions and murdered, two Holocaust survivors were finally getting reparations. They were in an assisted living facility run by a kibbutz, but they were home.

The Israel Museum in Jerusalem arranged for the heirs to attend the donation ceremony. After the dedication, Ben joined them for tea in a private room the museum maintained for generous benefactors.

"And this man," the woman asked, adding a sugar cube to her cup. Her fluffy white hair looked like the cotton wadding stuffed into the tops of pill bottles. "The one with our painting. He was arrested?"

"Murdered," Ben said. "Richard Pendleton III—it was his father who bought paintings from the Theodor Fischer Gallery in the wake of *Entartete Kunst*."

"*Oy gevalt*." She poured half a cup for her husband. "Who killed him?"

"The police have two suspects—his aide, Serge, had means and motive. Personally, I think a man named Thomas Benson did it, and the FBI have him in custody."

"So many thieves, so much death." The old man added

cream and sugar to his tea.

"There's more. The Theodore Fischer Gallery in Lucerne trafficked in stolen art. Richard Pendleton II sold munitions to Germany to finance his purchases of stolen art, and his son, number III, was murdered trying to legitimatize the theft by defrauding an insurance company. When all the criminals die, we call that *Frontier Justice*."

"I have watched this in your western movies." He stirred the cream and sugar into his tea. "But is it? Justice?"

"A poetic form, perhaps." Ben said.

"Then they are all dead?" She asked.

"Not yet. Some are unaccounted for. The thief who broke into the museum is still at large. She lost the painting she stole, and more, so there's some justice in that. I haven't caught her—yet. I'm still working on the case."

"Then I wish you good hunting." The man's hands shook, so he kept the saucer poised beneath the cup to catch any drips. Age spots and freckles had merged to give the tops of his hands the appearance of a deep-water tan. "Enough with the dead, already. Tell me about our painting. How did you find it?"

"By looking for another Renoir that had been stolen from Richard Pendleton III—the man who donated your painting to the Lowe Museum to gain respectability and defraud Coastal Insurance Company. He had help from the thief who stole it, Elizabeth Moynihan. I think defrauding Coastal Insurance Company was her idea."

"Another Renoir?" The lady looked surprised.

"Also part of Richard Pendleton III's illicit collection. His father's purchases from the Theodore Fischer Gallery formed the core of his collection; he couldn't sell the paintings due to the threat of war crimes reparations. Insurance fraud was a way around his problem—or so he thought."

His hands shook as he took a sip of tea. "As the *Torah* teaches us: 'He that does not bring up his son to some honest calling and employment, brings him up to be a thief.'"

"You sound like my father," Ben said. "He's a bit of an ex-

222

pert on the Santangel collection—"

"*Meyn gat!*" He grabbed Ben's wrist. "You can prove this? About the Santangels?"

"With pictures." He placed his phone in the center of the table so it faced the couple and tapped on the photo of the Santangel coat of arms. "*Beis Hei.* This is inscribed on the back of the frames of all of the paintings in their collection."

"You have more photos?" The woman leaned forward, opening the palms of her hands and holding them out to Ben in anticipation. Her husband put down his cup and gripped the edge of the table to keep his hands from shaking.

"This is the dreidel scratch on the frame of *Portrait of Señorita Santangel,* painted by Renoir in 1876. My great-grandparents had an art gallery in Vienna and it was rumored to have been part of their personal collection. It's been missing since *Kristallnacht.*"

He swiped a finger across the screen to show them a copy of the photo from *D'Erve's* money belt. "This is what led me to look through three tables-full of library books. When that didn't give me enough answers, I showed a librarian a black-and-white picture of a Paris Gallery full of Post Impressionists. It reminded her of World War II photos. A friend of hers remembered your family, which is how I was able to trace ownership of *La Grenouillère* to you."

"I don't understand," he said.

"Photos taken at *Jeu de Paume*: a museum in occupied France that turned into a sort of clearing house for stolen art." Ben used his thumb and index finger to enlarge the photo from *Jeu de Paume.*

"But I recognize some of these paintings." The woman slid the phone to the edge of the table so her husband could see.

He gasped; his hands shook. Tea spilled onto the saucer.

"What is it?" Ben asked.

"No," his wife gasped. "*Mishegas.*"

"*Shtum glik.* Could it be?" The old man asked.

"It's not impossible," she said.

"Craziness and dumb luck. Stranger things . . ." he raised both hands in a gesture of possibility.

"What is it?" Ben had seen this type of telepathic communication between older couples before, people who had been married long enough to share and read each other's thoughts. They even looked a little alike, as many couples did who had been together for most of their adult lives.

"Huh. The Santangel collection. Who knew?" she asked.

"*Yahweh*—God knows." He stood. "Come," he motioned for Ben to follow.

"The painting you so kindly brought back to us is not the first thing we have donated to this museum." The woman stood and linked arms with her husband. "We saved photos. Among them, a picture of your great-grandparents. Come. Our photo collection is on display in another wing of the museum."

They led Ben to a nearby room, stopping beside a photo of a young couple standing in a living room. In the enlarged black-and-white picture, paintings hung from the wall behind them. The young man and woman had their arms around each other and were beaming like newlyweds. She was visibly pregnant.

"You look just like him, *Rabbi Isaac Abrams*." He pointed a trembling finger at the young man in the picture. "You're the mirror image of your great-grandfather. And see here," he drew Ben's attention to the canvas hanging on the wall behind the young couple. "This is the same Renoir you showed me from your phone, *Portrait of Señorita Santangel*."

"Oh my God!" Ben forgot to breathe. He grew dizzy and placed his hand against the wall for support. The old woman asked if he needed a doctor.

"What is it?" The old man offered to lend Ben his cane.

"Look at the reflection in the mirror. You can see the photographer who was taking their picture. I recognize this man. He and his son were in Paris, standing in front of an art gallery."

"Solomon Santangel," she said.

"Did he have a daughter?" Ben asked.

"Both families had daughters. Your great-grandparents and the Santangels were neighbors. There were rumors that one of them survived *Kristallnacht*. Something about being hidden in a packing crate containing masterpiece paintings."

"*Grossmutter*. Which is why I would like to go to the Wall," Ben said, "so I can say *Kaddish* or *El Maleh Rachamim* for all of the departed souls in my family tree."

Mystery Island

Chapter 1: Thursday

Andrew Tate spent the longest night of his life watching his wife die. He did the best he could and felt like it wasn't enough.

She grabbed his hand so tight it hurt his fingers.

He wouldn't let go. The physical pain was nothing compared to what was coming.

"My halo's slipping," she said. "I'm seeing pitchforks."

"Means I'll get to see you again."

Maddie smiled through her tears; she'd been too weak to laugh for the last day or two. He'd lost track of time last week. The whole month had been an emotional train wreck.

"I want to see one more sunrise. You're gonna have to do the singing for me. Promise."

"I got the off-key part down pat."

She squeezed his hand, her last words a request for him to keep living.

He felt her death rattle in the bottom of his own lungs. He kept talking, anyway, and held her hand until the doctors turned off the machines.

Andrew Tate heard his wife singing as he passed through the thin veil between sleep and wakefulness. Seven months, two weeks, three days, and less than an hour since she had taken her last breath at daybreak. She had already let go; he couldn't stop hanging on. The time they spent together in his dreams was all he had left, and he lost a little more of her with every waking moment. He hummed the refrain to her favorite song until he donned his uniform: a sheriff who didn't believe in ghosts despite being haunted by the memory of his departed wife. He checked the mirror and adjusted his tie, straightened his shoulders and leaned closer to take note of how the latest set of worry lines had etched another toe in the crow's feet forming around his eyes.

Sheriff Andrew Tate kept the peace on a small barrier island off the Forgotten Coast. The indigenous people who preceded him had possessed enough sense to keep the location secret; massive shell mounds from smoked oysters and soft-shell crab documented an idyllic lifestyle spent beneath palm trees. Not much had changed over the centuries. Enhanced security for the inhabitants of St. Nicholas Island meant locking the front door. Sheriff Tate did most of his patrolling by monitoring social media on his cellphone; he got more call-outs by private message than police radio, because he kept the peace by staying a step ahead of trouble. It made him loved by those who knew him, feared by the few bad apples who were up to no good, and respected by the rest who fell somewhere in-between.

His phone dinged: one of the locals who gave guided tours posted another blurry picture and claimed it was the ghost of a shipwrecked pirate who misplaced his treasure. He ignored the warning; ghost sightings increased as the weekend drew near, and Mardi Gras was a bigger holiday than Christmas for the local guided-tour businesses. This sighting proved to be an exception, but he was set in his ways and didn't treat the post as a credible threat or future problem. Sheriff Tate spent his last uneventful day keeping the peace on an island too small for a traffic light and too big for a one-person police force.

Too tired to stay up; too antsy for sleep, he changed out of his uniform and headed for the beach. Walking barefoot on the sand gave him perspective; the vastness of the ocean leant itself to creative problem solving. He focused on the most pressing issues and let the answers drift in with the tide and swirl around on wave crests turned silvery-blue by moonlight. He hadn't planned on a ghostly intervention; he'd heard plenty of stories about ghosts and didn't believe any of them. Most accounts involved alcohol and he'd been stone-cold sober for a decade.

The apparition stood beside a clump of sea oats, looking out of place. Somebody playing electronic tricks on him? A hologram, perhaps? Must be—since there was no such thing as ghosts. He turned on his flashlight to cut through a projected, three-dimensional image. The light bounced off an emaciated man in tattered clothing. The whites of his eyes gleamed and Sheriff Tate was close enough to see the pupils constrict.

"What the hell?" Adrenaline surged through his body. His ears thrummed. Blood rushed to his fingers and toes. He raised his hands in a defensive position, widened his stance and felt the sand shift beneath his feet.

"Who are you? Speak up."

Rodrigo Luis Abravanel raised a skeletal hand to shield his eyes. The strange torch light blinded him.

"Hello? You're too early for Halloween." Sheriff Tate didn't put much faith in local legends of shipwrecked sailors locked in some kind of netherworld limbo. He didn't care much for Mardi Gras costumes, either.

"¿Qué? ¿Isaac? ¿Eres tu?"

"Huh? I mean. *Hola.*" The sheriff talked with enough maids and kitchen help to learn a smattering of Spanish. Most of their law-enforcement issues had more to do with paperwork than crime. He relaxed slightly, enough to move from an offensive to a defensive position.

"*Gracias a Dios.*"

"Not sure God has anything to do with it. Unless you're really a ghost and then I'm gonna join you in prayer." Making a joke was better than making an arrest when things got this weird. If he was having a nightmare, then it was past time to wake up.

"*¡Ayúdame!*

"Save you? Or help you? Never can keep those two straight. Er, *Que es,* um . . . something." Most Hispanic workers knew enough conversational English to get by, especially when motivated by a law enforcement issue. "Why? *¿Por qué?*"

"*Seferino.*" Rodrigo prayed to the true God of his fathers and carried a *seferino,* a small Jewish prayer book, smuggled in the lining of his coat.

"No *comprende.*" Sheriff Tate was in the habit of looking up the hard words on his cell phone; he was too stunned to remember it was still in his pocket.

Rodrigo was a learned man, a navigator. He opened the prayer book to prove his faith.

"Yiddish? What the hell?"

It had seemed so pragmatic to Rodrigo. Act as a Catholic on the outside and remain Jewish on the inside. When Queen Isabella ordered all Jews who refused to convert to Catholicism to leave Spain in 1492, Rodrigo escaped persecution by sailing to the New World. "*Y luego encontramos oro. El oro es una maldición.*"

"*Oro*: Gold. Something about it being your curse, maybe?" Dreams weren't supposed to be this hard. Nightmares, he was unsure about. The verdict was still out on hallucinations and drug flashbacks. Didn't matter. Time to cut to the chase. "Gold? Er, *Oro. ¿Dónde?* Where is it? *¿Comprende, amigo?*"

Rodrigo fell to his knees and began to pray when the horrors returned. He cursed the seas, first in Ladino and then in Spanish. Trading lives for gold was soul murder in any language. He lamented the greed which had cast him ashore in this distant land, for gold was the curse that doomed him to wander.

To keep reading: Mystery Island

Made in the USA
Middletown, DE
20 August 2022

71852443R00136